Love & Chocolate

Gail Cleare

Love & Chocolate
Red Adept Publishing, LLC
104 Bugenfield Court
Garner, NC 27529
http://RedAdeptPublishing.com/

First Print Edition: August 2018

Cover Art by Streetlight Graphics

This is a work of fiction. Names, characters, places, and incidents either are the product of the author's imagination or are used fictitiously, and any resemblance to locales, events, business establishments, or actual persons—living or dead—is entirely coincidental.

For Matthew, Justin, and Ryan.

You all turned out to be wonderful cooks.

Chapter 1

Cocoa shadows fluttered on the bedroom wall. A warm breeze sifted in through the casement windows. The moon floated high behind the trees, and bars of milky light spilled across the floor.

Silence filled the house. Everyone was sleeping. Everyone except Sarah.

A greenish glow illuminated her long, bare legs, splayed in front of her on the sheets. The laptop battery felt warm against her thighs, and her fingernails clicked on the keys, loud in the stillness.

A pop-up window appeared on the screen, white letters glowing inside a small blue rectangle.

HotNCold: *Coco, want to chat or... cyber?*

The avatar next to his name was a selfie of a firm, lean set of abs. She knew that lots of people were hooking up online at these dating sites. They called it "cybersex" or "sexting." It seemed perfectly safe, invisible, and anonymous. Wickedly spontaneous. She clicked to read his profile. "Single man 36 seeking single woman 30-45 for walks along the river, coffee by the fireplace, and whatever develops."

Sarah hit Reply, and the window expanded, with space for her to type a response. Her fingers hesitated.

She had signed in just now as CocoLvr, the account created by her cousin Paisley last night after they'd polished off too many bottles of merlot. Sarah had kept saying, "No, no—I'm not ready for this! I'm barely over the divorce," as she'd grabbed for Paisley's phone. Holding it aloft with a grin, Paisley had snapped a shot of Sarah's cleavage. She'd posted it with the caption "Sexy mama wants to paint you with chocolate sauce and you can imagine the rest, Big Boy."

1

"See?" Paisley had said. "You're only two years older than this guy and well below his expiration date."

They'd laughed until tears rolled down their cheeks, reminding Sarah of the carefree days before everything changed. Paisley had sent out a dozen silly messages, including one to this guy, whom she'd found on the page for new local members. Sarah figured if his face was half as gorgeous as his midsection, it must be amazing. But it didn't really matter what he looked like. She never planned to see him in person.

Too late to change her ridiculous profile now. This was irresistible. Just for fun.

CocoLvr: *Sure. Love to.*

Her pulse beat faster as she clicked Send.

Single since her ex-husband had revealed his true colors, Sarah ached for intimacy. But she couldn't see herself sitting down with a blind date, making awkward conversation while they checked each other out, or going to a bar to meet a stranger. An imaginary love affair seemed like the perfect amount of togetherness. Especially if it could satisfy her in more ways than one.

It wasn't as if they were actually going to touch each other. No condoms required, no embarrassment the next morning. The private message was all text, so he couldn't see her. He had no idea what her real name was. Nobody would ever know, and she was ravenous for a man's touch, virtual or otherwise.

CocoLvr: *Teach me.*

Her wrists tingled.

CocoLvr: *I'm a cyber-virgin.*

HotNCold: *OK baby have no fear, I'll be gentle. Tell me what you're wearing.*

CocoLvr: *Not much. Just a cami and bikinis.*

She inhaled sharply.

CocoLvr: *And you?*

HotNCold: *Just a big smile, baby.*

Her eyes opened wider as she read his reply. A shiver of anticipation shook her, and a trail of goose bumps popped up on her arms.

HotNCold: *Where are you right now? Want to picture it.*

CocoLvr: *In bed.*

HotNCold: *Alone?*

CocoLvr: *Of course.*

She searched the keyboard, looking for the plus sign.

CocoLvr: *Me + laptop.*

HotNCold: *Make room for me, baby.*

CocoLvr: *Okay, come on over.*

She leaned forward, her eyes fixed on the screen.

HotNCold: *<Sits on edge of bed and strokes his hand slowly up her leg, starting at the ankle>*

CocoLvr: *Oooh.*

She felt she was starting to get the hang of it.

HotNCold: *<Bends over to kiss her gently on the lips, while running his hand up, and up, and up.>*

Sarah read the words, and her imagination went wild. She licked her dry lips. This was just as up close and personal as making out in real life but without the actual touching.

Now her lap was hot for more than one reason.

"Mom?" The small voice came from across the hall.

Sarah gasped and jumped, feeling as if she were still sixteen and her parents had caught her kissing a boy on the front porch. She snapped the laptop shut and shoved it under her pillow. The room suddenly filled with darkness and the sound of Sarah's panting.

Or was that Hershey, her chocolate-brown Labrador? He lay on his pad across the room. She heard him hold his breath to listen, as she did, for the sound of that little voice to come again.

"Mom?" Devon called, his tone quavering.

"Coming." She swung her legs off the bed.

As she walked across the hallway to his room, her breathing became calmer. A guilty smile pulled at the corners of her lips.

His room was lit by a nightlight shaped like a star.

"What's up, sweetie?" Sarah asked, sitting on the edge of the bed to hug him.

"Bad dream." He rubbed his head against her shoulder.

"Want to tell me?"

He shook his head and sighed. "Gone now."

"Okay, buddy. Need to pee?"

Devon nodded. She took him by the hand and steered his wobbly form into the bathroom then lifted the toilet seat for him. He peed, yawning, and slammed the seat down as he flushed. After he ran his hands under the water in the sink, she dried them with a towel. Devon staggered back to his bed.

After he burrowed down under the covers, Sarah kissed him on the forehead and tucked him in. She left his door ajar and hurried back to her own room.

When she opened the laptop, the private message had disappeared. HotNCold must have thought she'd chickened out. She looked for him on the list of people online, but it no longer showed his name. He'd probably quit for the night.

Sarah lay alone in her big empty bed, with no one's head on the other pillow. No slow, even breathing to hear in the darkness. No warm body radiating coziness, pressed up against her under the sheet. Not even a virtual lover to soothe her with a sweet fantasy. A wave of bleak desolation rolled over her, and her stomach clenched as she swallowed the lump in her throat.

She shut down the computer, curled on her side, and hugged a pillow spooned against her. Then she reached over to pull open the drawer in her bedside table, the drawer that hid her guilty secrets. Her hand encountered a foil packet but rummaged further to find the plastic container. She pulled it out and peeled off the lid.

A dusky, delicious scent tickled her nose.

Mmm. Dark, sweet, and oozing, with just a little crunch for texture.

The best brownies on the planet, or so everyone at the restaurant said. The treat was another of Paisley's original recipes and one of their most popular desserts served *à la mode*. Cocoa, dark chocolate, and pecans, chock-full of the magic chemicals that made Sarah's heart beat faster and her body quiver with joy. The best high she'd ever felt. Well, nearly the best. Maybe chocolate wasn't really *better* than sex, but under the circumstances, it was a damn good substitute.

The sugar-laced chocolate bliss pumped through Sarah's body. Her anxiety began to subside. Maybe someday the right guy would come along, but in the meanwhile, she had to make sure Devon wasn't hurt by another of her flawed judgment calls. She never wanted to see that expression on his face again, as she had when she'd told him Daddy wasn't coming home anymore. It had broken her heart to watch Devon assume this was his fault. Too many times, Devon had heard Jim refer to him as Sarah's son, not his own. "Your son isn't normal," Jim would complain. "He's some kind of freak. Get him under control."

Sarah lay on the bed and watched shadows crawl up and down the wall as the trees outside moved in the wind. She imagined that someday a man might climb up to her window. A beautiful man, maybe one with a Zorro cape and a neat little mustache, intense eyes. He would stare at her through the casement window as she dropped her flowing silk nightgown to the floor, then she'd reach out to open the latch. His eyes would shine in the moonlight as he swung inside before standing tall and strong in front of her. His hand would stroke her hair as he leaned close to kiss her. Their tongues would touch, sweet, dark, and smooth with a spark of cinnamon. *Ahhhh.*

She swallowed and reluctantly put the remaining brownies back in their container then slipped it into the drawer. She slid down to rest her head on the pillow and stared into the darkness, picturing a naked man beside her, running his hand up her bare leg.

Up, and up, and up...

Chapter 2

Dark chocolate sour cherry fudge. Marbled black and white chocolate mousse in chocolate wafer cups. Devil's food cupcakes stuffed with coconut custard, sprinkled with chopped almonds.

Enveloped by the rich aroma of cocoa, Sarah sat on a kitchen stool and read the newspaper. Tarts and éclairs towered over her on stainless-steel rolling racks, waiting to be wheeled into the restaurant dining room and arranged in the display case.

Sarah wiggled her nose and inhaled deeply, her head spinning into paradise for a moment. The temptation to grab and gobble was nearly irresistible.

She swung her long blond hair behind her shoulder, turning her head slightly. She stared at the Almond Joy cupcake in the center of her field of vision. "Yum," Sarah whispered, hypnotized by the image. Her hand twitched, and she struggled not to reach out.

"Hey, pretty lady, you okay over there?" Jerome called out to her from across the kitchen. He slapped a bunch of fresh basil on the cutting board. Sarah looked up with a guilty quiver, and he winked at her. "Getting drunk on those chocolate fumes? I see those big blue eyes turning all glittery rainbow-colored, girlfriend."

"You just be careful and don't cut off your thumb!" She folded up the newspaper to read it more comfortably. "The customers don't like to find body parts in their food, you know."

"Ow!" Jerome cried in a falsetto voice, mincing herbs while he hummed along with the radio. Dressed in baggy kitchen-white chef's pants and a body-hugging sleeveless T-shirt that showed off his toned brown body, he had a red bandanna wrapped around his head to contain the long, kinky dreadlocks. Diamond studs twinkled in his ear-

7

lobes, smoky black eyeliner and gray shadow adorned his long-lashed eyes, and an ornate tattoo of a green dragon wrapped around his left bicep.

The second sous chef was his perfect counterpoint. Buttoned-up and tidy, Raoul was spotless in his traditional white chef's jacket and creased pants. He sliced potatoes into almost transparent disks while he talked a mile a minute in Spanish with his wife, Isabelle, on his iPhone, set to speaker and resting on the shelf in front of his workstation.

A delivery boy came through the back door with boxes of fresh produce stacked high in his arms, heading for the walk-in cooler. The big Hobart dishwasher hissed and gurgled as a cloud of steam belched out of its mouth. Jerome ran over to pull out a clattering rack of clean mixing bowls, leaving them to cool while he shoved in another rack and pulled the handle to lower the doors. It was bustling and noisy, as always on a Friday afternoon in the kitchen at The Three Chocolatiers, where everyone prepared for a busy night.

"I'm totally sick of so many Mexican recipes, Grandpa. Yes, they invented chocolate, but why can't we try something new? Let's be daring. Create our own innovations!"

Sarah's grandfather, Chef Emile Dumas, and her cousin Paisley—at age thirty-four, already a renowned pastry chef herself—entered from the bar and crossed to the tiny office at the back of the kitchen. In appearance, the cousins were like salt and pepper. Sarah, fair and tall, and Paisley, dark and small. They were just as great a combination when they paired their talents. Paisley cooked, and Sarah took care of sales, as they had since their first lemonade stand.

Her cousin looked over at Sarah now, sending a quick shrug and eye roll. Sarah held her tongue and gave Paisley a warning glance. As the junior members of the "Three" in the restaurant's name, they tried not to challenge Emile's authority. Sarah had joined the family business only three years ago, when she was laid off from a corporate marketing job. She was still learning and tried not to take sides.

"Paisley, you know the chocolate chili is always popular." Emile ran his fingers through his mane of white hair and tugged as his voice began to rise. "We must think of sales, *ma petite*! People are nervous about some of the more unusual dishes. What they really want is your fabulous desserts, of course."

Since Grandma Annie passed away last year, Sarah had graduated from bartender to take on the role of family peacemaker along with management of the dining room. She wondered if her diplomatic skills were going to be needed now. The two chefs faced one another with hands on hips.

Paisley backed down, flinging up her hands in surrender. "Okay, Grandpa. But tomorrow night, we make the chocolate tenderloin. We have a freezer full of beautiful grass-fed beef, and it's too good to grind into hamburger." She stomped away.

Sarah was absorbed in reading the local business news, and someone had entered and was standing in front of her, clearing his throat, before she noticed. She looked over her paper to see long legs in faded blue jeans, leading up to a brown leather belt with a silver concha buckle, and then farther up to a red plaid shirt covering a flat belly and broad chest. The shirt was worn unbuttoned at the throat to reveal a tanned neck adorned with a few nice curly brown hairs.

Following this fascinating path toward his smiling face before she could stop herself, Sarah recognized Blake Harrison, the manufacturer who supplied The Three Chocolatiers with its signature brand of premium double-chocolate ice cream.

He was in his midthirties with dark-brown hair and green eyes, and word on the street had it that he was currently single after a long-term relationship. Blake wandered through the kitchen once a week or so, meeting with Emile to take his order. He always wore his sleeves rolled up, as if he were ready for action. Sarah enjoyed imagining what kind of action that might be.

"Hi!" Sarah squinted up at Blake. "Nice, um, belt." She realized she'd been staring at his crotch, and her cheeks tingled with embarrassment. "Can I help you with something?" She cleared her throat and tried to look businesslike.

No point in giving him the wrong idea. She wasn't dating. She couldn't risk the heartbreak again. Better to stay solo and concentrate on being a great mom. That was what she told herself, anyhow, during the long dark hours before it was finally time to get up and make coffee.

Of course, Sarah did have totally normal, healthy urges, which sometimes pulled her in the opposite direction. Such as her current inability to stop staring at Blake Harrison with a goofy grin on her face, and the fact that her eyes kept wandering back to his belt.

"I'm definitely interested." He grinned at her, and their eyes locked.

"Huh?" Her mouth fell open. *Is he reading my mind?*

"Yeah, the chocolate wedding catering job sounds great. Count me in." He nodded and put his hands on his hips.

Her brain finally snapped into gear. "Oh, you got my email! Fantastic, the clients will be thrilled. Let me get my notes. Be right back."

She jumped off the stool and fled into the office to pull herself together.

THERE SHE GOES, RUNNING away again.

Blake admired Sarah's retreating form and wondered why she always seemed so skittish around him. Not that she didn't look great from behind, but he didn't have a lot of time for chasing women. He was a hardworking business owner.

For weeks now, he'd been hanging around the Chocolatiers kitchen, trying to catch a minute alone with Sarah. Blake was pretty sure Paisley knew what he was up to. She'd caught him staring at her cousin more than once.

He just wanted to take Sarah out on a perfectly normal date. With some perfectly normal sex at the end of it. What was wrong with that? They were both single, and both needed some social contact. A win-win as far as he could see.

But every time he found an excuse to start a conversation, she bolted.

He paced in front of the office doorway, watching as she shuffled through some papers on the table. Considering how he'd been dumped by his last girlfriend, right after paying the nonrefundable deposit on a Bahamas rental for their wedding, he should think twice about getting involved again. Hadn't he sworn off women when Mandy fled with their vacation fund and her trainer from the health club? He obviously wasn't good at this serious-relationship stuff. That was the second time he'd thought he found The One, only to be disappointed. Blake had thrown himself into work after that, struggling to fight off depression. Now he dated only casually. Very casually. As in, no spending the night and no promises.

A lot more opportunity existed for this lifestyle than he'd realized during the years when he was half of a couple. Women weren't at all shy about what they wanted these days. All he had to do was sit at a bar, and before long, some kind of invitation would appear. As long as he was totally honest and the woman knew what she'd signed up for, what was the harm?

That was his theory, anyhow. But while the uncomplicated sex was nice, he still felt lonely and unfulfilled. The lack of real love was downright depressing, and underneath his mask of cool self-assurance, anxiety buzzed.

Blake wondered what it was about Sarah that tempted him so. Why did he keep coming back for a closer look when she gave him no encouragement? That alone should have deterred him. Most women seemed interested in Blake, even the married ones. All ages, all types. Other women didn't run away. They even tracked him down and pounded on his door in the middle of the night. Well, that had happened once. Sarah's reaction to him was illogical. He wasn't giving up, though, because instinct told him she might be worth the risk.

He paced in the other direction, smiling when he caught her eye.

Was it that long taffy-colored blond hair, flowing down her back the way it was now or up in an elegant twist like a French pastry when she worked, showing off her graceful neck and the place behind her ear that he wanted to touch with his lips? Or maybe it was her tall, curvy shape. Or those little freckles sprinkled across the tops of her breasts like cinnamon on toast. He'd caught a good view of them when he stood over her just now, as she sat on the kitchen stool.

She made his mouth water. It was that simple.

It might even be serious if they ever got to the relationship part. There was an energy between them that he'd never encountered before. When he looked at her, he recognized a kindred spirit, with a lightning bolt of sexual attraction mixed in.

Last night, when he saw the new profile he'd been matched with at the online dating site, his intuition began to twitch right off the bat. CocoLvr and Sarah had the same cinnamon freckles and the same breasts, not to mention the same tiny starfish charm that dangled between them on a fine gold chain. What he had seen a moment ago confirmed it. Same interest in chocolate too, so it couldn't all be coincidence. He wouldn't have thought she'd be the sexting-with-strangers type, but things seemed to be going pretty well until she'd abruptly disappeared.

Even online, when she hadn't known it was him. So, it wasn't personal. Sarah ran away from everyone.

Blake had heard the stories about her ex. How the weasel ran off with some bimbo and left Sarah to raise their boy alone. A cute kid, whom Blake had seen playing Little League baseball. The guy obviously must be a jerk and an idiot. Who would walk away from all that?

Blake narrowed his eyes and watched her like a dog stalking a rabbit. Then he caught himself and tried to be cool. He stuffed his hands into his jeans pockets and leaned in the doorway.

Emile sat at a desk and opened mail while Paisley wrote on the specials board with chalk. Sarah looked up and smiled as she waved a yellow legal pad, and when their eyes connected, Blake felt his mouth smile back before he could stop it.

Damn! Grinning like a fool. Everyone will know I have a case for her.

He turned to one side and scowled, reaching for his cell phone to thumb through his messages and look busy.

"Let's go up front and sit at the bar to talk," Sarah said. "It's quieter there." She smiled and motioned toward the swinging door to the dining room, slipping past him with an accidental bump of her butt against his hip.

Blake's grumpiness melted, and he turned to follow her like a sleep-walker.

Beauty and brains. She'd more or less run the place since Emile's wife, Annie, died. And now she'd sold a chocolate wedding package to some rich foodies who wanted their own unique recipes created. Including a new flavor of his premium ice cream, packaged in custom-printed containers for local guests to take home in special insulated bags, along with cupcake versions of the wedding cake. All Sarah's idea, of course.

Pretty slick. Sarah was quite a tasty-looking cupcake herself. Come to think of it, now he had two ways to win her over, in person and online.

Maybe Blake could figure out how to have his cupcake and eat it too.

Chapter 3

Sarah started to walk through the swinging door to the dining room, but a funny gasp and a thump made her stop and turn around. In the office, Emile swayed and slid out of the desk chair, his face gray.

"Grandpa?" Sarah rushed past Blake into the little room. The old man lay on the floor, one hand to his chest and a confused expression on his face. "Are you okay? What's happening? Talk to me."

Emile's face was pale, and he sweated, breathing in fast, shallow gasps. Paisley hurried across the room and sank to the floor, taking his hand to feel for a pulse. Sarah knelt and tried to loosen his tight collar.

"Calling 9-1-1," Blake said from right behind her, phone already in his hand. He gave her shoulder a quick squeeze then turned away and spoke into the receiver.

"Here, Grandpa, let's use this for a pillow." Paisley took off her cardigan, folded it, and put it beneath his head. She gently stroked his hair. Her eyes met those of Sarah, whose eyebrows were drawn together in a worried frown.

Sarah had a lump of fear in her throat, and her hands shook as she finally managed to open Emile's collar. She had never seen anyone have a heart attack, but it seemed as though that might be happening.

The two sous chefs hovered in the doorway. Raoul twisted his starched toque in his hands. Behind them in the kitchen, salsa music blared until Blake found the sound controls and turned it off. He reappeared with a glass of water and a cool, moist towel, offering them to Sarah.

Supporting the old man's head with one arm, Sarah offered him a sip. Paisley gently blotted his face. Then there was an unnatural quiet, filled only with the sound of shuffling feet and Emile's labored breaths, which seemed to return to normal after a few minutes. His color looked a little better too. Sarah's frantic sense of panic diminished. Whatever was wrong, it seemed to be passing.

Sarah held her grandfather's hand. He looked around and blinked.

"Girls, am I lying on the floor?" he asked in a shaky voice.

"Yes, Grandpa." Sarah squeezed his hand, but he didn't squeeze back. "Are you in any pain? How do you feel?"

"How did I get down here?"

"I'm not sure, Grandpa. How are you? You don't look so good." Paisley stroked his forehead with the back of her hand.

"I think someone knocked me over. Did you hit me, sweetheart? I probably deserved it." He looked at Paisley and crinkled his eyes.

She looked at him with love. "No, silly Grandpa. I would never hit you, no matter how much you deserved it."

"Ha!" he said with a smile in his eyes.

Sarah heard a siren getting closer, and it stopped outside.

"They're here." Blake held the back door open, and two uniformed men rushed in with a gurney. Everyone stepped aside, and the EMTs checked Emile's vital signs and hooked him up to a portable oxygen tank. One of the men spoke on a walkie-talkie to his supervisor at the hospital, then he turned to Paisley, asking for Emile's identification and health insurance information.

"It looks like he may have had a heart attack or a mild stroke. Seems to be better now. The ER doctors will do some tests to find out. His vital signs are strong. Does he have any drug allergies? I'd like to give him some aspirin to prevent blood clots." When Paisley and Sarah both agreed, he gave Emile the medication.

Paisley rode along in the ambulance, where Emile was already trying to sit up, protesting that he was fine and wanted to get back to work. She promised to keep in touch with Sarah, who said she had to meet Devon's school bus in a few minutes.

When the ambulance doors closed, Blake put his arm around Sarah. She felt wobbly, and the friendly kiss he planted on the side of her head was comforting. With both hands on her shoulders, he turned her toward him.

"I'll check in with you later for an update, and please call me if you need anything, for any reason. Okay?" Radiating warmth and reassurance, his eyes filled her view. "I mean it."

"Thanks, Blake. That's really sweet of you."

"We'll talk about the chocolate wedding later."

"Okay, thanks for helping." He'd been nice and supportive. It was a little unexpected, considering how he was frowning and pacing while she'd tried to find her notes.

When the back door slammed behind him, Sarah and the two sous chefs looked at each other in shock.

"What about dinner? Is she coming back?" Jerome's eyes were wide and dramatic. "Who the hell is gonna cook, people?"

"What should we do? Should we close for the night?" Raoul had twisted his hat into a misshapen monster. He noticed and started trying to fluff it back into the proper shape.

Sarah raised one eyebrow. "You two can cook." The manager in her was taking charge. The best thing for Emile would be to know that everything was under control.

"Us?" Raoul seemed surprised. "But we usually just prep and make the easy stuff."

"Yeah, but we can cook, man, you know?" Jerome nodded. "It might be a little slow, but we could do it. 'All for one and one for all,' like the brother said." He punched Raoul in the arm.

"Well, the baking is all done..." Raoul said. "We could probably do it."

"Yeah, and we've got Freddy on the dishwasher and Leon busing, and they can both come in early to help us finish prepping, if you call them, man." Jerome looked at Raoul's cell phone and raised his eyebrows.

Raoul started to dial. "I'll call my sister to come in too. She can plate the salads and desserts."

"All right, then," Sarah said. "See what you think about making the specials. If it's too much, we'll skip them. Let me know, and I'll print out new menus off the computer. Business as usual, right, boys?" She projected an image of calm, cool collectedness, despite the burning in her belly.

"That's what the boss would want us to do, I think." Raoul's words held an emotional quiver.

"You said it." Jerome sounded determined. "I love that old man."

"I've got to warn you," Sarah said, "we're booked solid through ten o'clock, and this place will be jammin'!" A sense of excitement started to take hold. She still worried about her grandfather, but the thought of making him proud became a powerful distraction.

"Well, *bon appetit*, baby!" Jerome said, batting his eyelashes and posing like a runway model.

"We've got it covered, girlfriend. You go play with your fancy napkins and such," Raoul said, turning her toward the dining room and giving her a wave bye-bye.

Sarah ran to answer the telephone, which was ringing at the hostess station.

"Three Chocolatiers. I'm sorry, our tables are all booked, but you can sit at the bar if there's a seat available. You're welcome." She hung up the phone, and a disturbing thought flitted through her mind.

What about the chocolate wedding? If Emile was laid up for any significant period of time, they could be in big trouble. There was no way Sarah could supervise the service and the food by herself, and Paisley would need to focus on the restaurant. Satisfying the esoteric culinary demands of these temperamental clients required Emile's master touch. They would chop her up and sauté her for breakfast!

She didn't know enough about cooking to answer their questions or to run the event at their remote location. In her prior life as an advertising executive, Sarah had been the client at catered dinners plenty of times, but those days were long gone. She could probably charm the clients and supervise the waitstaff, but without a chef to take care of the food, the picture looked bleak.

Putting Sarah in charge of a chocolate catering job was like putting the fox in charge of the henhouse. Her ability to remain logical in the midst of cocoa chaos was extremely questionable, as her friends and family knew. She started snacking and got revved up, and pretty soon everything went to hell. Totally inappropriate things came out of her mouth, some of them rather funny, and she got into all kinds of trouble. Her corporate management skills were of little use under the circumstances.

She freely admitted her chocolate addiction and the bizarre effect it had on her thinking and behavior. The only reason she could cope here at the restaurant was that her family and coworkers kept an eye on her. Once the dinner hour arrived, Sarah avoided temptation by staying out of the kitchen. No little bites of this and that, here and there. No dipping bits of French bread into the *mole poblano* sauce. She made a point of saving her chocolate indulgences until after closing, when she was allowed one or two desserts, at most. She negotiated with herself, every night.

Paisley told her cacao contained a chemical called theobromine, a word derived from the Greek for "food of the gods." It affected most people similarly to caffeine, but Sarah knew others had a special sensitivity to it too. Many of the restaurant's customers agreed that the experience of eating chocolate was similar to that of sexual pleasure. The food of love.

No wonder Sarah was hooked.

The image of her grandfather lying on the gurney, pale and confused, returned to her mind. She hoped he would be home in a few days and back to normal. If not, maybe she still wouldn't have to tell the wedding clients what was going on. She didn't want to lose the contract since a lot of money was on the line, and it looked as though they were going to need it. Already, she could imagine what to say. The words echoed in her mind as her face relaxed, and she smiled.

If there was one thing Sarah had learned in the advertising business, it was how to put a positive spin on things.

No problem, she thought. *I can always fudge it.*

Chapter 4

After he left the restaurant, Blake drove his pickup to the old shoe factory that was now home to a variety of artists, artisans, and small businesses like his. Located at the end of downtown, alongside the river where barges once moved merchandise to market, the enormous brick structure had been in sad shape ten years ago when he and his brother, Jordan, bought it at auction. They gradually renovated the space and retrofitted it with modern technology, transforming it into a thriving hive of activity.

He parked in front of Blake's Ice Cream, located in the center of the busy loading dock. Tractor trailers were lined up on both sides to receive merchandise and deliver supplies, while workers stacked cartons on hand trucks and rolled them to and fro. Blake stepped out of his truck and surveyed the façade, always on the lookout for something else that might need fixing.

The ground floor housed a coffee roaster, a commercial bakery, a fresh salsa company, and a brewpub with a bottling operation. Blake and Jordan had worked hard to recruit the ideal tenants, and these specialty food companies were among the fastest-growing local businesses. They all profited from shared resources like administrative services, bookkeeping, sales reps, and consolidated shipping, which had allowed them to save money and work smarter. Grateful to his sharp, savvy younger brother for suggesting the incubator model, Blake thought it was a brilliant concept. It had given Blake's ice cream business a huge boost while ensuring a steady rental income for their partnership as landlords. Since Jordan headed the in-house sales team, representing all five companies, it was a profitable arrangement for everyone.

His brother's shiny black BMW spun into the driveway and pulled up next to Blake's dusty pickup. Jordan climbed out of the elegant car, slinging a messenger bag over his shoulder. He was neatly dressed for work, in gray slacks and a crisp blue dress shirt and tie. Tall, like his brother and father, he sported a stylish haircut and immaculately polished Italian leather shoes.

"Bro-ther!" Jordan flipped his sunglasses to the top of his head, reached out, and clasped Blake's hand in the series of arcane motions that had been their greeting ritual since they were kids. "What's up, man?"

"Not much," Blake said as they climbed the metal stairs to the loading dock and headed for the office doorway to the left of the freight entrance. He wished he could say he'd made a date with Sarah and frowned. "Emile Dumas collapsed of a probable heart attack in front of me today. Ambulance took him away."

Jordan whistled, low and slow, as they went inside. "Whoa, that's intense. Did the ladies freak out?"

"Those two are pretty cool in a crisis." Blake grabbed the pile of mail from the "In" basket on the shelf near the door. "Seemed like he was probably going to be okay, but they'll be shorthanded for a while."

Jordan put his bag on the tidy side of the big oak partners' desk in the middle of the sunny room lit by two huge windows in the brick exterior walls. "Everything on target for the chocolate wedding?" He loosened his tie and sat in his ergodynamic chrome-and-leather chair, which resembled a high-tech grasshopper.

"So far, I guess. We didn't have a chance to talk about it." Blake tossed the mail on the messy side of the desk, where a pile of bills and correspondence lay jumbled. He toed off his shoes and sat down, rolling up the sleeves of his plaid flannel shirt a little higher. "I'll call Sarah later to find out how Emile's doing. But it's probably too late for them to cancel without paying a penalty."

Jordan leaned back in his chair and steepled his fingers, his face serious. Shiny gold cuff links at his wrists flashed in the sunlight. "Did you order the mini-containers yet? If so, can we put them on hold?"

Blake preferred a sturdy, old-fashioned swiveling armchair that matched the desk. He swung it around and propped his feet on the side table. "I was planning to confirm with Sarah today," he said. "We'll wait and see before we order. Did you schedule the tastings at Hannaford's for next week?"

They started to talk about in-store promotions and were soon embroiled in a debate over what day and time were best for sampling each of the various products the incubator produced. A few minutes later, the door from the hallway opened, and their baby sister, Carrie, now twenty-one and much too hot for her own good, walked in with Blake's brown Lab, Kahlua, on a leash.

Blake looked behind him, realizing that the dog was gone from the corner bed where he'd been napping earlier. Not that it was unusual. Kahlua had a lot of friends in the building who welcomed his visits. The dog got around, especially when treats were on hand.

"I had him upstairs with us in Bookkeeping," Carrie said, anticipating Blake's question. "But those spreadsheets were driving me absolutely bonkers, so I took him for a walk along the river." She snapped the dog's leash off his collar, and he trotted over to Blake for a neck rub, his tail swinging lazily. "Can't you guys think of anything else for me to do? I'm not a data entry person, you know. I could be doing serious damage to everyone's records."

Jordan grinned and wagged his finger at her. "You'd better be careful, missy. Cooking the books is a serious offense."

She stuck her tongue out at him and rolled her eyes. "Jordie, I'd even do demos, if you'll let me. Anything to earn enough for school," she begged. "Mom promised you two would find me work." Carrie tossed her long auburn hair over her shoulder and hitched her hands in her jeans pockets, her green eyes flashing. She was the spitting image of their dad in female form, and Blake noticed it again when she spun around to wheedle him. "And how about you, big brother? I'd think someone in your business could find a little summer job for a hospitality management major like me, just like that." She snapped her fingers.

Blake thought of Sarah and her situation. Maybe she could use an extra hand with Emile out and a big event coming up. "I might know of something. Waitress or hostess. Interested?"

Carrie leapt forward and smothered him with a hug. "Oh yeah! Where?"

"Sarah and Paisley's place. Maybe. I can ask."

She flapped her hands up and down, her eyes beaming and a big white smile on her face. "The chocolate restaurant? Ohmigod, what heaven! You're not kidding, are you? Tell me you're not. It would be too cruel." She clenched her hands together, begging.

"I can ask, I said. We'll see." He told her what had happened to Emile.

She seemed encouraged and agreed to struggle along, entering information on the computer, until he had a chance to speak to Sarah. Carrie left to go upstairs, Kahlua settled down onto his bed with a sigh and a groan, and Jordan started making phone calls to customers.

Blake sat at his desk, a mountain of paperwork in front of him, and stared off into space. He couldn't help himself.

In his mind's eye, he replayed the moment Sarah had walked away from him that morning. Her shiny caramel-colored hair fell down her back in loose waves, clinging to her curves like hot butterscotch on a scoop of vanilla. Her waist nipped in just the right amount above rounded hips and a beautiful derriere. Her long, slim legs went on forever. And that sway when she moved, as graceful as a ballet dancer.

His body began to respond, and he shook himself alert, clearing his throat and grabbing the brass blade he used to open envelopes. He leaned forward and dug into the pile of mail, reading it carefully, making notes, and sorting it into the baskets on his desk. He worked steadily for the next hour.

All the while, he was thinking about something else entirely.

Chapter 5

Sarah drove home to her eggplant, turquoise, and teal-blue "painted lady" Victorian house and arrived just as the school bus was pulling away. She'd decided not to say anything to Devon about his great-grandfather's condition until she knew for sure what was happening. Devon tended toward the hyperemotional, and there was no point in worrying her son unnecessarily. When Sarah dialed her cousin's number, Paisley's cell phone rang and rang, eventually switching over to voice mail. Her hands gripped the steering wheel too tight, the frown lines deepening between her eyebrows.

Seven-year-old Devon stood at the curb, his poor little silhouette hunched over with exhaustion. His overstuffed backpack looked as if it was pulling him down to the ground. The full day at school was hard on him, and the school psychologist said that to help moderate his AD-HD, it was important he not get hungry or dehydrated. Sarah turned in to the driveway and stopped, opening the driver's window.

"Howdy, stranger," she said in a cowboy accent, tipping an imaginary hat. They'd been watching *Bonanza* reruns on TV lately, and Devon was fascinated by all things Western.

He turned and looked at her, his light-blue eyes and pale-blond hair nearly translucent in the sunlight. About to finish second grade, he was still small for his age and had the otherworldly air of an elf or an angel. When their eyes met, a spasm of love made Sarah's throat ache.

"Howdy, ma'am. Do you know where a cowpoke can get some cookies and milk around here?" Devon answered in a piping voice, letting the backpack slide off his shoulders until it thumped on the ground. His pants nearly went with it.

He ran over to her, one hand holding up his jeans and the other dragging the backpack by one strap like a ball and chain. His denim jacket was tied precariously around his waist by the sleeves. Devon pushed his glasses firmly onto the bridge of his nose, hitched his pants, and held the edge of the car door to tiptoe up and kiss Sarah hello, which she figured was probably considered okay because nobody was around to see.

"Meet me at the back door, sir, and I'll be happy to serve you in my saloon." Sarah looked down and noticed his hair already needed trimming again.

He hefted up his backpack and shoved it through the car window onto her lap then ran ahead across the lawn. Sarah drove into the detached garage and parked. She found Devon sitting on the steps outside the kitchen door, his head in his hands.

"You look tired, pumpkin." She automatically felt his forehead to check his temperature. She saw his leg jiggling and watched as his foot tapped.

"I'm okay." He shook off her hand and jumped up. "Just hungry."

"Coming right up, sir!"

"That's more like it." His voice was grumpy, and he scowled.

Devon opened the screen door and held it while she used her key. They could hear Hershey whining and grunting inside. Devon rushed in and dumped his jacket on the floor, heading straight into the bathroom and slamming the door. She brought his backpack inside and put it on the kitchen table then picked up the jacket to hang it on a hook in the entryway.

The chocolate Lab greeted Sarah with ecstatic kisses, dancing left and right. She let him out into the fenced portion of the backyard. He lifted his leg next to several bushes then raced over to the maple tree where a family of squirrels lived, barking in a deep voice as he chased them up into the branches.

Sarah loved her sunny country kitchen. Warm and inviting, it was the heart of the antique house that she had lovingly restored, bit by bit, over the past ten years. She remembered how it looked when she and her ex-husband, Jim, had first bought the 1890s Victorian. It had been falling apart and shedding paint from every peeling surface. Now there was only the guest bedroom left to renovate, and she had done most of the work herself.

Jim had never been interested in working on the place, but Sarah always enjoyed it. By now she had her DNA embedded into nearly every wall of the home she and Devon had made here in Ashford. Her blood, sweat, and tears, literally. She'd cut her fingers fixing broken window-panes and bled on the sills. She'd stripped wallpaper in her underwear during the dog days of summer and dripped sweat on the wood floors. And she'd cried into the paint tray on the night it finally hit her that Jim was probably never going to apologize and come home.

She'd called him that night as a last resort. When he answered, he sounded surly.

"Don't you want to see your son sometime?" she'd asked, trying to stop her voice from trembling.

"That weird kid is all yours. He may have a couple of my genes, but we're nothing alike. He's a total loser." He'd laughed, a cruel, mocking sound.

She'd gasped, unable to reply.

"Look, far as I'm concerned, we're done. I'll pay the child support. Don't expect any trips to Disneyland or father–son picnics, okay?" Then he'd hung up.

The tears had come next, everything she'd been holding inside. For her and for Devon. Her sweet, precious boy. He deserved so much more. She would give him what she could and keep him safe under her wing as long as possible. Someday, he would want to know more about his father, and she'd have to come up with an answer. But until then, she had windows to caulk and walls to paint.

Sarah's interior palette ran from earth tones on the ground floor to forest hues on the second floor to celestial blues on the third, where the bedroom and bath she rented out were perched. Their home was like a giant tree house with its roots in the soil and leafy branches reaching up into the sky.

Sarah ran a hand over the cool granite island as she walked to the fridge. She poured a glass of almond milk and put it on the serving counter with the cookie jar as Devon burst out of the bathroom, loped across the room, and climbed up onto one of the tall stools. After gulping the drink noisily, he put the glass down and breathed a dramatic sigh then pretended to collapse on the countertop. He gave a theatrical moan, turning up his eyeballs so the whites showed.

"Tough day, pardner?" Sarah observed, turning on the electric kettle.

"Very tough." He sat up and reached for a cookie, homemade by Sarah from a special new recipe. These oatmeal cookies were gluten free and sweetened with raw agave nectar, studded with pecans and a few dark chocolate chips. The high protein and low glycemic load was supposed to stop him from getting so hyper.

"What happened at school today?" Sarah opened the cupboard and got a mug, watching him out of the corner of her eye.

"Spelling test!" He spoke in dire tones, hiding his face in his forearm.

"I see. And this did not go well?" Sarah got a tea bag and calmly spooned honey into her mug, never very worried about Devon's actual schoolwork. Like lots of kids with learning disabilities who wondered why their fathers had suddenly disappeared from their lives, Devon was a child whose problems tended to be more social than academic.

"No. I only got a... A-plus! Ha ha!" He dropped his arm and grinned at her, bouncing on his stool.

"Woo-hoo! Congratulations! You were fooling me, weren't you?"

"It was a joke, Mom. Got you."

She ruffled his wispy blond hair, touched by how unbearably cute he was. "I'm proud of you, Devon. Good work." She looked him in the eye and nodded.

"I always get an A-plus in spelling." He grinned and swung his feet while picking the chocolate chips out of his cookies to eat them first.

"You're a great speller and a great joker. The greatest."

Pushing his luck, he glanced at her slyly from under his long bangs. "Can I watch a little bit of cartoons now? It's the weekend."

"Okay, old sport. What do you want for supper?"

"Macaroni and hot dogs," he said decisively. Then he finished the milk in one long swig and ran into the adjoining TV room to flop down on the couch and grab the remote.

"You've got it, my boy. Early supper and then dog walking with Miki. She'll be home soon."

Currently their third floor was occupied by a college student from Japan. Miki had ragged animé-style black hair that usually sported a few green, red, or purple streaks, and she shared Devon's obsession with video games. Sarah traded free room and board for childcare.

Sarah unzipped Devon's backpack and sorted through the papers inside. With the homework, crayon drawings, and the A-plus spelling test was a flyer printed on bright-orange paper:

Baseball Playoffs Start This Weekend!
Meet Your Coaches at Johnson School Field
Saturday at 10:00 AM

The flyer reminded her that Devon had a big game tomorrow, so she went into the laundry room to make sure his yellow team T-shirt had been washed. Moving one load into the dryer and starting another in the washer, she wondered again what was happening over at the hospital and wished her cell phone would ring.

Sarah went to the back door and called the dog in, telling him to "Sit!" for a liver snack. He gazed up at her adoringly, devoted slave forever. His toenails clicked on the floor as he crossed the kitchen to lie down by Devon in front of the television.

Taking her cup of tea, Sarah climbed the stairs to her cool, comforting bedroom and kicked off her shoes. Her room was shaded by the leafy limbs of an ancient oak that sheltered the south side of the house. The pale, translucent color of the green light bouncing off sage-green walls was wonderfully soothing. She breathed in the color and slowly let it out, noticing how the tension in her body released. After putting her cup on the lamp table, she threw herself across the bed. Her mind raced over the day's events. Blake Harrison's face hovered in her imagination, and she noticed that her lips had involuntarily curled into a smile.

Sarah yawned and rubbed her temples then wondered again how Emile was doing and reached for the phone.

This time her cousin answered right away. Sarah could hear voices in the background and the sound of an intercom. Paisley said she was in the emergency room, waiting for Emile to come back from having an ultrasound test on his heart.

"What are they saying?" Sarah asked, sitting up to pay closer attention.

"The blood test showed he did have a small heart attack, but it's probably not too bad. He has to take it easy for a while and take some new meds. It's a wake-up call. He's been working too hard, not exercising enough. They want to keep him tonight, maybe longer. They're checking for blockages or a valve problem. That could change the picture, if they find something."

"Give Grandpa a kiss from me, all right? Tell him not to worry. Everything is under control. The boys are going to cook. It will be fine. Take your time."

Paisley laughed, but she sounded nervous. "Those two in charge of the kitchen on a Friday night? Are you crazy? I can't tell him that. He'll have a massive coronary!"

"Okay, don't mention it, then. You know you're a terrible liar. Maybe he won't ask."

"I suppose they can do it," Paisley said. "Tell the customers we're having an emergency. Cut the menu down to the simple stuff. No souf-flés! And have Raoul make the chocolate chili tonight. He's done it be-fore."

Sarah tried to reassure her. "He's already working on it. The cus-tomers will be fine, so don't worry. Call me later, okay? After the rush? And call me right away if anything happens. I'll keep my cell on vi-brate."

"I'm sure you'll do great. Talk to you soon."

Sarah dragged herself off the bed to take a shower and dress for work in slim black slacks and a white tuxedo shirt. She smoothed her hair up into a French twist and anchored it securely then pulled a cou-ple of pale-gold tendrils down to soften the look. The big diamond studs that Jim had splurged on for her thirtieth birthday completed the picture. She stood in front of the sink to do her makeup, worrying about Emile and the night ahead. Her face looked pale and tense.

Despite the assurances she'd given Paisley, she was by no means cer-tain the evening would be a success. She hoped to be able to tell her grandfather the next day that she'd handled everything easily, and he could be proud of her. Luckily, for most of their customers, dinner was just a prelude leading up to the orgasmic moment of glory at the end of the meal—a flute of champagne and something dark, sweet, and smooth. The combination was pure magic, putting a smile on every-one's lips and sending them home to enjoy the heightened sexual plea-sure it inspired. As long as Sarah could supply plenty of Paisley's choco-late fantasies and the bar held out, customers would be happy. Every-thing would be *just fine*.

Weren't those famous last words?

Chapter 6

S arah smoothed the deep worry line between her brows, pushing with one finger. She carefully applied some blusher to her cheeks, then eye makeup. It was war paint, magical armor. Tonight she had to be strong, even if Blake stopped by to check on Emile and she was tempted to flirt. Somehow, she had to resist eating chocolate until later, when she went home.

The problem was, a chocolate high sent Sarah exquisitely out of control and filled her with yearning. While under the influence, she had been known to do things later regretted.

Like hooking up with her ex-husband, for example. The first time they had sex was on Valentine's Day, after he had wined, dined, and seduced her with incredible Valrhona truffles. She'd forgotten the sex by now, but she could still taste those truffles. It made her go all dreamy just to think of them, but then her eyes filled with tears.

Thinking about Jim always made her feel the same way it had when her father teased her about pimples or the braces on her teeth. A twist of anxiety throbbed in her stomach, with a sense of failure that brought tears to her eyes. She'd never been perfect enough for Dad. He hadn't cared that she got straight As, was captain of the debate team, and could sell ice to Eskimos. He got a little excited when she tried out for the basketball team, as she knew he would, but she hadn't been picked, and that seemed to make it worse. He was disappointed in her again. Initially, because she wasn't a boy, and next, because she wasn't an athlete. Sarah kept trying, but the things she was good at just didn't impress Dad.

They didn't impress Jim, either. In fact, it seemed to irritate him when she was promoted to the top level of executives at the ad agency where she worked after college. He made fun of her job, accusing her of using sex appeal to lure clients into signing contracts. Her intelligence and creativity didn't seem to count for anything with Jim. He'd belittled her accomplishments, bragged about his own, and changed the subject.

Just like her father, who had always made an embarrassing big deal of her shortcomings. She'd struggled to live up to his standards, but it was hopeless. Then one day, Dad left for work and never came back. He had a stroke at his desk, and his secretary found him dead when she delivered his lunch. Sarah never had the chance to make him proud. When Jim disappeared from her life too, it felt like history repeating itself. Once again, she had failed.

She never saw it coming. With a three-year-old in day care, an old house in mid-restoration, and her high-pressure job, she'd thought it natural for Jim to be taking business trips alone. She hired a housekeeper and a lawn service, and he went to Miami, Atlanta, Chicago, and Las Vegas.

Then one evening, the travel agency called. She could still replay the conversation in her head. They had a question about the ticket for Ms. Sherry Smith. Was that a round trip from Miami to Las Vegas direct, or via the same two stops that Mr. Westwood's ticket included?

Sarah said she had no idea, but it wasn't really true. She had a lot of ideas. She overflowed with them, in fact.

All night long.

The next morning, Sarah went straight downtown and withdrew all of their savings then set up a new personal account at another bank. She removed the contents of their safe-deposit box and took everything with her to the office, where her secretary locked it away. Then Sarah called the credit card companies and reported all their cards stolen, closing the accounts. She opened a new one in her name alone and had the card sent via FedEx overnight.

Then she waited.

It could all be undone if there was some mistake. He was due home in a few days.

Sarah's only mistake was not changing the locks on the house. He came in while she was at work and took away his things, the Oriental rugs, and all the sterling silver their families gave them when they got married.

But he left Devon. And that was worth so much more than everything else, Sarah had never regretted the way things ended up. Even though she'd been laid off from her corporate job and now struggled to pay the mortgage with only sporadic child-support checks and a much smaller paycheck than she was used to.

She went downstairs and found Miki and Devon playing a game on the wide-screen TV. They paused it to say goodbye to her.

"Don't worry. Have a good night!" Miki called out. Her hair had purple streaks today, and it matched her purple hoodie and striped socks.

"Night, Mom. Bring me something good." Devon loved the leftover food from the restaurant. Their home had the best-stocked refrigerator on the block.

"Will do, sweetie." Sarah gave him a hug and kiss, slipped into her denim jacket, and went to work.

BLAKE LOOKED AT HIS watch for the third time in ten minutes. He pushed Send on the private message window and closed his laptop with a snap. When Sarah checked her phone, a note would be waiting for her at the online dating site. She would likely check it pretty soon, because it was nearly eleven, and he knew the restaurant had stopped taking dinner orders at ten. He had happened to be passing by several times to walk his dog and noticed her routine. Okay, he'd been stalking her, but only in the nicest possible way. He was waiting for a chance to get her to open up. Tonight might be his chance, since they had shared a personal moment earlier and were both concerned about Emile.

He snapped a leash on Kahlua's collar and went outside then walked down the steps from his townhouse, just a few blocks from the restaurant. He broke into an easy jog, the Lab trotting by his side as they moved down the sidewalk toward the river. When they came to the restaurant, he stopped, standing in the shadows while he looked through the windows.

Sarah stood behind the bar, pouring herself a tall glass of water. She was still wearing her long chocolate-brown French waiter's apron, but she'd unpinned the updo she wore while working and let her hair flow free. It rippled down her back as she tipped her chin to drink. Blake tried to catch his breath from jogging, but the sight of her standing like that, her breasts thrust forward as she bent back her head, seemed to make it impossible. His pulse pounded.

What a pathetic doofus you are, he thought, simmering with frustration. *Get a grip!*

Two waiters wiped down the dining room tables and chairs, while a third ran the vacuum. They'd already turned off the lights in the front windows and foyer. At the back of the room, he could see through the open door into the brightly lit kitchen. Empty dish racks were lined up before the Hobart, which billowed steam from what looked like the last load. He could hear that somebody had turned off the dinner music and put on a mellow jazz CD. Jerome was singing along with the vocalist.

Blake pulled the dog after him to cross the street, walk toward the river, then cross back over to stand by the restaurant door. Now it looked as if he was coming from the other direction and had stopped on the way home to his condo down the street.

That's better, he thought. *Don't let her see how desperate you are.*

He resolved to keep his cool, no matter what. No matter how sexy she looked right now, for example, bending over to unload bottles from a case of wine.

Blake's self-confidence vanished in a flash, but somehow he managed to step forward and tap on the glass door.

THE EVENING HAD GONE well, and Sarah was exhausted. They'd been mobbed, and being two chefs short in the kitchen while the whole staff was distracted by worrying about Emile really put the pressure on everyone. She stood up, her arms filled with wine bottles, and took them behind the bar to slide into the wooden rack. Turning around to check on the cleaning crew, she heard a knock on the front door.

Blake Harrison stood outside on the sidewalk. Standing next to him was a chocolate Lab who looked a lot like Hershey, wearing a red collar and leash. The dog gazed at her through the glass and wagged his tail.

She went over and unlocked the door.

"Hey, buddy, who are you?" she said to the dog, patting his head when he nudged her hand. "He's beautiful, just like mine! I have a chocolate Lab too."

Blake continued to stand outside the open door. "Oh? Yeah, he's a good boy. Kahlua seems to like you." He held the leash taut so the animal's paws didn't cross the line into the restaurant, where pets were not allowed. "I just wanted to check on Emile. Took this guy for a walk down by the river, so we were passing by. How's your grandfather?"

The dog sat, and Sarah bent over to shake the paw he offered. "He's okay, for now. They're keeping him tonight, maybe longer. Paisley isn't back yet." She stood up, and so did the dog, tugging Blake forward with a jerk so that he stepped right beside her.

She inhaled the scent of something delicious. "Mmmm," she hummed before she could stop herself, her eyes falling shut. "You smell great. What kind of ice cream were you making today, may I ask?"

Her mouth watered, and she swallowed, then she opened her eyes and looked up at him. She was tall, but he was taller, and it was nice to be the little one for a change. Next to Paisley and Emile, the petite French side of the family, Sarah was used to feeling like a clumsy giant.

"Strawberry with fudge swirls." Blake's eyes glowed in the light from a nearby streetlamp, and he smiled. His shoulder muscles moved under his shirt as he controlled the dog, who bounced eagerly toward her again.

Before she had a chance to talk herself out of it, Sarah said, "Want to come in for a quick drink? We're just finishing up."

"Sure, let me just take this guy back to my place real quick. It's close."

Blake disappeared down the sidewalk, and she went inside, removing her apron then ducking behind the bar to get a cocktail shaker and two martini glasses. Just one drink, and then she would kick him out. She shouldn't, but he was so appealing. And it was nice of him to stop by and ask about Emile. She owed him this much.

Sarah's low energy level was crying out for chocolate and alcohol. She struggled with the craving for a moment then caved in. When Blake reappeared a few minutes later, she was assembling the ingredients for one of her favorite cocktails: crème de menthe, crème de cacao, Kahlua, vodka, and light cream, shaken with ice and served straight up, garnished with a thin curl of dark chocolate and a mint leaf from Emile's herb garden in the building's rooftop greenhouse.

Blake sat on a barstool and watched her mix the potion, one of his eyebrows rising higher and higher. When she threw in the third and then the fourth shot of liquor, his eyes blinked in obvious amazement.

"Whoa!"

"If you're only having one drink"—she put the lid on the shaker and rattled it briskly—"you may as well make it a doozy!" She told him the name of the cocktail, Mocha Mint Madness.

"Can't wait to try it." He leaned forward on his elbows. His sleeves were rolled up, as usual, and she noticed his muscular forearms were strong and defined. "I could use a little madness about now. I started early today." He rubbed his eyes with the heels of his palms.

Sarah held the strainer over the mouth of the shaker, poured the frothy brown liquid into the glasses and added the garnishes. They picked up their drinks and looked into each other's eyes across the bar. Sarah felt a fizzy electric charge shoot through her, starting in her brain and ending up in sparks all over her body.

Blake raised his glass. "To Emile, may he heal quickly."

"To Grandpa."

Their glasses clinked, and Sarah tasted Nirvana. The sugar and cream masked the bite of the spirits, and the dark flavor of chocolate lay smooth and rich under the refreshing perkiness of the mint. A moment later, the double kick of cacao and alcohol hit her, and she started to loosen up. Her cheeks grew warm, and she knew without looking in the mirror behind the bar that they were rosy. She unfastened the top two buttons of her tuxedo shirt.

Blake watched all of this with obvious interest. He dragged his gaze away from her flushed cleavage and scrutinized her face. "So, what do you like to do when you aren't working?" He put his hand on the bar, a scant centimeter away from hers, their fingers almost touching.

Tingling energy filled the space between them. His eyes were the cool deep color of shadows on grass, and Sarah started to float away into them, then she remembered he'd asked her a question.

"Me?" She smiled. "Oh, mostly I hang out with my son, Devon. I'm a single mom, you know."

"I heard. Just me and Kahlua at my place. He's chatty, but his vocabulary is limited."

"Woofs and growls can be very expressive. Hershey actually moans when I rub his tummy." She cocked one eyebrow, waiting to see if he'd take the bait.

"Hmmm. I can imagine why." He flashed her a sly glance and played along. "But the trouble is, my dog is addicted to *National Geographic* specials, and I prefer a good mystery."

"Me too. Sherlock Holmes is the best."

"Yes!" He nodded. "The old black and whites, with Basil Rathbone. Kahlua does like that fellow's name, especially the 'bone' part."

Sarah laughed. "*The Scarlet Claw. Hound of the Baskervilles.* He should love those."

They both grinned, and she giggled. The cocktails were slipping down very smoothly. She poured them each a tad more, emptying the shaker. Then she got caught up in watching the way the muscles in his forearm flexed when he picked up his glass and raised it to his lips. His fingers were long and slim.

"Where do you live, Sarah?"

She widened her eyes, coming back to reality as the zip of chocolate percolated through her veins.

"Up on Franklin. The old blue-and-purple Victorian. Come over for a tour sometime."

How about tonight? she thought. *I'll give you a personal tour.*

"The huge one?" he said. "With the fish-scale trim and the big porch? That place is enormous. How do you find time to take care of it?"

"I do my best. With whatever assistance a seven-year-old can offer, that is. He's great about pitching in, just kind of easily distracted."

Sarah thought about the last time Devon had tried to help her, when he'd had one of his meltdowns that ended with a crying jag. But this guy didn't want to hear about her parenting problems. He was probably used to single women with tons of freedom who could take him home to bed whenever the spirit moved them.

As it was undeniably moving her right now. She leaned toward him, noticing his eyes flicker to her breasts as they rested on her folded arms. A little bubble of intimacy had formed around Sarah and Blake, filled with the spicy scent of mint and cocoa.

"Yes," Blake said, "I remember that age. I was lost in fantasyland most of the time."

"At the moment, he thinks he's Little Joe from *Bonanza*," she said. "He wants me to get him cowboy boots and a pinto pony."

That's the way to play it, Sarah thought. *Focus on the cute things about having a kid. Maybe he won't be scared off right away. The stretch marks on my belly will take care of that, if he ever gets close enough to see.*

"Cool, he could keep it in the garage, right? And ride it to school?" Blake nodded with approval.

"You got it. Think of all the gas money I could save."

"You're lucky, Sarah. You know that?"

"I guess." She looked at him with wonder. *Lucky?* A painful reflex in the pit of her stomach signaled the memory of loss. Then she took another sip of her chocolate cocktail, and a warm glow eased the sensation.

Chatting about the townhouse he owned in the building next to the bank and how hard it was to remove old paint from woodwork, they finished their drinks and ate the chocolate curls, the cocoa butter melting on their tongues. Blake shivered, closing his eyes in an exaggerated swoon. Sarah watched him with a mixture of delight and fear.

"Hey, guys, how's it going?"

Her voice sounding hoarse and strained, Paisley walked in from the kitchen, followed by her current boyfriend, Wayne Gallaway, the restaurant's wine supplier. He was carrying a bottle of red under his arm and went behind the bar to pull the cork. Sarah and Blake shook their heads when he offered them a glass, while Paisley nodded and smiled. She gave Sarah a curious glance.

Paisley answered questions about Emile while Wayne poured the wine into two rounded goblets. He slid a glass over to her, and she took a sip. "Wow, that's great!"

"Our new Pinot." Wayne showed her the label. "When do they think he can come back to work?"

"They need to do more tests, but the echocardiogram went well. He definitely needs to take it easy. Real easy. He can't work in the kitchen until further notice, and he can't do the wedding job. That's the bottom line." She looked at Sarah. "I called my brother and my parents, by the way. Dad was going to call your mom. He offered to come tonight, but I said no, let's wait and see how Grandpa does. Dad can't just walk out on his job like that, and it's been a long time since he cooked professionally. He'd probably be more trouble in the kitchen than help. I can bake and cook, but I can't charm the clients and run everything. If you don't handle the chocolate wedding, we're screwed."

Sarah's stomach lurched, and her forehead started to sweat. "Um, okay, I guess. If you guys help me. I have no idea what's involved or even what the food safety issues are. We don't want to poison anyone, right?"

Paisley spoke in soothing tones. "That's my girl! We'll teach you everything you need to know, have no fear. You've always been a quick study, and nobody is expecting you to actually cook anything."

"That's a relief, huh?" Sarah remembered the last time she'd tried to help in the kitchen. She did not cook well under pressure.

Blake stood and excused himself, saying he had to be up early in the morning to make deliveries. He thanked Sarah for the drink and said how glad he was that Emile was feeling better. Sarah walked him to the front door.

"See you soon," he said with a funny expression on his face. His cheeks were flushed, and his eyes glittered in the dim light. He looked as if he had something else to say.

Oh no, Sarah thought, her heart pounding. *He's going to ask me out. I flirted with him, and now I'm in trouble. I like him, and he's so cute, but can I trust him? Will it end badly again?*

She quickly stepped inside and closed the door, waving cheerfully. His eyes stared through the glass as she turned the dead bolt, and he hesitated then raised a hand in farewell and turned away.

Blake walked down the sidewalk into the darkness, but as she stood just inside the doorway, watching him go, the tantalizing scent of strawberries and chocolate lingered on.

Chapter 7

Afer tossing and turning for over an hour, Sarah couldn't stand it anymore.

She pulled her laptop out of its case and switched it on. The melodic chord that sounded when she pushed the start button made her glance toward the bedroom door with a guilty wince, listening carefully. The house was silent, but she got up and tiptoed across the hall to Devon's door and peeked in.

He lay sprawled on his back, one leg under the covers and one leg out. With every exhalation, a cute little snore burbled from his lips.

Sarah sneaked back to her room and quietly closed the door behind her. After climbing into bed, she propped herself up on the pillows and slid the computer onto her lap. Telling herself she was just going to check on the restaurant account, she opened her iMail program and clicked on that mailbox. She had a few notes from vendors and customers who had heard about Emile's illness, and a little junk mail. She worked her way down the list then let her eyes wander over to the sidebar on the left. One unread email was waiting in her personal mailbox. She clicked on the icon, a prickle of anticipation flashing through her.

It said she had mail from HotNCold at the online dating site, and the subject line read, "Meet Me Tonight?"

Her throat clenched, and she stopped breathing for a moment, staring at the monitor.

But then her hand reached out, seemingly all on its own, and clicked the hyperlink. She logged in to the dating site as CocoLvr and read the note waiting there.

HotNCold: *Sorry to duck out, phone rang and had to go. Another chance? Promise you won't be disappointed.*

Sarah stared at the screen, tapping her fingernail on the keypad. It was really her fault for answering his message the other night. She had definitely led him on. No reason to be nervous. She was in control. And nothing had even happened. Not really. Not yet.

Just then, a small window appeared at the top of her computer screen, and a chime sounded as a message appeared in the window. "You have a private message from HotNCold. Do you want to accept?"

He was online right now, trying to contact her. Her hand shook as she clicked "OK," and his greeting appeared in the window.

HotNCold: *Hi Coco. How's it going?*

She fumbled as she slowly typed her reply.

CocoLvr: *Good. And U?*

HotNCold: *Good. Sorry about the other nite.*

CocoLvr: *Me 2.*

She paused while she tried to think of an intriguing remark. She remembered what he had said and wondered if he always slept in the nude. This thought swept all intelligent conversation right out of her mind.

HotNCold : *U online for a while? Want to play?*

Yes! she thought.

CocoLvr: *Sure, I guess.*

HotNCold: *OK. What's your pleasure?*

Sarah thought frantically, but her brain wouldn't cooperate. She kept picturing a man's naked torso lit by the green glow of a laptop, crisp white sheets pulled up to his slim waist.

HotNCold: *Coco? Lover? You still there?*

CocoLvr: *Be right back. I mean... BRB.*

She sat back and took a quick inventory of her conflicted emotions. On one hand, she couldn't believe she was actually considering going through with this. But being anonymous was fun and exciting, like going to a costume party while wearing a great disguise. She could tell him she was a twenty-two-year-old flight attendant, or a famous science fiction writer, or a Playboy bunny. Whatever she said or did wouldn't be real, anyhow, since this was all a fantasy.

HotNCold: *;-)*

When she saw the wink appear on the screen, she put her hands on the keyboard.

CocoLvr: *Back. Hi Hot, good 2 C U again.*

She added an emoticon kiss.

HotNCold: *Welcome home.*

He added a cyber-hug.

CocoLvr: *Did you miss me?*

She imagined skin on skin as she slipped into his arms and they pressed their bodies together.

HotNCold: *Oh yeah baby. Big time!*

She could sense the smile in his words and smiled back.

CocoLvr: *The other night... It was soooo frustrating.*

HotNCold: *Just when we got started, poof!*

She pictured his eyebrows rising comically.

CocoLvr: *Yes, I was interrupted by... someone.*

HotNCold: *The boyfriend?*

CocoLvr: *Sort of.*

She didn't want to get into details about her personal life, especially about Devon.

HotNCold: *You single, Coco?*

CocoLvr: *Yes. Divorced, actually.*

HotNCold: *I'm single too. Never married though.*

CocoLvr: *How come?*

Now she was curious and a little worried.

HotNCold: *We lived together for a long time, then she dumped me.*

Hercules/Tarzan started to transform into someone more human, though still wildly handsome and wearing a similarly scanty loincloth.

CocoLvr: *Bummer. Sorry about that.*

HotNCold: *It's okay. For the best, I guess. I was just going along, ignoring reality. I thought we'd get married when we were ready to have kids.*

Now Sarah was picturing someone a lot more brotherly, possibly wearing glasses.

CocoLvr: *So, what happened?*

HotNCold: *She fell in love with someone else. She's having his kids. Twins, actually.*

CocoLvr: *Wow.*

HotNCold: *Yeah. We liked each other a lot, but we weren't really in love.*

She was impressed by his philosophical attitude.

CocoLvr: *So were you, like, devastated?*

HotNCold: *Disappointed. But in a way, relieved.*

Sara's mixed emotions about her breakup came back to the surface when she read his words.

CocoLvr: *I can relate to that.*

HotNCold: *Same for you? It's weird, isn't it? It's over and you fight it, can't stand for it to end, but then it does and you're secretly happy.*

Sarah remembered when she was finally able to begin leaving Jim's betrayal in the past and get on with her life.

CocoLvr: *You're not glad it happened, but you're sure glad it's over.*

HotNCold: *I hear you, sistah!*

CocoLvr: *LOL!*

She actually did laugh out loud.

HotNCold: *Coco? I have to work before the crack of dawn tomorrow. And here I've wasted all this time talking about myself... will you forgive me?*

Don't go! she thought.

CocoLvr: *Oh, sure. I mean, I enjoyed it.*

HotNCold: *Mind if we continue tomorrow night? Sorry I wandered off the subject.*

CocoLvr: *It's been fun to get to know you, Hot. We can have sex any old time, right?* :-)

HotNCold: *<Putting one hand on each side of her sweet face, he kisses her gently on the eyelids, the nose, then the lips.>*

CocoLvr: *Good night, Hot. C U tomorrow night.*

Sarah felt a goofy grin form as she stared at the screen, dreamy-eyed. He was such a nice guy. What a great vibe.

HotNCold: *<Slipping his tongue between her lips, he gives her a gentle taste of what is coming tomorrow night.>*

CocoLvr: *Yummy.*

Sarah smiled into the darkness of her bedroom, which was filled with his invisible presence.

HotNCold: *Bye, lover!"*

After that last message, his screen name disappeared from the Members Online list as he quit the program.

Sarah gazed at the inactive chat window for a minute while, in her mind's eye, Hercules/Tarzan closed the lid of his laptop and lay back in bed, his strong arms crossed behind his head. Moonlight shone on his skin and glinted off his dark eyes as he pictured her lying in her bed. How did he imagine her, she wondered. Blond? Brunette? African-American? Latina?

However he saw her, that was cool. Sarah was happy to look any way he wanted her to, in his mental pictures. And whatever they both looked like in real life didn't matter, because something else was drawing them together.

Their minds were attracted. She could sense him out there, on the other end of the keyboard somewhere in cyber-land, and she knew he could feel her too. It was powerful and electric, like being wired directly into each other's brains.

She had never experienced anything like this before. Absolutely intimate and as drop-dead sexy as hell. Her body pulsated, an ache between her legs.

After shutting down her laptop, Sarah put her hand into the drawer of her bedside table and pulled out a small plastic bag. Inside was a piece of almond bark candy made from marbled white and dark chocolate, scavenged from the kitchen at work. She popped a piece into her mouth and savored the flavor as the chocolate encountered her body heat and melted, spreading across her tongue. Closing her eyes, she trembled with pleasure.

Dark, sweet, crunchy... ecstasy.

A rush of blissful sensation flowed over her. Paisley had told her that the theobromine in cacao caused the same chemical response in the brain as sexual orgasm. According to her cousin, the connection between sex and chocolate wasn't mythological or urban legend but scientific fact. Whether or not this was true, Sarah had found chocolate to be downright addictive.

Her social life was getting more and more interesting every day. Honestly, it was enough to keep a girl up all night, wondering what was going to happen next.

JUST AS SARAH WAS DRIFTING off to sleep, Hershey suddenly barked, a single sharp explosion of sound. His toenails clicked as he raced from his bed to the open window, and she heard him sniffing. When they both heard the sound of scraping metal outside, the dog raced down the stairs, barking with passionate intensity. His deep voice echoed through the house.

Sarah sat up in bed, disoriented. The thud of Miki's feet hitting the floor came from upstairs, and Devon's sleepy voice called, "Mom?"

Sarah jumped out of bed and ran into the hallway as Miki thumped down the stairs, carrying her lacrosse stick. Devon appeared in his bedroom doorway, his eyes huge.

"Why is he barking, Mom?"

She didn't want to frighten him. "Probably just a skunk or something."

"I don't smell one, do you?" His voice was very high and squeaky.

"No, but—"

"What was that?" Miki said and jumped as they heard something crashing at the back of the house.

"The garbage cans. See, it's just an animal. Raccoon, maybe. They love to eat trash."

"Let's go find out," Devon said bravely. He glanced at Miki, who was waving her improvised weapon aloft. "Wait a second, Mom." He ran into his room and got his baseball bat. Carrying it in one hand, he slipped the other into Sarah's. "Okay. Ready."

They trooped down the stairs in a tight pack, turning on lights as they went.

Hershey continued to bark hysterically. When they arrived in the kitchen, he was throwing himself against the back door, frantic to get outside.

"Quick, open it!" Devon rushed to pull on the door handle.

"No, wait. If it's a porcupine, he might get hurt. Just hold on," Sarah said, turning on the outside lights. The two garbage cans that normally sat under the kitchen windows had tipped over on their sides and were rolling around in the driveway. No creatures were in sight.

"Looks like Hershey scared them away." Sarah got a leash from the hook by the door and snapped it onto the dog's collar. "Here, hold him while I see." She handed the leash to Miki.

After unlocking the back door, Sarah stepped outside. She looked both ways and peeked under the bushes. She saw no signs of raccoons, skunks, or feral cats, so she lifted the garbage cans up, straightened their lids, and dragged them back to their place.

Sarah noticed that one of the azalea bushes next to the foundation had some bent branches hanging down.

"Wonder what would do that." She went inside and locked the door behind her then moved to the window and pointed out the damage to Miki, who shrugged.

"Good boy!" She patted Hershey's head. He panted and grinned.

"Cookies 'n milk?" Devon suggested, his eyelids already drooping.

"No way, kiddo. Back to bed." Sarah picked him up and carried him up the stairs, noticing how heavy he had become, his long legs dangling as he lay over her shoulder.

Miki let Hershey off the leash and turned out the lights, following them. They wished each other good night, and Sarah took Devon to the bathroom for a quick pee before she tucked him under the covers.

Back in her own bedroom, Sarah sank down on the pillows and was soon asleep, unconcerned.

Chapter 8

The next morning, Blake woke up with a sense of purpose.

Last night's heart-to-heart proved that his attraction to Sarah went much deeper than how his body reacted when she walked across a room. He hadn't opened up like that to anyone for a long time. His style ran more to small talk and an air of coolness. He didn't like for people to get too close right away. The weird thing was that last night, it felt good. Not embarrassing at all. He wanted more.

Blake was definitely going after her, it was clear in his mind.

In person and on the internet, if necessary. This woman must be taken, under any circumstances. Taken and held. No way was he going to blow this chance. Strategy was required.

Maybe he could try to become more like the kind of guy she was looking for. Intuition said this was someone sensitive and loyal. That part would be easy. He already fit the description. All he had to do was peel back the gruff mask and let himself show. He could do it, with a little time to work up his courage.

But she probably also wanted someone cultured, intellectual, into French food and all that. A snappy dresser, like Jordan. Somebody who would take her to the opera.

Shit, that's never going to happen.

He'd have to get by on his good looks and amazing performance in bed.

Blake hummed a cheerful tune as he showered and shaved, grinning at himself in the steamy bathroom mirror. Then he realized how stupid he looked and tried to scowl. It didn't work, and all he could manage were puckered eyebrows and a silly smirk.

Whistling as he walked, Blake left Kahlua in the townhouse and drove his truck over to the Downtown Diner, where he was meeting his dad and brother for breakfast. When he went inside, he spotted them sitting in the usual booth, up front by the window.

"Yo," he said as he slid in next to Jordan. He smirked again, on purpose this time.

Jordan and their father looked at him suspiciously. His father put down the newspaper he'd been reading. Just turned sixty, with a long, lean body and only a few silver strands in his full head of brown hair, Blake's handsome dad still made female hearts flutter wherever he went. Even now, dressed for work at the construction site, he managed to look like a Ralph Lauren model. Blake wondered if he could get some of that to rub off real quick and thought of his wardrobe of worn clothes with a twinge of dismay.

"Feeling okay, son?" Sam Harrison grabbed his coffee cup by surrounding it with his big hand and lifted it to his mouth for a sip. He examined his oldest son's face. "You look... happy?" He tilted his head and raised his eyebrows.

Jordan leaned forward, holding his arms up to avoid dipping his immaculate cuffs into his scrambled eggs. He examined Blake's face and nodded. "I know that look. It means trouble." He turned and called to his buddies at nearby tables. "Lock up your women, boys! Blake's got the look!"

"Shut up, pipsqueak." Blake pulled his eyebrows together and managed a decent sneer, looking down from his two-inch advantage.

Jordan pulled back his head, rolling his eyes. At only six foot two, he was the smallest of the Harrison men, and Blake never let him forget it.

Sam lifted one finger and subtly signaled the pink-uniformed waitress, who jumped, blushed, and scurried across the room toward them. She stepped up and took Blake's order for waffles and bacon then poured him a cup of coffee before she moved away to refresh the other customers' cups.

"Something you want to talk about, son?" Sam tucked a napkin into the top of his shirt and took up a fork to dig into his pancakes. He paused, waiting for the reply.

Blake shook his head and lifted his cup the same way. "No, sir. Nothing special." He sneered at Jordan again, just to make his point.

Jordan threw up his hands in surrender.

Then as Blake began to daydream again about his two-pronged plan of attack, his father and brother chatted about the energy-efficient house Sam was building down by the river for a client. They had just moved on to talking about the proposed addition onto the Shoe Factory, as everyone still called it even though the sign out front said Riverside Commons, when Blake's breakfast arrived, and they all paused for a few minutes of serious eating. For the Harrison men, this meant consuming every bite at record speed and wiping the plate clean.

"Blake." His father got his attention. "Your mother asked me to deliver a message."

"Oh?"

"Get your sister a job at that fancy restaurant, or else."

"Or else what?"

Jordan answered. "You'll be on the Black List." He shivered.

"God forbid, son." Sam looked at him with sympathy, shaking his head.

Blake sighed, thinking of his mother, Maggie, and her dramatic Irish temper. "Yes, sir. I'll go over there right away." He realized this was a perfect excuse to put his plan in motion. He'd check on Sarah, chat her up. "No problem. Want to find out how Emile is doing, anyhow."

Jordan looked at him with a slightly confused expression, as if he'd caught a whiff of something he couldn't quite identify.

Blake threw some bills on the table and stood up, saying goodbye to his dad with a slap on the shoulder. He sneered at his brother one last time for good measure. "See you later, pipsqueak." He walked across the room, whistling, and flipped Jordan the bird on his way out the door.

She'd be in the kitchen about now, getting ready to print out the specials and check the phone messages. He knew right where to find her, and this time, he wasn't going to let her run away.

Chapter 9

Two days later, Emile was released from the hospital. That morning, Paisley went to bring him home, and Sarah planned to meet them at his apartment above the restaurant.

Originally built in the early 1900s, the brick building had a wine cellar and storage area in the basement, the restaurant and kitchen on the ground floor, Emile's spacious apartment on the second floor, and Paisley's tiny studio on the top floor, where a door led outside onto a flat rooftop. The chicken coop and greenhouse there supplied the restaurant with fresh eggs, herbs, and greens.

Whenever Sarah entered her grandparents' home, she thought of Grandma Annie. Despite the fact that this venerable lady had passed away more than five years ago, Annie's apron still hung on a hook in the kitchen, her perfume and silver combs still adorned the bedroom dressing table, and her loving spirit lingered.

Sarah imagined she felt the brush of a ghostly kiss against her cheek when she walked through the door, as if the space had welcomed her. She tidied up and changed the sheets on Emile's bed, listening for the sound of the elevator coming up from downstairs. The peculiar silence that came just after a voice had finished speaking vibrated in her ears as she moved from room to room, preparing for Emile's arrival. It was as though Annie were there with her, holding the other end of the blanket and helping smooth the pillowcases.

"Okay, Grandma. I get it. We need to watch him carefully, or he'll be downstairs, baking brioches at five o'clock in the morning."

The atmosphere seemed to swell and warm as the sunshine brightened, and a tiny waft of cinnamon led Sarah to the kitchen. She filled the kettle and put it on to boil then cleaned out the refrigerator and threw away everything that had expired. She took the garbage down-stairs to the dumpster in the alley, picked up a plate of Paisley's choco-late scones from the kitchen, and climbed back up the stairs.

On her way, she checked to make sure Blake Harrison wasn't lurk-ing around again, as he had been the past couple of mornings. They'd already discussed the chocolate wedding and his sister's need for a job. Yesterday, she'd hired Carrie to work as hostess for the summer so Sarah would be free to deal with other things during Emile's absence. There really wasn't anything left to talk about, except town gossip or the weather, but Paisley was betting he'd be back today, anyhow. The idea both delighted and terrified Sarah. She was relieved when she reached the apartment without bumping into him.

Her flourishing new cyber-relationship was about all the intimacy she could handle right now. Meeting HotNCold online had become a nightly ritual, but they still hadn't come around to actual cybersex. The incredible dialogue they were having kept them together until late. At that point, a quick emoticon kiss was the best farewell. But tonight was going to be special, he had promised. She wondered what he had in mind.

Sarah heard the elevator coming up from the ground floor parking lot entrance, bringing with it the sound of her cousin and grandfather arguing. Reassured by this familiar dynamic, Sarah waited in the sec-ond-floor hallway. As they approached, she could make out what they were saying.

"Grandpa, we're going to do exactly what the doctor said."

"But... the wedding? We'll lose our shirts."

"I told you, we've got it covered. Nothing to worry about. You trained us well."

"Paisley, dear, it's too much for her to learn so quickly..."

Their voices paused as they reached the landing, and the gears en-gaged to open the door. They were frozen in an awkward tableau as it slid to the right, their faces suddenly smiling when they saw Sarah waiting there.

She knew what they'd been talking about, of course. The idea that in just a few weeks she could learn enough to run a big chocolate catering job was crazy. The thought made her break out in a sweat.

"Grandpa! Welcome home." Sarah stepped forward to kiss him.

He folded her into a hug and patted her on the back. She felt him trembling slightly and reached around to support him. With Paisley holding one arm and Sarah on the other, Emile entered the apartment living room and sank into his favorite armchair in front of the window. Sarah had already put the newspapers from the past few days on his lamp table.

"Glad to be home?" Paisley pulled up the footstool for him and covered his legs with a knitted afghan.

"Ah," he said, sinking into the cushions. "That's more like it." A blissful smile creased his face, lined by many years of living life with gusto.

Sarah went into the kitchen and returned with chamomile tea and scones. She put the tray on a low table and passed around steaming mugs then sat on the sofa with her legs curled beneath her.

"Heaven," Emile murmured. "Though I'd rather have a glass of pinot noir."

Paisley gave him a stern but loving look. "Grandpa, you know what the doctor said. No alcohol." She turned to Sarah. "He can't drink at all anymore, no caffeine, and he's on a low-fat, low-salt diet. There are two new medications for him to take. More tests coming up soon."

Emile sighed and pouted. "How can you expect a French chef not to cook with butter? It's ridiculous."

Sarah teased him. "You and Devon can have a pity party. He's not thrilled with his dietary restrictions at the moment, either. He's off sugar, lactose, and gluten."

"Between the two of us, we can't eat anything at all! It's a conspiracy to starve off all the men in the family. How can we ever manage this?" Emile looked stricken, his eyes tearing up.

Paisley patted his hand. "Don't worry so much, old man. The women of the family have everything under control, right, Sarah? New recipes are in progress as we speak. We're very creative!"

"At least we can still cook normal food for the restaurant, so my fifty years of experience isn't all wasted," Emile said.

His granddaughters exchanged a glance.

"About the restaurant," Paisley began, but she seemed to chicken out. She looked down and fiddled with her fingernails then glanced at her cousin.

"Since you can't work in the kitchen for a little while"—Sarah spoke in a confident tone, though she was totally winging it—"it's a perfect time for you to tutor me. You know I'll never be able to run the chocolate wedding without lots of help, Grandpa. It's going to be a ton of work."

He stopped grumbling and seemed to consider what she had said.

"I suppose there is quite a bit of organizing that I can do right here, from this chair."

Sarah encouraged him. "That's right! You'll be the brains. I'll do the running around and handle the crazy clients."

"But don't think you just get to sit on your *derrière* the whole time," Paisley said. "We've got to get you out walking every day too. Doctor's orders."

"Maybe Hershey can help with that," Sarah suggested. "He loves to stroll around downtown and visit the shopkeepers, but he needs a chaperone. It sounds like a win-win to me."

Emile started to look less anxious, his face relaxing. "Brilliant. You two are quite a pair of conspirators, aren't you?"

"We love you, Grandpa." Paisley leaned toward him. "You should let us take care of you."

"All right, then. Sarah, bring me everything from the top shelf of the bookcase, and I'll give you some reading assignments. Paisley, get down to the kitchen and start figuring out what you're going to cook for lunch that won't make me gag. I suppose we'll get through this."

Sarah put her hand on top of his, and Paisley added hers on top of both, a ritual from their childhood. Their fingers intertwined in a three-way squeeze, and Sarah realized that now she was really going to have to go through with it.

Crash course in food safety and cocoa cookery, coming right up, she thought. *But what if I'm not good enough? What if I ruin everything?*

Inside Sarah's head, Grandma Annie's voice was like the sound of a distant bell.

"It is what it is, dear," Annie had always said.

I know, Grandma, Sarah thought. *Don't worry. I'll try.*

A shaft of sunlight shot in through the window and dazzled her for a moment. She squinted, and when she looked at her grandfather, a glowing shape seemed to embrace his shoulders for a moment, gilded by the backlighting. Then it flickered and was gone.

Focused on the wedding, Emile and Paisley were already making lists and discussing an electrical plan to accommodate the lighting and refrigeration needs. Emile dog-eared several chapters in his books and handed them to Sarah, peeking at her over his reading glasses.

"We'll discuss these tomorrow at lunchtime," he said. "Start paying attention when Paisley cooks. She'll teach you a lot if you watch and ask questions."

"Okay, I'll start on the books tonight, my night off. But Devon has a game this afternoon, so I need to get home."

Remembering her "date" with HotNCold tonight, Sarah wondered how to manage everything. She didn't want to let Emile down, but no way did she intend to miss the closest thing she had to a social life.

Luckily, she had always been an excellent multitasker. And it seemed appropriate that she'd be reading about chocolate and having a virtual love affair at the same time. All she needed was some dark, delicious goodies to munch on, and she'd be in cocoa paradise. Her heart beat a little faster at the thought.

After kissing Emile and giving Paisley a hug, Sarah ran down the stairs to raid the kitchen on her way out, making sure she had plenty of supplies for an evening of education and indulgence.

Chapter 10

A crew of professionals had painted the exterior of Sarah's antique house back when Jim was still paying half the expenses. It was a massive project, but the ornate pattern of teal-blue fancy trim and aqua fish-scale details against the main color of dark-purple clapboards was utterly fabulous. The front door was violet, and the ceiling of the wide, curling front porch was a serene light blue. When she reclined on a chaise and looked up, she felt as if she were floating in the sky. Some of her favorite afternoons had been spent out on the porch with a good book and a pitcher of iced tea—when she could take the time off from renovation work, which was a never-ending process.

Sarah scrutinized the front porch as she rolled into her driveway, noting the area near the wisteria vine where paint had started to flake. Her fingers twitched, longing to attack it with a scraper. She pushed the thought from her mind and parked in the driveway. Stepping out of the car just as Devon erupted from the front door of the house like a yellow cannonball, already wearing his baseball T-shirt, she steeled herself for his well-meaning onslaught.

"Mom, hurry. We gotta go!" He bounced up and down, on a hyper-jag.

"Okay, sweetie. We're right on time. Take it easy." She soothed him as she walked toward the house, and he hopped alongside. "I just need to change and get my things. We'll be fine."

"But HURRY UP! Please?" He grabbed her arm and yanked it up and down as he jumped.

"I will, Devon. Calm down. Now." Sarah struggled not to drop the bags of food she was carrying, tempted to snap at him. She knew he was just excited about the game, but it was a challenge to hold her temper. Using her foot to prop the door open, she successfully maneuvered everything and the two of them inside the front hallway.

Devon looked at her wild-eyed and scrambled off toward the TV room. Sarah ran upstairs and quickly changed into jeans and a hoodie, pulled her hair back into a ponytail, and grabbed a yellow baseball cap with the team's logo on it. She hurried down to the kitchen to help Miki stock their cooler with drinks and snacks, then they all piled into the car, including Hershey.

"You guys are totally gonna tear 'em up, dude." Miki sat in the back seat to help reassure Devon, who was practically bouncing off the ceiling. Her hat matched Sarah's, and the streaks in her hair today were yellow, in honor of the occasion.

"YEAH," Devon shouted, "we're gonna murder 'em."

"Quiet down, honey. And don't forget good sportsmanship." Sarah hoped he would be able to concentrate on the game. His position in the outfield wasn't high pressure, but he did have to focus on the ball. At the moment, he was so worked up she doubted he could stand still. "Miki, why don't you give him a protein bar and some water?" The pediatrician had warned Sarah that valleys and spikes in Devon's blood sugar made his excitability much worse, and he'd recommended frequent high-protein snacks. It did seem to help.

"Okay, here you go, kiddo."

He settled down to chew the treat, but in the rearview mirror, Sarah could see his legs still jiggling.

Devon and Sarah had gotten used to being a family of two. She knew that her son missed having a dad around to cheer at baseball games, take him on camping trips, and squeeze into the teeny tiny elementary school chairs for parent–teacher conferences. But Devon wasn't the only one in this situation, and that helped.

It had surprised Sarah how many of the students at Devon's school were being raised by single parents. The motley crew of grown-ups all sat together at the baseball games and cheered for each other's kids, filling in for the missing ex-spouses. There was a real sense of belonging to a community. The kids blossomed, and the parents felt supported. Sarah had good friends to count on when she felt like talking. She'd become buddies with some people she would never have dreamed of befriending otherwise. Sticky Mason, for example.

Sarah was afraid to ask how he'd gotten the nickname. The balding, stocky, middle-aged guy with bushy black eyebrows wore a dark-blue windbreaker with his name embroidered on the pocket and "Mason Foreign Autos" printed on the back. Big and loud, Sticky goaded the other team—and the other team's coaches—with obnoxious remarks. Occasionally he was thrown out of the bleachers. Supposedly he had a wife, but she never showed up for any of the games. Rumor had it that she was a Russian mail-order bride. His son, Jimmy, was on Devon's team. Tall and wiry, the kid ran like a rabbit and was impossible to tag out. During tryouts, the two boys had competed for the same position. Sticky had called Devon every borderline-profane name imaginable. Her son was so shaken up, he dropped the ball.

Sarah had changed seats and moved over to sit right next to Sticky, tossing her hair and batting her eyelashes as she smiled at him. She'd put her hand on his leg above the knee and leaned over, getting his full attention.

"You see that boy," she'd said sweetly, "the one with the blond hair and glasses?"

"Yeah. Puny little runt can't run for shit."

"That's my son." Sarah had put her mouth right next to his ear. "And if you don't shut up and let him have a fair turn, I'll knee you in the balls first chance I get, do you hear?"

Sticky had turned and looked at her with new respect. "Yes, ma'am! I hear you, that I do. And some great ball player he is too. Look at the arm on that kid!"

He'd whistled and cheered when Devon successfully blocked the next hit, catching the ball before it hit the ground. After that, Sticky was Sarah's admirer and Devon's loyal supporter. She was looking forward to his running commentary on the first game of the playoffs today.

When they pulled into the line of cars parked at the school playing field, the place was bustling with families unloading folding chairs and picnic baskets. A game was just ending between two of the other teams in Devon's league. Sarah saw green T-shirts that said Sheehan's Pub on the back and purple ones bearing the familiar name Blake's Ice Cream.

Devon ran to join his team, while Miki stood on the sidelines with Hershey on a leash, and Sarah dragged the cooler up into the bleachers, where the whole gang was already seated.

"Blondie!" Sticky greeted her with a wolf whistle. "Where ya been? I was gettin' lonely with just these Desperate Housewives for company." He gestured toward Sarah's pals, who were neither desperate nor housewives and who booed and showered him with popcorn. They greeted Sarah and offered her hot coffee from a thermos bottle.

Ellen was a loan officer at the local bank, divorced mother of Jenny, the red-haired spitfire in pigtails who played shortstop. Bailey was a speech therapist, widowed since her husband had passed away from cancer last year. Her son Ben played center field. Several of the single fathers had shown up as well, and the group was obviously well on its way to a hot dog high. Sticky leaned over and offered Sarah a shot of whiskey from his flask, to spice up her coffee, which she gratefully accepted.

The kids who had just finished were leaving the field. She noticed Blake passing the stands, wearing his team's purple T-shirt, a whistle hanging from the lanyard around his neck. Sarah caught his eye and waved. He climbed up the stairs to chat, and her friends watched with interest, listening to every word.

"Hey, Sarah! Thought I might see you here. Your boy plays for Bob's, right?"

She caught a whiff of something sweet on the breeze that blew toward her. "Right," she said. "How did your team do? I just got here. Are you coaching?"

"We won. I have fun helping out... assistant coach. If you guys win this game, we'll be up against each other in the playoffs."

"Holy crap," Sticky interrupted. "Who knew? A juxtaposition of opposites! Be still, my heart." He clutched his chest dramatically.

The women one row up hooted and showered him with popcorn again.

"Just ignore him, Sarah," Bailey advised. "You go ahead and chat with the hot guy all you want. And if you're not interested, send him over to my house."

"Yeah," Ellen called. "Has he got an older brother?"

"No, but maybe his dad might be available," Sticky shot back. "Or his grandfather."

More popcorn throwing ensued.

Sarah winced and looked at Blake. "Sorry about that. I think the junk food has gotten to them."

"No problem." Blake grinned. "Room for one more?" He raised his eyebrows, and she moved over.

Sarah introduced him to the gang, and they all turned to cheer as the yellow team ran onto the field to warm up. The opposing team, wearing navy-blue shirts that said Lions Club, was huddled with their coaches for a last-minute pep talk.

Blake sat down, and his thigh lined up parallel to Sarah's. There was plenty of room, but his warm, solid bulk pressed up against her like a Labrador begging for attention. She glanced at him from under her lashes and saw he was pretending not to notice, his eyes fixed on the field ahead. Then he reached down and very deliberately placed his hand on her knee, turning his head toward her.

She looked directly into those cool green eyes as the heat between them began to travel up her body, past her chest, and into her cheeks.

As he watched the blush rising, his face flushed too. Her mind went completely blank.

BLAKE SAW SARAH'S FACE get redder and redder and finally took pity on her. He started the kind of casual conversation he'd been instigating with her recently as part of the master plan. "I'm glad we ran into each other, Sarah." He turned to look out at the field.

"Me too," she croaked then cleared her throat.

He gave her knee a squeeze, and she quickly took a sip of coffee. Blake saw that Bailey and Ellen had noticed his gesture. They mugged at Sarah, and Bailey fanned herself, pretending to faint. Sarah stuck her tongue out at them and turned to give Blake a friendly pounding on the back. Then the game started, and they were all swept up in the action, hooting, whistling, and hollering.

It was a close contest, with several tense moments, but in the end, the yellow team prevailed. Devon didn't get a hit when it was his turn at bat, but he didn't disgrace himself, either. In Blake's book, it was a good day. Sitting next to Sarah, sniffing the occasional hint of flowers that radiated off her hair, made it even better. Her friends seemed to like him. Even Sticky Mason, who slapped Blake a high-five whenever the team scored and offered him a swig from his flask.

By the time the game ended, Blake felt as if the two of them had become fused at the hip, and when they stood up to walk to her car, his left side felt oddly cold, exposed and vulnerable.

Sarah seemed thoughtful, her eyes downcast, and then she spoke. "We have plenty of chocolate chili from the restaurant at home. You're welcome to come over. It's my night off."

Score! he thought, careful to keep his expression bland.

"Sounds great." He grinned then remembered his obligation to run the tenants' meeting at Riverside Commons that evening.

Crap, there's no way I can get out of it. Jordan's on the road.

But he could still see Sarah online later. She had mentioned a "cute guy" she'd met at work, and it seemed possible she meant Blake. Tonight she might reveal more, something he could use. "Wow, really sorry, I have another commitment. How about a rain check? I'd love it another time." He sounded, and was, genuinely regretful as he opened the tailgate of her car to load Hershey inside.

Miki and Devon jumped into the car, and Sarah started the engine. Leaning in through the driver's window, Blake wished them all good night. His face swooped closer, and for a second he considered kissing her on the cheek, but then he stopped himself and said goodbye instead. From the expression on her face, she was disappointed. He stepped back to wave as they drove away.

Blake whistled as he walked to his truck. He was getting to her. It wouldn't be long now. He really liked this woman. His hurt feelings over Mandy's desertion had begun to fade into distant memory. It felt good. In fact, he hadn't been this happy in a long time. Now he just had to be careful not to drop the ball.

SARAH DROVE HOME WHILE Miki sat in the front passenger seat, texting on her phone. "That guy is cute," she observed while Devon listened to his iPod, oblivious. A jagged lock of yellow hair hid her eyes.

"I know him from the restaurant. It's a business thing." Sarah shook her head, trying to snap out of it and get a grip on herself. She needed to focus on work, not daydreams. Emile had given her a huge amount of reading to cover tonight.

"Oh, he's not one of them, then."

Sarah stopped at a red light and turned to look at her. "One of who?"

"The guys you and Paisley were messaging the other night." Miki spoke casually.

The light changed, and Sarah drove on, a puzzled frown on her face. "How did you know about that?"

"Oh, I hang out at dating sites sometimes too. Mostly the ones for gamers. You probably wouldn't recognize my user name, but I noticed yours in the list of new members the night she came over and set up your account. You two were pretty loud, so I couldn't help hearing. Unless CocoLvr is her account?"

"No, it's mine," Sarah muttered and felt her face getting hot. It seemed her cyber-flirting was not so private and anonymous after all. How humiliating to be caught by her babysitter! But Miki didn't seem to think much of it. Maybe in her circle, an internet social life was normal.

"You can meet some cool people online," Miki said, her fingers flying across the tiny keyboard on her phone. "But you gotta watch out too. My girlfriend met this guy who turned out to be a real creep. A creepy creep, if you know what I mean."

"Like, creepy how?" Sarah glanced at the girl as another flurry of keystrokes erupted from her slender fingers. Miki stared at the small screen and smiled, reading. Sarah snapped her fingers to get her attention. "Hey, Miki, like what?"

"Oh! Sorry. Well, she made a big mistake. After they'd been sexting for, like, a year, she agreed to meet him IRL—in real life. It didn't go well, and he found out where she lived. Then the guy stalked her for months. She ended up getting a restraining order to stop him from coming to her apartment in the middle of the night."

Sarah turned in to their driveway. She noticed the peeling front porch again and was distracted by a vision of her new paint scraper. "Really?" she mumbled, not paying attention. "She gave him her address? That seems unwise." Sarah pulled into the garage.

"Well, yes. But that's easy for anyone to find, Sarah."

"It is?" She was paying attention now.

Devon burst out of the back seat and flipped the tailgate open, releasing Hershey. They raced into the yard.

Miki looked at her askance. "Sarah, don't you know there are a million cyber-search tools out there that can find anybody from just a name, a place, a phone number, or even an email?"

Sarah met Miki's eyes and swallowed, thinking of all the personal information she had shared online. For example, that she lived alone with her young, vulnerable son.

"Tell me."

"I'll do better than that," Miki said. "I'll show you."

AFTER THE DINNER DISHES had been cleared away, a load of laundry was in the washer, Hershey had been walked, and Devon was settled down in front of the television for his favorite shows, Sarah crawled up the stairs to her bedroom. What Miki had shown her online was a real shocker, and the sickness in the pit of her stomach wouldn't go away.

Flopping onto her bed, Sarah moaned and pulled a pillow over her eyes. The chocolate books on her nightstand nagged at her, but for the moment, she needed to lie on her back and think about what to do.

Letting Paisley enter her favorite user name had been a huge mistake. The email address "CocoLvr@3Chocolatiers.com" was listed all over the internet as the contact for the restaurant. A quick search brought up a score of web pages where its physical address appeared. Busted!

Sarah and Miki had typed in the name of the restaurant, and on the first page of results was a link to an article in the *Ashford Gazette*. Sarah, Paisley, and Emile were all mentioned by name. There was even a photo of them standing in front of the pastry case.

Then Sarah found that her phone number and home address were listed in the Whitepages telephone directory online. When Miki copied the address into Google Earth, the view zoomed in from a satellite overhead, and Sarah could see her house in full digital detail. Her car was parked in the driveway, and Hershey was standing in the yard. He looked like a smudgy brown cigar, but it was definitely her dog.

Big Brother was watching Sarah.

Who knew? Everyone else, apparently. She felt stupid for not being better educated.

Hopefully, HotNCold wouldn't put it together. He'd never pressed her for information or indicated he knew where she was. He certainly seemed more interested in talking about other things, especially what they intended to do when they met later for their fourth cyber-date. Sarah would be much, much more careful from now on. In any case, the cat was already out of the bag if HotNCold was motivated to chase her down IRL.

She switched on her bedside table lamp, plumped up the pillows, and settled back against the headboard. Time to read up on the technical details of cooking with chocolate. She was scheduled to meet with the wedding clients in a few days. They were paying a bundle for something totally unique, and she had to make sure they got it. She stared at the pages until her eyes glazed over, and she drifted off, her head nodding. When the home phone rang, she thought it might be Paisley and answered groggily, but nobody was there. Probably a wrong number.

Too tired to resist, Sarah closed her eyes again. Just a quick nap, until it was time to put Devon to bed. At least she didn't have to shower and get all dolled up for her virtual date. That was convenient. No worrying about which jeans made her butt look fat. She flashed back to the last time she had met HotNCold online, and a burst of affection washed over her.

He was a genuinely nice guy, not a weirdo. He sounded so lonely and sweet. Her instincts told her everything was okay. But now that she had seen the big picture regarding online relationships, she certainly wasn't going to tell him anything that might lead to trouble.

Thank goodness Miki had educated her about how easy it was to track someone down, before it was too late.

Chapter 11

HotNCold: <*He kneels between her legs and leans forward to kiss her hello.*>

CocoLvr: *Hello, HotNCold. I missed you.*

HotNCold: <*Showing her how much he missed her too, he rubs up against her, and she realizes there is something cold and hard in his hand.*>

CocoLvr: *I would prefer something* warm *and hard, sweetie.*

HotNCold: *It's a bottle of Dom Perignon, nicely chilled.*

CocoLvr: *Oh, that's perfect! Yum.*

HotNCold: <*He pops the cork, and they each take a swig.*>

CocoLvr: *No crystal flutes? Not very elegant.* :-(

She added the frowning emoticon just for fun.

HotNCold: <*Raising one eyebrow with a devilish grin, he drips a few drops of champagne into her belly button.*>

Sarah pushed her mind into cyberspace and pictured a man's naked torso lit by the glow of a laptop. She felt a connection between them made of tiny electronic blips, as though their minds were hooked up to a personal wireless network.

CocoLvr: *Wow! Chilly, but I can handle it.*

She tried to keep her mental distance by joking, but she felt herself being drawn into the fantasy world, deeper and deeper.

HotNCold: <*Bending his head, he licks the wine from her navel, presses his lips against her skin, and sucks, his tongue probing the sensitive opening.*>

Sarah jumped and sat straight up in bed, the computer bouncing into the air. She grabbed it quickly, gasping, and settled it back into her lap. She stared at the screen before slowly typing her response.

CocoLvr: *Mmmm... wow!*

HotNCold: <*Lifting his head to smile at her, he fills her navel again and dribbles a trail of champagne down her body, ending right between her legs.*>

CocoLvr: *I'm getting all wet, Hot.*

HotNCold: <*He follows the trail with his tongue... flicking it back and forth... sliding his body down to rub against her leg.*>

CocoLvr: *Is that a banana in your pocket, or are you just glad to see me?*

HotNCold: *We're naked, Coco, remember? No pockets.*

CocoLvr: *Oh. I guess it's the latter, then.*

HotNCold: *Always glad to see you, baby. Are you ready for me?*

Sarah thought she knew what was coming next, and it totally freaked her out. A flash of heat rose from her stomach to her face. She stalled with another joke.

CocoLvr: *Always ready for you, even when the silk sheets are getting drenched and I'm freezing to death.*

HotNCold: <*He covers her with his body, warming her with his energy.*>

CocoLvr: *Oh yes, much better.*

HotNCold: <*They kiss, tongues rubbing together, as he pushes against her, proving that he is very, very glad to see her.*>

Sarah closed her eyes for a moment, trying to imagine Hercules/Tarzan bending over her, *sans* loincloth. She licked her lips. A flame of arousal shot from her mouth to her belly, spreading south from there to follow the imaginary champagne trail. Her skin felt electrified, puckering up in tiny bumps.

But then, there it was again. That twitchy paranoid fear of being caught doing something wrong. Like when her high school prom date took her behind the curtains on the stage to put his hand down the front of her dress. The guilty reflex. It neutralized everything in a flash and left her empty, sad, and lonelier than ever.

So. Looked like this cybersex thing was apparently not going to achieve liftoff. Not for her, not tonight, anyhow. Maybe she could work up to it. Or maybe she just needed some... help.

Sarah reached over, opened her bedside table drawer, and pulled out a small white cardboard box. She lifted off the top and revealed three perfect dark chocolate truffles, round and plump. While she read his next line, she popped one into her mouth. It melted into creamy ecstasy when it met the heat of her tongue, and her eyes narrowed as the cocoa thrill swept through her body. Time for the theobromine to work its magic. Her pulse throbbed. Her mind wandered off as she zoned out.

HotNCold: *<He deepens the kiss.>*

Sarah spun into a dream, floating on a cloud of bliss as he continued his description. She pictured the hard, muscular chest of a man hovering over her. As she popped a second truffle into her mouth, her imaginary eyes turned up to watch his imaginary face as it approached to kiss her again. A dark, handsome face that looked strangely familiar. The green eyes swooped closer, and she groaned, recognizing Blake Harrison's face instead of Hercules/Tarzan's.

What is he doing here? Talk about a buzz kill.

Sarah's throat tightened, and tears leaked out of the corners of her eyes as she stubbornly put the third truffle into her mouth. She sat up in bed and chewed until it had all melted away, then she wiped her eyes with her hands and dried them on the sheets, leaving chocolate fingerprints behind.

CocoLvr: *HotNCold?*

She interrupted his sexy narrative, which had become more explicit.

HotNCold: *Yes?*

CocoLvr: *No offense, but I don't think it's going to happen for me tonight. I feel kind of weird.*

There was a moment of blank screen before he replied.

HotNCold: *Coco, I hope I haven't said the wrong thing. I thought you wanted this?*

She typed her answer quickly.

CocoLvr: *I did. I do, I mean. Just... it's not working so well right now. I don't know why. You were very good, very... um... romantic. It's not that. It's me.*

HotNCold: *OK. Don't know what to say.*

Sarah didn't want him to be upset.

CocoLvr: *Please don't worry. I'm just, kind of uptight I guess. And old-fashioned.*

HotNCold: *So no cyber-sex until we're officially engaged, is that it? :-(*

She burst out laughing. The guy did have a great sense of humor, for sure.

CocoLvr: *I'm sorry, Hot. But we can cyber-neck, just a little. If you still want to after my rude behavior.*

HotNCold: *Coco, I get off just talking to you, don't you know that? This conversation is more intimacy than I've had in months. You're a total sweetheart.*

Sarah smiled.

CocoLvr: *That's quite a compliment. You're a great guy.*

HotNCold: *I wish we could, you know, see each other. I have this image of you in my head.*

She shook her head no, no way.

CocoLvr: *Yeah, I have images of you too! LOL!*

She thought of the two men's faces she had just pictured and registered that the real HotNCold probably didn't look like either of them. She tapped her fingernails restlessly on the laptop.

CocoLvr: *Well, I'm not sending you a photo, so you can forget that idea. With me, what you don't see is what you get.*

HotNCold: *Will you give me another chance, Coco?*

Sarah stared at the screen. Her feelings were so mixed, she didn't know what to answer. She was starting to regret this whole thing and wanted to log off now. HotNCold seemed like a nice guy, but it didn't look like cybersex was going to be the answer to Sarah's relationship problems.

She had enjoyed flirting with him, saying outrageous things she'd never dare say in real life. She loved Coco, the character she had created. Someone strong, assertive, independent, and sexy. So *not* the way Sarah actually was. It was fun to masquerade as that person, to have a secret life.

CocoLvr: *Sure.*

She thought about her response for a moment before she hit Send.

HotNCold: *Great. What do you say we take a night to cool off and then meet again and see what we think? Same time and place?*

She thought about it for a moment and decided, *What the heck?* She could say yes now and not show up if she changed her mind.

CocoLvr: *Sure.*

HotNCold: *Night, Coco. See you soon.*

IN THE DARK, SARAH perched on the window seat and watched as rain beat down on the sleeping neighborhood. The streetlights were bright oases in the gloom. Their golden glow reflected in puddles and on the wet leaves. Everything outside was dripping.

Hershey snored on his mat in the corner, a warm, homey sound. But Sarah couldn't seem to stop thinking and relax. She huddled with her feet pulled up under her bathrobe to watch the lightning flash, counting the seconds until thunder grumbled. First came the warning, then the tempest.

Had she ignored a warning tonight when she went to the online dating site despite what Miki had told her about the dangers? Was she asking for trouble?

Sarah looked across the street and noticed an unfamiliar dark-colored car parked in front of the Victorian that was for sale. The place had been vacant for months. It seemed kind of odd that a vehicle would be parked there in the middle of the night.

Through the mist, she saw a small flame appear inside the car. Somebody was sitting in the driver's seat. A smoker, she guessed. Sure enough, a few seconds later, an even smaller red blur flared as he or she puffed on the cigarette. *Disgusting. Makes the car stink,* she thought. Sarah wondered what the driver could be doing over there. Maybe they just stopped to wait out the rain. The storm was pretty bad.

Lightning flickered, turning the view into a film noir. This time, Sarah only counted to two before the booming crash sounded. The rain beat down even harder, battering the pavement and flooding the sidewalks.

Across the street, an engine started up, and the car slowly pulled away from the curb. The funny thing was, its headlights didn't turn on until it was way down the block, nearly to the intersection. Almost as though it was sneaking away.

Weird. Kind of spooky.

Whipped by the wind, rain spattered against Sarah's windows like a volley of gunshots. She jumped and caught her breath then ran to her bed and slid under the covers.

In a few more hours, she could get up and make breakfast.

Until then, she'd just have to try to absorb some more chocolate trivia. She turned on the reading lamp and picked up another of Emile's books. She read that chocolate was made from a large pod that grew on the trunk of the cacao tree in hot, humid regions close to the equator.

The Aztecs believed it was a gift from the gods. They made a drink from the ground seeds to give courage to the volunteers at human sacrifice rituals, while the officiating priests drank it to fall into a murderous trance. Luckily, chocolate didn't make Sarah feel murderous, though the boost in serotonin and endorphin levels definitely put her into an altered state. For her, a chocolate high was much more about sex than murder.

She read that cacao contained phenylethylamine, an aphrodisiac to which Sarah obviously had an extreme sensitivity. First brought to Europe by Spanish explorers, cacao was rare and terribly expensive. Accessible only by the aristocracy, it became famous for its mood-altering and passion-inducing effects. Unscrupulous French royalty used sweetened hot chocolate to seduce innocent virgins. Okay, that was something Sarah could believe. Death, sex, and chocolate. Throughout history, the three went together.

Sarah's eyes began to close, and she slumped down on the pillows. She dreamed of a strange red mist glowing in the street and yellow eyes that watched her through the bedroom windows.

Chapter 12

Blake got into his pickup and sat there, staring into space. Time for another day's work. Somehow it didn't seem challenging and fun, as it usually did. A gray cloud hovered over his life, and everything looked a little less shiny. He sighed and immediately wanted to kick himself in the butt for being such a pussy.

Get over it, he thought. *What made you think this would be easy? You've been asking for trouble.*

He looked over at Kahlua, sitting in the passenger seat like a person, his head level with his master's.

"What do you think, buddy?" He reached over and patted the dog's back.

Kahlua turned and gave him an adoring look, the tip of his tail wiggling.

"Oh yeah? You think we struck out pretty bad last night. But you like me, anyhow, don't you?" Blake treated him to a little head scratching, with special attention behind the ears. The dog grunted, and his rear leg began to thump.

Blake started the engine. Maybe he shouldn't go straight to the factory today. Nothing worthwhile ever came without some effort. He'd learned that long ago. And he wasn't a quitter. Sure, he'd failed at pleasing her online—for exactly what reason, he had no clue. The scenario he'd described seemed incredibly erotic to him. In fact, the sensual images had stuck with him all night, he hadn't slept much, and this morning, he was strung out. But he was determined to change his tactics and keep trying. The campaign was far from over. Perking up, Blake revved the engine. He pulled out into the street.

What if he stopped to see her on the way to work? Just for a minute. He could make up some excuse, try to sense how she felt this morning. Maybe he could even comfort her if she was upset about their lousy online date. After last night, it didn't seem that she would be wooed and won over the internet. He should go back to plan A.

Yes, he thought, *a little face time will be just the thing.*

He felt better immediately and sang along with the radio as he drove down Main Street. By the time he got to the restaurant, he was grinning from ear to ear, swaying with the music.

Blake parked under a shade tree in the rear. The morning was cool and cloudy, so he rolled all the windows down and told Kahlua to stay in the truck. He entered the restaurant through the back door. As busy as always, the kitchen reverberated with the whoosh of the Hobart, the hum of the walk-in cooler, the hiss of the espresso machine, the clink of glassware and plates, and the cheerful sounds of music and voices. The air was scented with fresh coffee, baking bread, warm sugar, and choco-late. Raoul slid a sheet of steaming baguettes out of the oven while Jerome sprinkled confectioners' sugar on top of a row of little dark-brown cakes. Paisley went out of the office as Blake was walking inside, and she grinned when she saw him.

"I called it," she said to the sous chefs, holding out her hand for a high five.

Jerome looked around and spotted Blake, meeting her palm with his. "You sure did, missy." He frowned and scolded Blake, "Y'all need to be a little more subtle, brother. Like the *b* in 'subtle,' hear me?"

Paisley and Raoul laughed, but Blake didn't get the joke. He was pretty sure it was at his expense, though, and cringed. Subtly.

Raoul came over and put a friendly arm on his back. "Don't worry, *mi amigo*. It's a good thing, to have an open heart." He pounded a fist against his chest, his eyes tearing up.

Blake looked at him like a horse that saw a snake. His face burned, and he suspected it was turning red. How did they all know what he was up to? He turned to Paisley, thinking fast. "I'm just here to see the boss. Is Emile up to visitors? Dad sends his regards. We thought he might want a little company."

That's the way. Throw them off track.

She stared at him for a second then stammered, "Well, yeah. He'd love it, as a matter of fact." Her eyes narrowed as she seemed to be thinking. "Sarah's not here yet, you know." Paisley watched his face.

Blake shrugged and shook his head, trying to keep his expression blank. "Oh? Promise I won't wear him out. Is he upstairs, at home?"

She nodded, and he strolled out the door into the stairwell, hoping he looked casual. *Close call,* he thought, wiping the sweat off his forehead. Paisley didn't seem to mind that he was trying to date her cousin, but it was embarrassing to know they were all talking about it. And the last thing he wanted was sympathy. No way. He wasn't *that* pathetic, though sometimes he was undeniably the world's biggest jackass. If people were talking, pretty soon Jordan would find out what was going on, and then it would be all over. The teasing would never stop. Sarah would be embarrassed too, and that would put an end to the whole thing.

Upstairs, he knocked on the apartment door. Emile called, "Come!" so Blake went inside. The old man was settled in an armchair by the window, surrounded by stacks of books and newspapers. He wore droopy black sweatpants and a green plaid robe, with his slippered feet propped on a footstool. His thick white hair stood up in the back, flattened on one side, and it looked as though he hadn't shaved for days. Half-glasses perched on his nose, and he looked up from a yellow pad, where he'd been writing.

"Well, well, what an unexpected delight!" Emile broke into a wide smile, wrinkles circling his eyes like nested parentheses. He remained seated, his lap covered with an afghan.

Blake quickly crossed to stand before him, hand outstretched. "My friend," he said warmly, shaking Emile's hand, and took a seat on the sofa, where the old man indicated he should sit. "How are you, Emile? The whole community has been wondering. My father sends his regards."

"Oh, many thanks. I'm doing great, nothing to be concerned." The old man's accent still lingered, a hint of music behind the words, even after fifty years of living in the US. His eyes looked worried. "Please tell everyone, it's fine. The girls have everything well in hand."

Blake understood Emile was concerned about the restaurant's reputation. As the senior partner and original founder when the place was just a little French bistro many years ago, he was regarded as the heart and soul of the place.

"Of course they do," Blake said. He nodded solemnly. "I'm glad to see you looking so well."

Emile lifted one side of his mouth in a half smile, and his eyes crinkled with humor. "You'd better stop now, *mon ami*. You're a terrible liar. I'm going to start thinking you're trying to butter me up."

"No, no! Really, I mean it. Most guys would look a lot worse after what you've been through." Blake returned the smile, settling back against a pillow and crossing his legs. "So tell me, what have you been up to since you got home?"

The old man took his glasses off and waved them in the air. "Oh, a little of this, a little of that. Tutoring my granddaughter in the finer points of cooking with chocolate and catering a large event. We've a wedding coming up, *n'est ce pas?*"

"Yes, the ice cream is all organized." Blake nodded. "We've ordered the custom-printed containers and insulated bags."

"*Bon.* Hopefully everything else will go smooth. Sarah will be in charge on the site, and she's a little nervous. Paisley will cut the wedding cake herself, after the bride and groom do the first slice. Will you send someone to serve your *crème glacée* and hot fudge sauce?"

Blake realized this was another opportunity and answered quickly. "Actually, I thought I'd better do that myself, Emile. Just in case, you know, they need some help from… a friend." He felt his face pulling into a guilty smile and tried to reorganize his expression.

Emile watched him with a knowing look. "Yes," he said slowly, nodding wisely. "That sounds like a good idea. We want to take good care of her, my precious Sarah." He sent Blake a warning glance. "You know how important she is to our family and our business."

Now Blake was worried that the old man had caught on to him too. What was it with these people? Were they psychics? Or was he that obvious? Really, he must get a grip on himself.

"Yes," he mumbled. "Of course."

Emile glared at him with apparent mistrust for a moment, leaning forward. A dazzling burst of sunlight shone around the old man's shoulders where he sat near the window, highlighting the tips of his silver locks. He looked distracted then shrugged and sat back, smiling. The movement stirred up dust motes that sparkled and swirled in the air. The old man turned his face into the light, closing his eyes as the glow covered his shoulders like a comforting embrace.

Blake stood up and cleared his throat. "I'll be going to work now, Emile. So glad you're feeling better." A breeze brushed his cheek, but the window was shut, so he wondered where it had come from. He caught the faint scent of cinnamon and turned but saw that the front door was still closed.

Emile watched and smiled. "Ah, she always did like you, my boy. 'That's one to watch,' she said."

"Pardon?" Blake thought he was talking about Sarah, but it didn't sound quite right.

"*De rein,*" Emile said and waved his hand. "Better get going. Give my best to your father, Blake. It's been good to see you."

Blake went to the door and opened it then paused on the threshold to look back. He raised his hand in farewell. "I'll come again another day. Let me know if you need anything."

But the old man had turned his face to the light, his eyes closed again. Rays of sunlight shot across the room now, pooling at Blake's feet, and the scent of cinnamon was stronger. Had someone been baking up here today? One of the cousins must have made breakfast for Emile. That was it.

Despite the thinly veiled warning Emile had delivered, Blake left the apartment feeling happy and reassured. Now it was official. He would attend the chocolate wedding to help Sarah. Emile had requested it, so how could he say no?

Chapter 13

That afternoon, Sarah sat at Emile's desk in the restaurant office and looked around with a sinking sensation. Papers were scattered helter-skelter, and nothing was in file folders. A pile of mail covered a stack of purchase orders, and she spotted the printouts she'd intended to give Blake Harrison the day her grandfather collapsed. Glad to have an excuse to postpone sorting through the mess, she stuffed Blake's documents into an empty file folder and went out the back door into the alley that led to Main Street.

It was a gorgeous day, and she loved to walk downtown. The broad street was lined with shops and little cafés, with pretty flowerbeds at the intersections and encircling the fat trunks of ancient maples. She greeted her fellow merchants, many of whom had set up clothing racks and tables of merchandise right on the sidewalk. Foot traffic was heavy as the downtown community turned out to enjoy the nice weather.

At the end of the row of shops, the street curved off around a small park, and behind that was Riverside Commons, where Blake's ice cream company had its headquarters.

He was standing on the loading dock when she approached, his hands on his hips and his sleeves rolled up. He signed something on an outstretched clipboard, and the driver turned, went down the steps, and climbed into his truck.

Blake squinted into the light and shaded his eyes, his face breaking into a grin. "Well, if it isn't the chocolate queen!"

Sarah bobbed her head and smiled, clutching the folder of papers in front of her chest. She stood below him in the driveway, her head tilted back as he towered above her. From this angle, his legs looked ten miles long, and his silver belt buckle flashed in the sun like a lighthouse beacon. The message it sent wasn't a warning, though. It was a demand for attention.

"Hi, Blake, how's it going?" She pushed her sunglasses up more securely, keeping her eyes hidden so he couldn't see where she was looking.

"Not bad." He came down the stairs and stood next to her in the driveway. "So, what's up? I stopped in to see Emile this morning. It was good to see him feeling better." Blake seemed in a very good mood, beaming in fact.

It was sweet of him to visit her grandfather, thoughtful. This guy might have serious potential... *if* she were interested in a relationship, that was. If she ever dared to trust again.

Blake stepped a little closer, and she held her ground, even though the hairs on her arms stood up when he moved into her space. She inhaled the sweet scent that seemed to float around him like an aura. Her skin tingled.

"Thanks," Sarah said, enjoying the advantage of being able to look into his eyes while hers were still hidden by the shades. "I'm sure Grandpa enjoyed the company. He's getting a little antsy, not being allowed in the kitchen."

His eyes are the most amazing green. Dark but saturated, the color of shadows on grass.

He flicked them over her body, so fast it was like a blink.

She smiled. "By the way, I forgot to give you these the other day."

"Thanks for thinking of me." He reached toward her.

She handed him the folder, and their fingers touched. A little zap of energy shot up her arm, and she lifted her foot to step away.

He held her there with his eyes. "Want to come inside?"

"I'd love a tour! I've never seen how this is done." She settled her sunglasses on the top of her head, and they stood toe to toe, with just a few inches of air between them. It seemed to shimmer with tension.

A slow smile stretched his lips. "Lovely." His gaze slid over her face. "Let's go in this door." He put his hand against her back and guided her toward the stairs.

The spot right above the curve of her bottom burned from his touch, and she fought the urge to shiver. It was the most intimate sensation she had felt in ages. She smiled at him, dazzled, and let him steer her into the shipping entrance.

Blake showed the way into a wide, chilly hallway lined with metal doors. "This is where we pack the ice cream into shipping boxes, sorted by customer, and move them into the storage freezers for transfer to the refrigerated trucks." He stopped to explain the importance of never letting the ice cream warm up and refreeze, as the texture would be ruined by crystallization. This explained why everyone she saw was rushing around. They all seemed cheerful, though, smiling and joking with Blake as he led her through the area.

"Just now we're making banana fudge swirl." He put a hand on her shoulder and steered her through to the next room, where she saw the machines that churned the liquid ingredients into frozen custard. The temperature in here felt even lower than in the shipping area, and the workers were dressed for it. Containers printed with Blake's elegant foil-embossed logo were filled and sealed then moved immediately into the hardening freezer.

He offered Sarah a sample on a small wooden tasting spoon. She rolled the cold, fruity cocoa sweetness around in her mouth and was immediately transported back to when she was a little girl, sitting at the counter in the local diner with Grandma Annie, who was a major fan of banana splits.

"Good?" Blake watched her enjoyment, his eyes appreciative. "You like?" He reached out and touched her cheek, where a strand of hair had strayed.

She looked up at him and smiled, wanting to pull away but unable to move. Something inside her loosened and unfurled, like a rose in the sun. "This is amazing," Sarah said and meant it. "Delicious and great... um... texture."

Then Blake showed her the beginning of the production line, where a mixture of milk, cream, sugar, and vanilla chilled in an enormous stainless-steel tub, constantly circulating.

"We make a huge batch of this every morning. It's the base for all our flavors." He showed her the natural ingredients that were added to various mixtures. "After it's almost done churning, we mix in the nuts and chunks. You can add just about anything you want, as long as it doesn't freeze so hard it'll break a tooth." He offered her a sample of the special chocolate chips he used, with a high percentage of cocoa butter so they would stay softer when frozen. When he popped one into Sarah's waiting mouth, his fingers touched her lips, and the sensation was mesmerizing. She stared into his eyes.

If he told me to cluck like a chicken or bark like a dog right now, I'd probably do it! I'm totally falling for this guy.

She wasn't just turned on. She was impressed. It was refreshing to talk to someone who was in love with his job. Aside from Paisley and Emile, who were devoted maniacs about cooking, most of the people Sarah knew were working their way toward something better. They were hoping for a windfall, not pursuing a true passion. Blake was different. He was a *grown-up*, something her ex-husband would never be, even when he turned eighty.

The tour ended in the office, where Blake showed her his overflowing desk. He threw the file folder down on top of a pile. "I'm afraid I don't spend as much time sitting here as I should," he said with a shrug.

"That's okay." Sarah soothed him with a hand on his back. "You should see Emile's desk. It's a disaster area!" She felt the hard muscles move under his shirt as he turned and reached toward her waist, his eyes wide with interest and more than a little heat. Just then the phone rang, and he changed course at the last second, picking up the receiver.

Sarah's pulse raced, and her head spun. By the time he had finished the call, she was composed and standing near the doorway, waiting politely and poised to run.

Her heart was pounding madly, but he probably couldn't hear it from across the room. "I really must be going," she said, slipping toward the exit sign and waving her hand. "Time to set up for dinner!"

"But wait—" He reached toward her.

"Good to see you, Blake. Thanks for the tour. Bye!"

She nearly ran down the front steps of the building and hit the parking lot at a fast clip, afraid to look back. That was a close one. One more minute, and they would have been making out, right there in his office. Anyone could have walked in. And Lord knew what could have happened next. *Ohmigod.*

Sarah's legs shook as she rushed down the sidewalk toward the restaurant, but her lips curved in a broad smile. She hadn't had this much fun in ages. She giggled.

What if he had touched her, after all? What if nobody had been around, as if it were after hours? What if he'd kissed her and bent her back onto that paper-covered desk, leaning over her and pressing his body against hers? What if she were wearing a skirt instead of pants and he slid his hand up under it? No, not that one. Maybe the short black pencil skirt. Yes, that was the one. Now, what if she weren't wearing any underwear?

"You look like you're having a good day, little sister," Jerome said as she walked past him into the kitchen, totally oblivious.

"Huh?"

"What's that evil grin on your face about?" He raised one eyebrow and grinned back at her, as though he knew exactly what was happening in her mind. "If I didn't know better," he said, following her across the room, "I might think you were coming back from a rendezvous with a gentleman caller, if you know what I mean. Where you been at, girl?" Addicted to gossip, he leaned closer and beckoned.

"Just cooling off with a little... fresh air." Not to mention a stroll through Blake Harrison's ice cream freezers.

He squinted at her suspiciously, his hands on his hips.

"Really," she said. "Just *chilling*, honestly."

"Okay, baby, that's cool."

If you only knew how cool *it was,* she thought and went to make sense of Emile's random filing system before the first customers arrived.

THAT NIGHT, SARAH WAS filling in for the bartender, who had a brand-new baby at home. After the early birds had paid their dinner checks and headed out the door, laden with boxes of cupcakes and éclairs, she noticed someone familiar standing alone at the back of the line for a table. He was hard to miss—a dapper, handsome guy in his midthirties wearing a suit and tie. She made eye contact and called to him.

"It will be about fifteen minutes if you want a table. I can serve you at the bar right away, if you'd rather."

He showed her a dazzling smile, his teeth bright white against an olive complexion. His hair was black and cut short, his figure trim and his clothes stylish. He looked like a model for a men's fashion magazine. She thought she'd seen him before but couldn't place him. He walked over and took a seat at the bar. She noticed an onyx ring on his pinky but no wedding band.

"Welcome," she said, putting a placemat and silverware in front of him. "Don't think we've met. I'm Sarah. Your first time here?" She handed him a menu. He was really quite handsome—movie-star quality, in fact. It made her nervous to look at him up close.

Then he tipped his face down to glance at the menu, and when the light gleamed on his prominent forehead, she realized why she felt as if she knew him. He was the spitting image of Hercules/Tarzan from her fantasy.

In the flesh. The very lean, strong-looking flesh. He took off his jacket and hung it on the back of his chair, and she watched in fascination. Big muscles rippled under the white shirt, which was fitted to hug his slender waist. The fingers that reached for hers were long and slim, and his eyes were the color of dark chocolate.

"I'm Alonzo, hi. Good to meet you, Sarah." He pressed her hand between both of his.

"Can I start you off with a cocktail or a glass of wine?" she asked automatically, staring in fascination.

"The pinot noir, I think. Thank you. How is the special tonight? It looks... unusual." He gestured toward the chalkboard that stood inside the front entrance.

"Well, yes, one hundred percent grass-fed organic beef tenderloin with a chocolate and port wine sauce is one of our chef's most unique dishes. It's seasoned with rosemary. The aroma is divine. You'll love it."

"It sounds beautiful, Sarah." He somehow made it sound as though he was complimenting her instead of the food, his eyes roaming over her face. He chose the rest of his meal, and she handed his order to a passing waiter and headed for the kitchen.

She poured Alonzo's wine and put the glass in front of him.

"*Salut!*" he said and raised it toward her, nodding his approval after he took the first sip. "So, this is the famous chocolate restaurant I keep hearing about!" He looked around, nodding toward the dessert display case.

"My cousin Paisley is the pastry chef here. She won Best of Show at the regional chocolate festival the past five years in a row."

"Tell me, how does it work? Are there independent judges who make the decisions?" He watched her avidly as he sipped his wine, as though chatting with her across the bar was the most important item on his to-do list.

"No, this is more of a people's choice–type award. People pay for admission and get to sample free from each booth, then they vote for their favorites. It would be hard to find qualified judges who weren't already participating in the competition, so this works better."

"I see. It sounds fabulous. I'll have to check it out. The perfect event to bring a young lady to. I'll bet there are a lot of happy chocolate lovers getting together that evening, afterward, if you know what I mean."

Sarah felt her face glowing when she saw his sly expression. "Well, um, yes, of course. All that chocolate, it does evoke a certain... mood."

Alonzo laughed. "You mean, nine months later the maternity wards are very busy? I'll just bet they are!"

"Hmm, I've never really investigated that question, but I wouldn't be surprised." She grinned at him, interested to see he was taking a small spiral-bound notebook and a pen out of his pocket.

"Can't forget to line up a date," he said when he saw her watching. "I don't suppose you're available, are you... love?"

Sarah felt her face getting warm again. "No, um, I probably have to work at our booth, you know. Duty calls. But thanks, anyhow." Not to mention, she wasn't dating. Anyone. At all. She sighed, hiding it behind her hand.

Hercules/Tarzan/Alonzo smiled in response as she was called away by a waitress standing at the service station with drink orders. Sarah felt him watching her as she worked behind the bar. His beautiful dark eyes smoldered. It was exactly the same look that the Ape Man gave to Jane right before he carried her off via swinging vine to their sleeping nest high in the trees. Sarah's pulse quivered, and drawn like a fly to sugar, she was about to go back and engage him in conversation again, but then a thought popped into her mind.

What if it was *him?* The actual, original Hercules/Tarzan? Alias HotNCold, her online lover? What if he had tracked her down and come to make contact IRL, as Miki had warned her might happen?

A quiver of nerves tightened her stomach, and she hesitated, looking at him again as he ate his tenderloin and wrote something in his notebook. Maybe it was better not to interrupt him. He looked preoccupied. Give the guy some privacy to enjoy his meal in peace.

It couldn't possibly be HotNCold. That was just ridiculous paranoia talking.

Sarah gave herself a mental shake and tried to focus on bartending. When she turned around with a martini shaker in her hands, she caught him staring at her, and their eyes met, but he seemed totally unembarrassed. There was no mistaking his intentions toward her, that was for sure. When she cleared away his empty dinner plate and handed him the dessert menu, his fingers brushed hers, then his eyes lit up with pleasure as he was clearly captivated by the list of chocolate delicacies.

"I've heard a lot about your pastries," he said excitedly, scanning the menu. "What do you like?"

He settled on a slice of white and dark chocolate marbled cake with ganache drizzled over it. "May as well go all the way," he said and added a scoop of double-chocolate ice cream to the order.

"A man after my own heart," Sarah whispered as she passed him on her way to the pastry case, where she plated the cake and bent over the freezer to scoop his ice cream, giving him another long look at her from the back. He was really very sexy, in a *metrosexual* kind of way. When she turned, she was disappointed to see that he hadn't even noticed her, preoccupied again with scribbling notes in his little book.

"Terrible memory." Alonzo shrugged when she stood waiting for him to pocket the notebook so she could put the dessert in front of him. "I was on the road pretty early today. Things are getting fuzzy around now."

"What do you do for work?"

"I sell HVAC, heating and cooling systems," he said as he sampled the ice cream with interest. "Fascinating, right? Don't worry. You don't have to ask me about work. You're very polite, but I know how boring it is." He laughed and dug into the cake, obviously savoring the smooth and spicy flavors. "This is outstanding," he said, rolling his eyes in apparent ecstasy.

Something nibbled at the back of Sarah's mind while she stood next to him and watched the pleasure on his face. It felt as though she was intruding on a very personal, intense experience. Then it all came together and hit her. Up early... heating and cooling... hot and cold... HotNCold!

Ohmigod, it's him.

Sarah jumped away so fast she nearly tripped a waitress coming out of the kitchen with a full tray of food. Without another word, she rushed into the back and found Paisley, who was plating five different dinners all at once, her colorful garnishes making each one a work of art.

"I need you," Sarah said earnestly, holding her cousin's arm. "I think I'm in big trouble. You have to help me!"

Paisley quickly read her face then finished what she was doing and put the plates up on the ready-to-go counter. "What is it?" she asked quietly, steering Sarah toward the office, out of the kitchen chaos.

"Remember that guy online I told you about? He's here, or well, I think he's here tonight. Sitting at the bar. He... it's just like Miki said, he tracked me down. You should have heard what he was saying to me."

"Wait a second. How do you know this is the same guy?" Paisley stroked Sarah's arm and pulled her down into a chair.

"It's got to be him. He was dropping all kinds of hints. It's him. He's stalking me! Should I call the police?" Sarah felt her eyes open wide, and she started to breathe too fast.

"But you're really just guessing, is that right? He hasn't actually said he's the same person you've been talking to online?" Paisley's calm voice began to soothe Sarah, who clutched her cousin with both hands.

"Right," Sarah said. "But he said almost exactly the same things and was talking about sex and chocolate. I hope he doesn't have my home address!"

"Sarah, what if he's just some guy who thinks you're pretty?"

"I doubt it," Sarah said, shaking her head with a frown. "I'm just an old mom, and he's gorgeous. I mean drop-dead gorgeous, like Tarzan and Hercules and Zorro and Jesus Christ all rolled into one. Here, come and see."

She beckoned and brought Paisley back into the kitchen to look through the window into the dining room. They hid behind Jerome and Raoul while they scrutinized the bar area, but Sarah couldn't see anyone sitting there anymore.

"Son of a..." she sputtered, racing out through the swinging door for a closer look. "If he stiffed me for the tab, I'll—" She stopped short.

Under the empty dessert plate was a hundred-dollar bill with a heart drawn on it in ballpoint pen.

"Will that cover it?" Paisley asked, placing a calming hand on Sarah's shoulder.

"Oh yeah," Sarah said. "More than. Nice tip, in fact."

"Probably just some guy, Sarah. Right?"

"I guess so." Sarah slumped, a little embarrassed.

Paisley patted her back. "Take it easy. It's really not an emergency every time some guy makes a pass at you, honey. You can handle it, and we're all right here with you."

"Okay. I was being silly."

"And you're not just some old mom. You're a red-hot mama with the longest legs on Main Street and hair like a Viking princess. Speaking for all the short, dark women of the world, I hate you." Her cousin pretended to scowl, raising her fist.

Sarah grinned, and they hugged. "Thanks, P. It probably wasn't him."

"That's right, cuz."

"I mean, what are the chances?" Sarah said, and they both laughed.

Her online life and her real life were safely compartmentalized, she thought, relaxing. One would never spill over into the other. The idea was ridiculous.

Chapter 14

Blake rolled into his parents' driveway for family dinner night forty-five minutes late. He parked his unassuming Ford pickup behind Jordan's elegant BMW, Carrie's perky red Jeep, his mother, Maggie's, efficient Prius, and his dad's practical hybrid SUV.

You are what you drive, he thought. *Maybe I should get a new vehicle.*

He headed across the lawn toward the flagstone patio that lay stretched out in the evening sun behind the early 1700s farmhouse that was the Harrison family home. Every time he came back, Blake felt a sense of safety, stability, and grounding. It was like drinking from a cool fountain. He knew Jordan felt the same. Carrie was still living here, the last kid at home. After she graduated next year, she'd be off on her own too. It was weird to think of his parents here alone. But they would all come back for his mother's family dinners, and for holidays, so the house would still be home to everyone, no matter where they all lived. His parents had said they were planning to stay on in this big house, and someday soon, hopefully, the next generation would start to fill the place up with grandchildren.

"I can be patient," his mother had said, a gleam in her eye. "But not forever."

A newer addition on the back of the original old building embraced the pool and gardens, and when he went around the corner, Blake saw them all assembled there, sitting on the Adirondack chairs that he and Dad had made together last summer. The sun was going down. It was nearly eight, and deep buttery-yellow rays slanted across the scene.

Carrie spotted him first and held up a hand and shaded her eyes. "There he is! Thank God you finally showed up. Can we eat now?" Her ginger hair looked bright flaming-orange in the tinted light.

Jordan stood up and tossed an empty bottle into the recycling barrel, his aim precise. "Brewski, bro?" He reached into the cooler by the picnic table and pulled out two Heinekens. Handing one to Blake, he hip-checked him a hello.

"Son, glad you could make it," his father said, smiling at Blake while he flipped sirloin strips on the grill.

Blake went straight to his mother and bent over to kiss her cheek as she hugged him around the neck. "Hi, Mom, how's it going?"

"Terrific!" She smiled, crinkling the corners of her eyes. "Especially now that you're here." Her masses of dark curly hair, shot with a few strands of silver, looked wilder than ever as the breeze lifted them off her shoulders. She was still a beauty at fifty-five, and her forget-me-not-blue eyes saw much more than most people's. She patted his leg when he sat down next to her. "How about you, darlin'?" She looked at him carefully.

Knowing that her famous X-ray vision would see through any story he might make up, Blake took a long pull of his beer and answered, "I'm okay. Let's talk later."

She smiled, satisfied, and began to change the subject, but his brother stepped up and interrupted. He gestured with his beer, a wicked smile on his face.

"Later? Thought you'd have other plans for later, right, bro?" Jordan took a swig, swaying a little.

Blake frowned, sensing trouble. "Give it a rest, buddy, whatever it is."

His brother grinned and gave a complicit wink. Blake wondered how many empties were in the recycling barrel and tried to distract everyone from whatever embarrassing scene Jordan was about to create. The kid was looking for a chance to hassle him, just as he had when they were younger, but nowadays that got annoying fast. Luckily, right then Carrie came over and started talking about her new job at the restaurant. Jordan backed off and took his beer over to hang with their dad by the grill.

"I start tomorrow. It's so cool! I can't wait." Carrie tossed her long curls over her shoulders and bounced on her feet, as though ready to get right to work here and now. "Sarah says she's going to train me as a waitress first, then hostess, so I can fill in wherever they need me. They do catering too. She said something about a wedding. Oh my God, this is so much better than data entry, you simply cannot imagine." She laughed and shook her head.

Blake saw her happiness and felt a quick tug of emotion. "Glad I could help," he said in a gruff voice.

She jumped over and locked him in a fierce hug. "Thank you, big brother!" She smiled up at him brightly then went off and lit the hurricane lanterns on the long glass table set with fresh flowers, Maggie's blue china, cloth napkins, and old family silver.

Everyone pitched in to take the prepared food out from the kitchen. Big bowls of potato salad and coleslaw, a plate of thick-sliced heirloom tomatoes with fresh basil, a green salad from the garden. Sam carried over a platter of perfectly grilled steaks, which all the men especially appreciated. Blake and Jordan eyed their choices and dove for their forks.

The little weasel is such a brat. He'd better watch out for his hand! It was all in fun, right? A game? Blake swooped in on the perfect piece of steak, snatching it from under his brother's fork.

"After you, please," Jordan said with an angry expression. He leaned back with his arms crossed in front of his chest, staring at Blake. "You're probably in a hurry to get back to your stalking activities."

Blake froze with his fork in midair, slowly turning his head to gape at his brother. His jaw literally dropped. He sputtered, "What the F are you talking about?"

"Oh, I think you know what I mean," his brother said, raising one eyebrow. But Jordan stopped there, zipping his lips with another stage wink.

Blake got the message. Jordan somehow knew he was after Sarah, and he might be prepared to make it public knowledge. He must have talked to Paisley today. It was blackmail, plain and simple.

After dinner, they stood at the sink together, rinsing their plates.

"So, what do you want?" Blake spoke quietly.

Jordan smiled. "Oh, maybe you have to mow Mom's lawn this week and next. And clean the pool before Carrie's birthday party. I hate doing that."

"That's it? Really?"

"Why, you would have paid more? Okay, you can take the garbage out now too." Jordan tied a knot in the top of the bag and handed it to Blake. "Get outta here, knucklehead. I'm not really an asshole, you know."

Blake cringed. He'd been so defensive, he'd lost his sense of humor. "Hey, man, sorry. I know you aren't. It's just, kind of a sore subject, I guess. And I really don't want to be having this conversation, you know what I mean?"

Jordan nodded and reached out for a high five. "Brother, I feel your pain. I too have been a fool for love."

"Okay, so just shut up about it."

"Right. No problemo." His brother patted him on the back soothingly, shushing him.

"I mean it, twerp!"

"Yes, yes, I know." More patting ensued as Jordan steered them both out to the patio, where Maggie was waiting with a nice blaze going in a bowl-shaped metal fire pit. He pushed Blake down into the chair next to their mother, gave him one last pat, ruffled his hair, then kissed her good night and left.

Blake and his mother sat side by side, watching the thin red line on the horizon, all that remained of the sun. Little bats ventured out of the old barn and swooped around the garden and fields, catching insects. Lightning bugs glowed, vanished, glowed, vanished. The evening was nearly silent but for the rustle of the long grasses and the bubbler in the pool.

"So, tell me." Mom didn't turn her head. She just said it in a matter-of-fact voice, as though they were picking up an ongoing conversation.

"I met someone. Re-met, actually. Already knew her, sort of." He paused, surprised it had slipped out.

"That's good!"

"Thing is," he continued, "I don't think she likes me very much. I'm not sure what she wants."

His mother turned toward him and nodded. "Yes, you do, honey. Think about it. You know what she wants. You're just afraid to give it to her."

Confused, he shook his head and frowned. "I thought I knew. I did. But then it got, well, really confusing, and now, I'm just not sure."

"Blake, in every relationship, somebody has to go first. Somebody has to take the risk, reach out, and declare themselves. I'm betting that's what she wants, because it's what *all* women want. We want to be *adored*." She smiled and drew a flirtatious hand up her cheek, fluttering her eyelashes. They both laughed.

"Okay, so what does that mean I should actually do?" Blake asked, still puzzled.

"My darling boy, it's very simple. Show her how you feel."

Thunderstruck by her words, he tried to process them. It was a simple, direct, yet terrifying and potentially devastating idea. There were pros and cons. But one thing was certain. It would end this dancing around, trying to be two fascinating people at the same time and failing at both. He was scared shitless, but he kind of liked the plan. Blake started to cheer up.

She continued. "Everything will always turn out fine as long as you are your honest, true self. That's what every woman wants too. Just be yourself."

Blake froze in horror, as what she had said soaked in. He hadn't "been himself" at all, had he? He'd been two different fake people, both of whom were tricking poor Sarah. His spirits sank like a deflated balloon, settling down into the gutter of depression he'd been slogging through lately.

"Oh, Mom," he said, rubbing his face with his hands. "I wish I'd talked to you a month ago."

She grinned and laughed. "So, my advice is that good? All right!" Watching his face, she still had a shadow of concern in her eyes.

"Always the best, Mom. I have to try to make things right. I need to think about it, figure things out. And then I'll do what you said—show her and tell her."

"Good," she said and kissed the side of his head. "You're a good boy, Blake."

"Thanks, Mom."

"Nighty night, sweetheart."

He walked away into the darkness, and through the trees, he saw a pink moon rising. The blood moon, they called it. People used to think it signaled the end of days. Maybe it did. The end of this relationship, anyhow. He could just give up and walk away. Was it really worth all this trouble? This irritating, shitty feeling in his gut? Something was very wrong with the situation if it made him into such a loser. And now he had to find the courage to tell Sarah everything, according to his mom, who was always right when it came to matters of the heart. That was another giant bummer, to top off all the others.

Blake went home even more depressed than when he had arrived. But he knew what he had to do. Getting up the courage to do it was another story.

Chapter 15

When Sarah got home from the restaurant that night, the house was dark except for the small lamp on the hallway table, and Hershey stumbled down the steps from upstairs to greet her with sleepy eyes.

"Good boy," she murmured, scratching his neck underneath the leather collar, making him groan and thump his leg. He panted, grinned, and wagged his tail, gathering himself for a big sloppy shake. His ears flapped noisily, his toenails scraping on the tile floor. Dog hairs flew in all directions, and Sarah stepped back, laughing. "Easy, mister! You'd better go outside." She led him over to the kitchen door and opened it, flipping on the floodlights in the backyard.

The dog ran over to his favorite squirrel tree and lifted his leg then stopped and looked toward the house, sniffing the breeze. His hackles rose, and a low growl rumbled in his throat as he stared into the shadows beyond where Sarah stood in the doorway.

She took two steps down the path toward the dark bushes on the side of the house and stopped to listen. Aside from Hershey, she heard nothing. Then there was a snap-crack sound like a stick breaking, not far away, and she turned and ran.

"Hershcy! Come!" she called, leaping back into the doorway and clapping her hands for the dog. Dragging her eyes back and forth between the dog and the bushes, she tried to whistle, but her lips were too dry. He trotted over to her with a malevolent glance at the driveway, coming reluctantly, inch by inch. She finally grabbed his collar and hauled him inside then slammed the door shut and bolted it.

She plunged the kitchen into darkness and looked out the windows. Nothing stirred except her heart, still pounding in her chest.

"What the heck was that, boy?" She swallowed and decided to leave the outside lights on all night. "If it's raccoons, maybe they'll be scared away."

Hershey panted and smiled then turned to go upstairs. He stopped to look back at her over his shoulder as if to say, "Coming?"

"Right behind you," she answered, and they climbed up the stairs to bed.

THE NEXT MORNING, SARAH awoke to a frantic rush, getting Devon up, dressed, fed, and ready for school and onto the bus on time. On Fridays, he had to hand in a whole week's worth of writing assignments, his "portfolio," and he had a terrible time keeping track of all the papers for five days. But now they were all safely ensconced in a big manila envelope, labeled with his name and the teacher's name, zipped inside his backpack. Sarah pulled herself up onto a barstool at the kitchen island and quickly drank a cup of coffee, trying to replace the energy she'd just burned through.

Miki came downstairs and dumped her lacrosse stick and messenger bag near the door. Still wearing yellow streaks in her hair out of loyalty to Devon's team, she went behind the counter and poured coffee into her hot-pink travel mug, which featured a Hello Kitty motif. "Do I need a jacket today?" she wondered aloud, going over and checking the thermometer mounted outside the window. "Holy cow, Sarah, did you see this?" She stared down as Sarah came over to see what she was looking at.

The bushes under the window were trashed, much worse than before. Something big, like maybe a bear, had almost completely flattened them. The empty trash cans had tipped over and rolled against the side of the garage, a good six feet away from where they usually were.

Sarah and Miki stared in silence.

"Well, looks like whoever emptied the garbage cans made a big mess," Sarah finally said. She frowned. "I'm going to call the trash collectors and complain. This is unacceptable."

Miki nodded. "Those guys didn't have to ruin your landscaping. What a bunch of jerks." She grabbed her things, waved goodbye, and set off down the sidewalk toward campus, just a few blocks away.

"Unacceptable," Sarah echoed, looking at the damage again. She got her lopping shears out of the garden shed, trimmed off the bent branches, and threw them onto the compost heap. Then she went back inside and got dressed.

When she was about to leave, the phone rang. She dropped everything to rush over and answer it, just in time to hear a click as the call was disconnected. The caller ID said Private Caller. Probably just another telemarketing call. Amazing how many times recently she'd answered to find nobody there.

WHEN SHE GOT TO THE restaurant, the atmosphere in the kitchen was unusually somber. Jerome had lowered the radio volume to what most people would consider normal, and Raoul chopped vegetables silently, his back turned to the room. Neither one of them greeted her. The smell of burnt chocolate hung in the air. Sarah sensed trouble.

She walked through the kitchen toward the office, where Paisley sat at the big table, surrounded by paperwork. She wore a soiled white apron over blue jeans and a T-shirt, and her short hair stood up in the front as though she'd been tugging at it in frustration. After punching numbers into a calculator with the eraser end of a pencil, she entered the result into the accounting ledger. The expression on her face was dire.

"What's the matter? What happened?" Sarah approached warily.

Her cousin looked up with a scowl. "I'm just no good at this multitasking, Sarah. I did the whole page wrong and had to start over. Then I forgot what was in the oven and ruined the cakes. Had to start them over too. Hopefully the smell will be gone before tonight, or our customers will think we're incompetent. Which"—she twisted her mouth—"we are. Without Grandpa, it all tends to fall apart."

"No, it doesn't. You're brilliant!" Sarah went around the table to comfort Paisley. "You just have too much to do."

"But what's the answer?" Paisley turned up her face, and Sarah saw tears in her eyes. "I can't just clone myself or something. And neither can you."

Sarah sat down next to her. "Well, we'll have to hire someone to do the bookkeeping, I guess."

Paisley shook her head with a mournful expression. "We can't afford it. According to these numbers, anyhow. We're carrying Grandpa's salary, with none of his production. It just doesn't compute."

Sarah thought for a moment. "What if we each take a cut, you and me?"

"Can you afford that? I could probably pay my bills, but can you? What about your mortgage on the house?"

"No, not really." Sarah's shoulders slumped. She thought harder. "Is there any way to cut expenses? Get a better discount on supplies? Maybe buy some less expensive vegetables or meat? Cut the pricey wine off the menu?"

"Grandpa has always stuck to the rule of nothing but the best ingredients. It's how he built our reputation. We might get away with a few substitutions, but if he finds out, he'll have a fit. And don't think he won't know. I caught him down here first thing this morning, snooping around."

Sarah nodded, picturing it. "Not surprised. It was inevitable."

"My brother called this morning, by the way," Paisley said. "Checking on Grandpa."

"Well, that's it. That's the answer. One answer, anyhow." Sarah grinned.

"You want Lucas to work here?" Paisley's mouth hung open. "For free? Are you out of your mind? He already has a job, in case you forgot. And a wife and family in New York. Not to mention, he's a terrible cook."

"I know, I know, but he did say to ask if we needed any help with Grandpa, didn't he? And it's not that far away." Sarah urged her to think more creatively.

"True, true. Actually, maybe you have a good idea there. He's a whiz with math. What if we gather all the paperwork every week and FedEx it down to him? He could handle the books. Probably only take him a few hours, since he isn't numerically challenged like I am." Paisley had already started to brighten up.

"Yes! Exactly. And maybe I can come up with some promotions to help us generate more income. Like a special menu several nights a week. Fixed price, for a whole meal, with wine included." Sarah began to wave her hands in the air. "Something super profitable, though the customers won't know that. I can make it sound fabulous and special. They'll be knocking down the doors to get in."

"Okay, that could work." Paisley was getting excited now. "I can come up with a unique dessert to go with it. Maybe something like tasting portions of several things, all on one plate, kind of like a dessert *dim sum*." She grinned.

"Wait, wait." Sarah jumped out of her chair and swept one hand across in front of her as though reading a banner. "What about a whole meal of luscious tidbits? We can unload the odds and ends from the freezer. Or a buffet-style evening, with all-you-can-eat chocolate chili and whatever else is cheap to make? You know we'd generate serious cash on that."

"Okay, sounds great. Let me take a look in the basement and see what we have. I'll talk to Wayne about getting some decent discontinued wines. And I'll call Lucas today." The worry lines between Paisley's eyebrows were gone. "It's time he pitched in, anyhow. But I really don't expect he'll mind. He's been offering, whenever we talk on the phone." She looked at Sarah. "But, honey? You know what this means, right?"

"What?"

"You really have to hit the ball out of the park with the chocolate wedding. We need the money, and the good publicity, more than ever."

Both cousins nodded, their faces serious.

"Yep," Sarah said. "You can count on me for that, P. I'll get upstairs now for my next lesson with the master. We'll talk more about this later. You'd better get to baking, and just leave the bookkeeping until Lucas comes this weekend."

"Good idea. I'd just screw it up, anyhow." Paisley stacked the papers and put them on Emile's desk. "We'll be fine, right?"

"All for one and one for all." Sarah waggled her eyebrows.

Paisley shot her an evil grin. "Where there's a will, there's a way? It is what it is?"

"Okay, enough with the clichés, darling. No moping allowed, and no more burning things in the kitchen." Sarah gave her a hug and went to gather some goodies for her grandfather.

SARAH GRABBED A PLATE of fresh-baked croissants and took them upstairs to Emile's apartment. She planned to spend the day with him, preparing for her meeting with the Chocolate Bride next week. When she knocked on the door, he called "Come!" and she entered.

Emile sat in his chair by the window, surrounded with books and newspapers. He was still wearing his bathrobe and flannel sleep pants, and his hair looked as if it had been combed with a handheld mixer. But he looked at her with a bright, alert expression and smiled. "*Bon-*

jour, ma petite! A beautiful day for my beautiful granddaughter. Come and give an old man a kiss." He held out his arms.

Sarah bent to kiss him on both cheeks, and he did the same. She felt a cinnamon-scented breeze touch her face. *Good morning, Grandma,* she thought. *I love you too.*

"How about a cup of decaf?" she asked. "I found some nice French roast for you at the food co-op. They're making a lot of different blends now, decaffeinated by the Swiss water process. It's quite good." She put the plate of pastries on the coffee table and walked toward the kitchen.

He followed her with his eyes. "Okay, I'll try it. Maybe I can get used to fake food. Can you use it to make espresso?"

"I don't see why not."

"*Bon!* Every day, something new. Life is an adventure, *chérie.*"

If you only knew, Sarah thought, keeping it to herself.

She went into the kitchen to make two cups of espresso and, after grinding the beans to fine powder, packed them into the basket carefully and tamped it down. It dripped out of the machine like dark syrup, just the right consistency. When she carried the cups into the living room, Emile had straightened up the mess and cleared a place for her on the sofa.

"Ah," he crooned when she handed him his small cup and saucer. He took a sip. "Not bad! The flavor, at least, is the same. Guess I can live without the kick."

"That's a good way to phrase it." Sarah used her scolding voice. "Since 'living' is the whole point."

He gave her a sheepish look from under his scraggly eyebrows. "Yes, yes, I know, *ma petite.*"

Sarah sat down across from him and pulled out her notepad. They worked for several hours, then she went back to his small kitchen at noon to make sandwiches and more coffee. After lunch, Emile gave her a quiz, and she answered all the questions correctly. At that point, she was beginning to think she might be able to fake expertise if a chocolate-cooking demonstration wasn't required. Then her grandfather started on food safety regulations and all the intricacies of producing a big event at an off-site location. Soon, she realized how easily the whole precarious stack of cards could collapse in front of hundreds of people. She would need to be confident and a good negotiator to get along with the staff at the wedding venue. Emile warned her there was always a sense of competition in the air when he took his crew into a place with existing food service, like the country club booked by the Chocolate Bride.

"You have to see it from his point of view," Emile said, speaking of the club's chef. "The client loves the location but has rejected his cooking. It's like spitting in the eye! He's not going to like you, *cherie*, no matter how adorable you are."

"What can I do, then? He could sabotage the whole event. I can't watch everything that happens in the kitchen and on the floor, all at the same time!" Sarah's stomach twisted, and her upper lip began to sweat.

Emile looked thoughtful, staring into space. "True, very true. I was planning to manage the kitchen while you ran the service, like we do at home. We'll precook everything here to plate and finish on site, so we need someone to take my place behind the scenes. You can concentrate on making the clients and their guests happy."

He picked up the phone and called Paisley, who was downstairs in the kitchen. A few minutes later, they heard the elevator approach and stop, the doors rumbling open. Sarah went to open the apartment door, and there stood her cousin, carrying a heavy tray.

Sarah's mouth watered as she sniffed the Black Forest cake and saw the teapot covered with their grandmother's favorite knitted cozy. "Yum," she whispered, closing the door behind Paisley, who set down the tray after Emile moved his books off the table.

"Just a small slice, Grandpa," Paisley cautioned. "There's a whole lot of stimulation packed into this cake. We don't want your heart racing."

Emile frowned, but he nodded. "One small piece," he agreed. "The doctor said that one modest transgression every day won't hurt if I follow my program the rest of the time. I walked this morning, and I'm taking Hershey and Devon to the dog park later. So don't worry, I'm being good. Probably the first time ever."

Sarah got cups and saucers, and everyone helped themselves, followed by a few minutes of communal silence while they ate and drank. Then Emile brought up the subject of the wedding, and they presented their concerns to Paisley.

"Obviously, I need to be at the country club with Sarah. Can't Raoul and Jerome handle the kitchen at the restaurant?" she asked. "They did it the night you went to the hospital. It'll be fine if Raoul's nephew comes in to help. Louis is a good prep chef. We've used him before, on Valentine's Day."

"Brilliant!" Emile clapped his hands. "The perfect solution. You see, my dear. Nothing to worry about." He put his arm around Sarah and squeezed.

She nodded but wasn't convinced.

"Girls," Emile said, leaning back and looking dreamily out the window. "Did I ever tell you about the day I met your grandmother? You know, I owe all my happiness, and your very existence, to a *soufflé au chocolat!*"

Paisley smiled at her cousin with a wink, since they had both heard the story many times. "You were working as sous chef at a little restaurant in Paris called Chez Joseph, right?" she said, piling the dirty dishes onto the tray.

Sarah continued the tale. "One night, a beautiful young lady came into the restaurant with her extremely wealthy upper-class gentleman, and they ordered a dessert soufflé, but the chef was indisposed and had left early."

"The lady was so ravishing, you couldn't help spying on her through the swinging door," Paisley added as she waved away Sarah's move to help and carried the tray toward Emile's kitchen. "She had long golden hair like a fairy-tale princess, and the bluest eyes you ever saw."

The sunlight coming in the window behind him glowed through his thin white hair as Emile picked up the thread. "The *patron* tells me to make the soufflé. It is an important guest, and we must not disappoint. I have never done this before, but I am very careful, following the recipe, and it comes out of the oven absolutely perfect."

Sarah smiled. "Grandma was so impressed, she came back into the kitchen to congratulate you, and it was love at first sight."

"Yeah," Paisley called from the kitchen, where it sounded as though she was loading the dishwasher. "Who needs a rich boyfriend when you can have Emile Dumas?"

"And all the chocolate soufflé you can eat," Sarah said. "Don't forget that part."

"It's a powerful dessert, truly." Emile gestured with his hands, raising his voice. "It brought us together. The love of my life, thanks to a *soufflé au chocolat*. Remember this when it's time for some magic in your lives. A little chocolate can make miracles happen."

Any wonder I'm so addicted? Sarah thought as she tidied up the books and papers, smiling. *It runs in the family.*

The faint scent of cinnamon drifted past her nose again, like the ghost of Christmas cookies past. Then it was gone, and she looked up to see her grandfather enveloped by a bright radiance, draped around him like a blanket of light as he sat in front of the sunny window and closed his eyes, drifting off into the past.

Bye, Grandma! Sarah thought as she and Paisley tiptoed out of the room.

SARAH TAGGED ALONG as Paisley headed upstairs to her studio apartment to kick back for a while and change clothes before the dinner shift.

At the top of the stairs to the third floor was a door that led out onto the flat roof that covered most of the building. At the far end were a greenhouse and raised vegetable beds that supplied the restaurant with fresh organic greens year-round, and the chicken coop that provided their eggs. The circle of life was in full operation here, since the manure from the chickens fertilized the veggies, the scraps from the restaurant fed the chickens, and the chickens gave back eggs and, occasionally, one of their older sisters, who would discreetly disappear and turn up in Emile's *coq au vin* pot a few hours later.

The rest of the third floor consisted of an itty-bitty one-room apartment, where Paisley lived. Sarah always said it was a good thing her cousin was short or she'd never fit. She wondered how it worked when Paisley's boyfriend, Wayne, slept over. The guy was well over six feet, and if he lay down, his feet would probably be outside. Well, maybe that was a slight exaggeration, but the place was definitely small. When the two women stepped in through the sliding glass doors, Sarah felt a twitch of claustrophobia and automatically ducked.

Paisley did keep her nest very tidy, a good thing considering there was nowhere for clutter to accumulate. Her Murphy bed folded up into a cupboard, leaving space for a small sitting area that could be pushed back against the wall when the bed was in use. The kitchenette was divided from the living space by a short counter with two barstools, and the bathroom had a slender stall shower, a compact sink, and a tiny toilet that reminded Sarah of those on a train. She was always afraid she would sit down and break something.

"Seltzer?" Paisley asked, flipping open the door of her compact refrigerator.

"Sure." Sarah nodded and sat on the love seat. "So, what do you really think?"

"About the wedding job or about Grandpa?" Paisley handed her a cold Perrier and sat down in the little slipper chair.

"Both."

"I think the wedding will be fine. I have utter confidence in you." Paisley lifted her bottle for a toast, and they clinked.

"What about Grandpa, then? Do you think we're doing everything we should? I'm kind of worried about his diet. I saw a pint of heavy cream in his refrigerator just now. How can we keep vigilant without pissing him off?"

Paisley frowned. "Where did that come from? Not downstairs, do you think?"

Sarah shrugged. "Who knows? His car is right out in the parking lot. He can go to the store whenever he wants. We can't stop him."

"And we can't watch him all the time, even though I'm right here. He could have slipped out just now, and we'd never know it."

"Yes, he has to police himself."

Paisley sighed and held the cold bottle to her forehead. "Okay, I'll talk to him about it. And you do it too."

"We'll double-team him." Sarah smiled, remembering many times from their childhood when they'd used the same strategy with great success.

Paisley seemed to remember the same thing and grinned. "The power of Salt and Pepper?" She used the nicknames they used to call each other.

Sarah leaned forward to wrap her cousin in a hug. "Thanks for being you, P." Her throat needed clearing, and her voice wobbled.

"Nothin' to it, easy peasy. You okay, Sarah?"

"Mmmpf," she replied, her face buried in Paisley's shoulder. She wanted to talk about Blake and her experience with sexting, but it all seemed so lame. "I'm fine. Just a little emotional from the soufflé story. Gets me every time."

"I know. Me too."

They hugged for another minute then said goodbye, and Sarah went home to meet Devon's bus.

Chapter 16

That night on the way to work, Sarah came to a reluctant conclusion. The online dating scenario just wasn't working for her, no matter how sweet HotNCold was. She couldn't handle the risk of letting down her guard with someone who might turn out to be something other than what he'd appeared. She'd been there before, and it sucked. The idea of possibly dating Blake in real life was scary but somehow less so than it seemed before. At least he was a known quantity.

Sarah had assumed that dating someone via computer would be totally safe and anonymous. Now she was involved with this man, even intimate in a bizarre way. She didn't even know for sure that the fabulous abs in his photo were his or that "he" was even a guy, for that matter. Anyone could be sitting behind that keyboard.

How do I break up with someone online? What's the etiquette?

She didn't feel right about dumping the guy by disappearing and never responding to his messages again. He hadn't done anything to deserve it. In fact, he'd been totally accommodating. He showed respect for her. She should return the favor and let him down easy.

She needed to explain.

When she got to the restaurant, Sarah went straight into the dining room to her "office" behind the bar then tapped out a note on her phone. She pushed Send.

WHEN BLAKE CHECKED his phone after work that evening, he found Sarah's message. He stood in the parking lot outside the factory and read it with his key in the door to his truck, distracted in midmotion.

She was ditching him. That much was clear. She wanted to meet "one more time" online to talk about why she couldn't "see" him anymore.

Blake stuffed his phone into his pocket and got into the truck. Resting his forehead against the steering wheel, he closed his eyes. His failed attempt at being sexy in writing had obviously sealed his doom. He'd seen it coming. Stupid of him to think this could work.

The only good thing was that maybe now he didn't have to humiliate himself by confessing his double identity after all. He'd been trying to figure out how to pull that off without losing her completely. If she was dumping HotNCold, then why shouldn't Blake benefit, and none the wiser? The conflict and competition would be over.

Maybe he'd never have to tell her. His mom wouldn't approve, but it would be a hell of a lot easier. Jordan had obviously noticed he'd been hanging around the restaurant and chatting her up, but he didn't know the rest. It could stay a secret.

Blake sat up and typed on his phone.

HotNCold: *Sorry to let you down, Coco. Guess I'm not very good at this.*

He clicked Send, and she must have been checking her phone, because a few seconds later came the reply.

CocoLvr: *Don't say that, you're great. It's not you, it's me.*

Blake couldn't help smiling.

HotNCold: *Hey, I've heard that line before! LOL*

CocoLvr: *LOL! No, really, I mean it.*

HotNCold: *OK, so why is it you? What's wrong, Coco, if it's not my crappy sexting?*

There was a pause. He waited, watching his messages.

Then the screen blinked, and the chime sounded as her reply appeared.

CocoLvr: *Sorry, I'm at work. Had to pour wine. It's kind of a long story, Hot.*

HotNCold: *And you're working, I get it. Never mind.*

CocoLvr: *No, I mean it. It started with my father, if you really want to know. Then my ex-husband continued the tradition. Bottom line is, I have issues with trust.*

Blake held his breath. She was opening up now. She must really like him, or she wouldn't tell him all this.

HotNCold: *It's understandable. But not every guy you meet online is out to hurt you, Coco.*

Another pause.

CocoLvr: *I know, Hot. It just makes me too nervous. I'm a wreck. I even started imagining someone is watching my house.*

Blake frowned. *What is she talking about?*

HotNCold: *For real, Coco? What happened?*

She told him about the noises, the truck across the street, and the trampled bushes. A surge of protectiveness made him want to rush over and patrol her neighborhood.

HotNCold: *You should call the cops if that happens again.*

CocoLvr: *Oh, I don't think it will. I'm probably making it all up. That's the point.*

HotNCold: *I see. Look, Coco. I don't want anything from you that you don't want to give, so relax. I'd love to stay friends, if you're open to it. But I'll back off now, give you some peace. You can message me if you want to talk. I'll be here for you.*

Next came a longer pause, and Blake was actually driving out of the parking lot when the next message made his phone chirp. He pulled over to read it.

CocoLvr: *You're the sweetest guy I know, Hot. Thanks for understanding.*

He sighed in relief. He'd been able to really turn it around. *Now, don't push it.* He grinned before typing his reply.

HotNCold: *No sweat, kiddo. Stay in touch!*

CocoLvr: *I will.*

HotNCold: *Bye now.*

He added a red heart and a smiley face, since he knew women loved those weird little pictures.

She sent back a lipstick print and a hand waving.

Well, it wasn't a real kiss goodbye, but it was the online equivalent. It was the most he could expect, considering.

Every lady in distress needs a hero to protect her, he thought. It sounded as though somebody was messing with Sarah. Even if it was paranoia, as she thought, she would still appreciate a knight in shining armor.

Tomorrow was the last game of the baseball playoffs, and he knew Sarah would be there. *The perfect opportunity,* Blake thought. He headed home to polish up his shield and sword.

IT WAS A SLOW NIGHT at The Three Chocolatiers, and Sarah spent most of the evening behind the bar, playing Bubble Mania on her phone while she thought about Blake. The memory of that moment in his office when he'd reached for her, right before the phone rang, still made her breathless. If only she hadn't been so nervous.

After the last customers said good night, Sarah took off her long brown apron and went to lock the front door. She stepped outside for a breath of air. Looking up and down the street, she saw no signs of a tall man and a brown dog, so she hugged herself and sighed.

One moment she'd had two men pursuing her, then she pushed them both away and was left with nobody. How would she ever find the right guy if she kept this up? The internet was cool, but it was time to give old-fashioned socializing another try. She was totally fed up with being lonely and miserable.

Sarah went home, let Hershey out, started the dishwasher, and climbed the stairs. She checked on Devon and found him lying with the covers thrown back to let the breeze coming in the window cool his skin. She kissed his cheek, careful not to wake him.

Sarah went into her room, where Hershey had already curled up on his mat.

As she undressed in the dark, she thought about Blake again. He would be at the playoffs tomorrow, since his team was competing against Devon's for the championship. She'd have a chance to see if he was still interested. Something needed to change, that was certain. Even with a great kid, a wonderful, supportive family, and good friends, she still had an empty place inside that hungered, all the time, no matter what she did to distract herself. Dreams and fantasies certainly weren't going to help.

Sarah collapsed into bed, pushed her face into the pillow to muffle the sound, and let the tears come. A few minutes later, she rubbed her face on the sheet, sat up, and reached into her bedside table drawer, but it was empty.

Of course, it's downstairs, she thought and swung her legs out of bed.

She padded down to the kitchen on bare feet and found the white paper bag she'd left on the countertop. Inside was one of the most decadent, satisfying cupcakes in the world, Paisley's devil's food chocolate lava cake. She put it on a plate and slid it into the microwave. While it warmed, she got a glass of milk and a fork. Hershey had followed her downstairs and sat at her feet, watching expectantly.

"No way," she told him. "Chocolate is dangerous for dogs."

The bell dinged, and she took out the cupcake, her mouth watering at the sight of melted chocolate bubbling up from the middle and flowing down the sides of the pastry. Just as she was about to take a bite, something brushed against the window screen, and Hershey barked.

He ran over and stood with his front paws on the windowsill, looking outside. Sarah switched on the outside lights and looked around, but just like last time, nothing moved. Hershey lost interest, dropped back onto all fours, and went over to sniff around the island for crumbs. It was probably just a big moth.

Determined not to be a scaredy-cat, Sarah switched off the lights and took her cupcake and milk upstairs. But before she left the kitchen, she double-checked the back door to make sure it was bolted securely.

No sense in inviting trouble, she thought. *Even if it's imaginary.*

Chapter 17

Blake finished brushing Kahlua, snapped on his bright-red collar, and made him "sit!" for a crumb of cheese. The dog would do anything for cheddar, so Blake usually carried some in a little baggie. He found that even when the treat got all dried up and funky, it still worked. Maybe it even worked better. When it came to chewing and chewing, to extract every last iota of flavor, Kahlua showed obsessive concentration.

In many ways, Blake identified with this.

For example, today he was chewing on how to convince Sarah that love in real life beat cybersex with a stranger, every time. After thinking and rethinking and rerethinking all night long, he kept coming back to the same notion that was the basis for his company's marketing strategy: a free taste demonstrates quality. He and Sarah would be terrific together if he could just persuade her to try a sample.

The erotic pictures that popped into his head inspired him to be persistent. Imagining all the ways he could please her was as stimulating as a double-chocolate hot fudge sundae. When a shell-pink dawn finally illuminated the horizon behind the thin screen of trees, Blake sat with his coffee on a lounge chair in the small garden behind his condo. He watched the sun swell up from the fiery edge of the world and wished Sarah were here, her bare legs dangling as she sat on his lap, arms around his neck, as they welcomed the new day together.

Maybe not today but soon, he vowed. *Possibly tonight.*

Blake knew there was a sleepover for the kids on Devon's team at Jimmy Mason's house tonight. He'd heard Sticky talking about it at the last game. A golden opportunity like this didn't appear often, and he wasn't going to blow it. If she didn't invite him to dinner again, he would ask her.

A flame of anticipation kept him charged up as he showered and dressed, and he whistled as he grabbed Kahlua's red leash and threw some supplies in a shopping bag then stowed it behind the seats in his truck.

Just don't act like a total fool. Everybody knows what's going on, but try not to advertise it.

Kahlua jumped into the passenger seat, smiling and panting as Blake climbed behind the wheel. The dog was obviously having fun already. Hopefully, the human would soon achieve the same karmic bliss. A vision of Sarah wearing nothing but a sheet had been chasing him around in his dreams last night, and it appeared before his eyes again now. Blake shook his head and gripped the steering wheel tighter.

Steady. Stay focused.

"Okay, buddy, here we go." He pulled on his purple *Blake's* baseball cap, popped a disk into the CD player, and sang along with Willie Nelson's "On the Road Again" as he pulled out of the parking lot. He had a good feeling about this day, despite the undeniable danger of making a giant jackass of himself.

SARAH PUT THE LAST of the beer, juice, and water into the cooler and dumped ice on top of the drinks then closed the lid. Paisley and Emile were bringing the food, so she just had to throw some chips and gluten-free treats into a bag. Miki helped her carry everything to the car and load it into the cargo hold, while Devon sat in the back seat, dangerously quiet and still.

Sarah went around to his window and examined his face. It looked a little gray. "You okay, punkin?"

He nodded, his jaw clenched and his expression grim.

Sarah automatically reached in to feel his forehead, and he brushed away her hand with a scowl. She tried to encourage him. "It'll be fine. You'll see. You'll do great and have fun."

Devon had been so anxious since last night, it was painful to watch. He was probably afraid of blowing it during this last, most important game of the season. Especially considering his long history of public humiliation, times when he was younger and totally lost it at the mall or a grocery store. He was less impulsive now, but the social pressure was even greater.

Miki put Hershey in the back of the car and closed the cargo door. Today he was wearing a bright-yellow collar and leash in honor of Devon's team. Sarah and Miki were similarly decked out with caps, shirts, and matching yellow sneakers that Miki had found at the dollar store. They piled into the car and pulled out of the driveway.

Devon was silent on the ride over, and Sarah checked him in the rearview mirror every few minutes. Miki offered him a protein bar, which he munched while staring out the window. When they arrived and parked, he leapt out of the car and sped over to where his team was gathering, immediately lost from view in a blur of yellow shirts. Sarah could tell he was struggling to stay calm and doing a pretty good job.

Time to let him grow up, she thought, suppressing the urge to go over and speak to the coach. She took one end of the cooler to carry it into the stands with Miki, while Hershey followed obediently at their heels.

The first thing she noticed when they went around the end of the bleachers was Blake Harrison, sitting by her friends and family with his cute chocolate Lab. Her girlfriends saw her and cheered, beckoning. Sticky Mason and the other fathers smiled and nodded. Blake took off his purple cap and waved it at her then climbed down the stairs, signaling he would help with the cooler. The two dogs greeted each other like long-lost brothers, sniffing thoroughly, relaxed and mellow, tails wagging.

Miki praised Kahlua and petted him, taking the leash from Blake to free his hands. "I'll hang out with these good boys over here. Don't worry, we'll be okay," she said and strolled along with both dogs toward a grassy area on the sidelines.

"Hey," Blake greeted Sarah, his eyes taking a split-second trip down to her feet and back up to her face.

So, he's still interested. Maybe I didn't ruin it after all.

She smiled, and he looked surprised but pleased then hoisted the cooler up onto his shoulder and brought it to where her family was already seated.

"Sarah! Come explain to me this game, *ma petite*. All I know is three strikes and you're out." Emile had a yellow bandana tied around his neck. He wore a wide-brimmed straw hat and sat on a comfortable padded seat.

Paisley looked cute in her yellow sundress and sandals. "Grandpa used to play soccer when he was a boy in France. Did you know that, Sarah?" she asked, standing up to give her cousin a quick hug.

"Yes, but it's much different from this," Emile said in a bright voice. Sarah hadn't seen him this upbeat since his illness and was glad she'd insisted he come. "The great American sport! I really should learn about it, since I am American now. And so I will, thanks to my great-grand-son." He beamed, radiating pleasure.

Out on the field, the two teams were warming up. One of the yellow coaches threw a high pitch toward the outfield. Teetering as he watched the ball falling directly toward his outstretched mitt, Devon held his ground and waited. Sarah's friends went wild when he caught the ball and managed not to drop it.

"Great catch! We'd better watch out for that kid," Blake said, grinning. "Guess I'll have to stop fraternizing with the enemy for now." He stood up and bent close to Sarah's ear. "Don't let Sticky drink all the beer." His lips tickled, and his hand was warm on her shoulder.

She brazened it out. "Sure thing, coach. No offense, but I won't wish you luck. Go yellow!"

He smiled and doffed his cap, heading over to where the purple team had gathered. As if in a dream, she watched him walk away, fascinated by those long legs striding and those wide shoulders bulging as the muscles moved when he clapped his hands and whistled for the kids.

This was a man who probably wouldn't be scared off by the fact that she had a son. He actually *liked* kids and came from a solid family. His parents and siblings were great. Paisley used to date Jordan back in high school, and they were still friends now. Emile adored Blake's parents, who enjoyed a romantic dinner at the Chocolatiers every few weeks. On the surface, everything looked perfect for something good to happen with Blake. She just had to stay cool and not get freaked out.

Not every guy is like Jim, she thought. *Maybe this could work, for me and for Devon.*

For a moment, her eyes blurred, then she blinked and heard her friends cheer as the two teams lined up and the game began. Purple won the toss and was first at bat. That meant Devon had to be ready to repeat his spectacular catch if necessary. Sarah started to sweat at the thought.

Two hours later, they were all hoarse from yelling, the beer was gone, and Paisley's amazing picnic had been devoured. It was close, but the yellow team won, and Devon managed to get through the whole game in relative obscurity. Everyone was still congratulating him for his big catch during the warm-ups, which was more positive reinforcement than he'd ever received before. Sarah watched him bump shoulders with his teammates as they congratulated one another, and she started to relax for the first time all day.

She volunteered to drive as many of the kids as she could fit in her car to the celebratory sleepover party at Sticky Mason's house. Devon's sleeping bag and backpack were in the back of the car, ready and waiting. With a party to look forward to on top of winning the game, he was beside himself with joy.

"You understand what you're getting into?" she quietly asked Sticky, who was loading his own vehicle.

He looked at her and nodded. "You bet, Blondie. Jimmy's got two older brothers. I'm the king of sleepovers. No sweat." He threw a few more backpacks into his minivan and slammed the tailgate shut. "Anyhow, my sister and her hubby are coming to help. No way would I do this alone."

"He can't eat sugar, caffeine, or gluten. You have to remember, or he'll be bouncing off the walls. You know he has ADHD, right?"

Sticky nodded and put his arm around her shoulders. "Don't worry, princess. My oldest kid was the same way. Now he's in college and going to be an accountant. All things must pass." He patted her on the back.

Tears leaked into her eyes, and her throat hurt as she tried to suppress the anxiety. "I know he'll turn out okay," she said, her voice cracking. "It's just hard to watch him find his way by bumping into things."

"There, there, Blondie. Now man up, er, woman up and get a grip. You're embarrassing the kid and ruining my reputation as the town asshole."

"Okay." She sniffed, smiled, and pulled away. "Sorry about that."

Sticky laughed. "Listen, kiddo, I've got your number. Any problems, I'll call. Now let's drive these champs over to my place, then you go home and take a nice bubble bath, or whatever it is you females do for Me Time." He patted her arm again and turned and climbed into his old minivan, full of rowdy yellow-shirted kids.

It looked as though Devon had loaded up the back of Sarah's car with friends too. There were heads bobbing and happy voices, and the radio was blaring. Miki stood by the open passenger door with Hershey, entertaining the crowd with her dance moves. Families found their cars and loaded up, while others paused to say goodbye to their friends. Sarah quickly wiped her eyes and saw Blake coming toward her through the crowd of parents and kids with his dog, a puzzled expression on his face.

"Everything okay?" He ran his hand down her arm and squeezed her hand.

The electric path of his touch made goose bumps rise up on her arms, and she tried not to jump. It took every ounce of control to keep from squeaking. "Yes, it's fine," she said, breathless. "Just nerves. It's Devon's first big sleepover party tonight, at Sticky's house."

"Ahhh, I see." He nodded, his beautiful eyes smiling, lingering.

Her mind began to wander to those deep, green pools. Suddenly nervous, she broke the eye contact and turned to walk toward her car. He followed, walking by her side.

"I remember my first sleepover." Blake slung his arm around her shoulders. "At John Sheehan's house. We stole his father's beer and got wasted, then Freddy Spence threw up all over Mrs. Sheehan's new couch. It was great."

"Not for Mrs. Sheehan!" Sarah objected, laughing. His hand was on her shoulder, and she snuggled against his warm arm, enjoying the way her shoulder fit perfectly right beneath his armpit and how her long stride matched his. Their bodies probably fit together in other ways too. Sarah was more and more eager to find out exactly how good a match they were.

They reached her car as a wave of baseball fans began to cross the parking lot. Miki ran to the back with Hershey and handed the leash to Sarah, then she walked around and got into the front passenger seat before slamming the door. Now the car was actually rocking a little, left then right, as a good-natured wrestling match broke out in the back seat.

"So, Sarah," Blake began, turning her to face him then stepping back to let a mother with two toddlers pass by. He stepped toward her again. "I was wondering whether you might..." Another group of people approached, and this time he stepped forward as they walked past. Now they stood toe to toe, while the two dogs looked up at their masters and grinned, tails wagging. "I mean, if you're not busy..."

"Mom! Time to go. We're missing the *whole party*!" Devon jumped over the back seat and yelled at the top of his lungs as he slid out the open cargo door. He grabbed her hand and pulled it up and down as he jiggled. "Let's go, Mom." The dogs got excited and began to prance along with him. Voices inside the car sang "Rock You," and it did, from side to side. The back seat was a swarm of yellow as air guitars and drums were played.

Skittish already from the closeness and the intoxicating scent of something sweet that radiated off Blake's body, Sarah jumped and turned to caution her son with a finger. "I'm coming. Right now. Calm down."

She turned to Blake and smiled, distracted. "Sorry, I really have to go. They won't wait any longer." Blake stepped back as another young family crossed between them, then a teenager pushing a bike.

Blake laughed, apparently defeated, and shrugged. "Okay, I'll call you later if that's all right."

"Yes, thanks." Sarah grabbed Hershey, boosted him into the cargo hold, and slammed the door shut. Then she ran around to her door and slid into the driver's seat.

Chaos reigned in the back seat. Yelling at them to fasten their seat belts, she started the car and carefully wove her way out of the busy parking lot. All the way across town, young voices uttered piercing cries, whistles, bizarre noises, and the sounds of various bodily functions. One kid had the sound of a motorcycle engine down pat. Another one could say, "Zap ban doody," while emitting a long belch. They laughed uproariously, and through the insanity, Sarah smiled. It was loud and obnoxious, but it was the sound of normal kids having normal fun.

She stopped for a red light when they were almost there and looked in the rearview mirror. Devon was sitting in the middle, a big grin on his face. Every time he laughed, his nose crinkled up, and he slapped his knees with both hands as his buddies on both sides jostled for space. He was in heaven, clearly.

The contagious joy spread through the car, and Sarah turned to Miki with a smile. "Can I drop you at campus on my way home?"

"Sure, thanks. Big party in the dorms tonight. You working?" Miki had the night off since Devon was otherwise occupied.

"No, I hired a new girl this week, and she's doing great, so I'm actually taking the night off myself. It's been intense lately." She thought of her first appointment with the Chocolate Bride, coming up this week, and shivered.

They made it to the Masons' house and offloaded the passengers. Sarah waved goodbye to the back of Devon's head as he raced into the house. His backpack dragged along behind him. Relieved and a little hurt by his snub, she drove toward home and stopped to let Miki out along the way. Pulling into her driveway, she once again noticed the peeling paint on the porch and was starting to think about finding her scraper and stepladder when she glanced into the rearview mirror again. She frowned, blinking.

Hershey was still there, standing way back in the cargo hold, looking straight at her over the back seat. He was panting and smiling as usual. Something looked different, though.

After parking in the garage, she got out and opened the tailgate. The chocolate Lab jumped out and stared at her intently, making an urgent noise in his throat. She confirmed that his collar and leash were unexpectedly but undeniably bright red.

"Kahlua?"

The dog snapped to attention, sitting at her feet.

"Ohmigod. You poor boy!" She went down on one knee and petted him, scratching behind his ears and stroking his glossy brown head. He put his ears back submissively and gazed at her with sad, soulful eyes. "What did you think was happening? We left your man behind in the parking lot, didn't we? And you just sat there and cooperated. Good boy, Kahlua. What a good dog."

She held the leash and led the dog, whose tail was now wagging, to the fenced-in backyard. After opening the gate, she let him inside and snapped the leash off his collar. He ran across the yard, sniffing happily, and raised his leg against the squirrel tree.

She closed the gate with her hip, went inside through the kitchen door, and pulled her cell phone out of her pocket and dialed Blake's number, which was listed in her contacts under Ice Cream.

"Hi, Sarah."

"I'm so stupid!"

He chuckled. "I was wondering how long it would take you to notice. You had a carload of distractions."

"I dropped everybody off and got all the way home! Can you believe it?" She flipped the switch on the electric teakettle and opened a cabinet to reach for a mug.

"It took me a couple minutes to realize what happened too. Your boy is very well behaved, by the way. He got worried when you drove away, but he trusted me and came along nicely."

Looking out the window, she watched her visitor making himself at home. "Kahlua is a perfect gentleman. He's enjoying our fenced yard at the moment, introducing himself to the squirrels."

"So, can I come over and make the switch?"

She caught her breath, suddenly adding it all up in her mind. *If anything is ever going to happen, it will happen now. This is my chance to find out.*

"Wonderful. Want to stay for dinner?" She opened the fridge to inventory the contents, thinking fast. "I've got some nice salmon, if that's all right."

"Sounds perfect. In about an hour?" He sounded excited.

"Great. See you then."

Sarah went over a mental list: *Change sheets and towels, clean bathroom, shower, shave legs, touch up pedicure, pretty underwear, sexy sundress, uncork a nice bottle of red, set the table on the patio and put out fresh candles... condoms?* She fished around in her wallet to find the packets Paisley had stuffed there the night she signed Sarah up for online dating. Yes, she was all set.

It would be her first real date with a man she found attractive in all these years since the divorce. Hard to believe this was actually happening. She wasn't worried about having forgotten what to do, though. Her body was already telegraphing detailed instructions to her brain. And the best part was this time it would be live, up close and personal, in real life. Actual touching and, hopefully, actual orgasms.

With a smile on her lips and a nervous tickle in her throat, she ran up the stairs to prepare for the seduction.

Chapter 18

Blake ran a hand over his freshly shaved chin for the third time in ten minutes and popped another mint into his mouth. He'd been showered, dressed, and ready for anything when she'd called, but then he puttered around for a while to give her some time. Growing up with his sister and mother had taught him that women needed to perform their ablutions before a social event. The rituals enhanced their self-esteem, and he wanted Sarah to be totally comfortable when the evening began, to help erase the damage done by her father and that jerk, her ex.

Now that he knew what was behind Sarah's fear of men, Blake could try to reassure her. It stood to reason if he generated enough positive vibes, they would cancel out the negative ones that haunted her. She'd said something about feeling like a failure, not good enough. So his plan was to make a list of all the totally legitimate, wonderful things about her and try to say something nice about each of them without sounding like a con artist. It would be tricky but worth a try.

Meanwhile, way at the back of his mind, a tiny red beacon of guilt flashed.

He heard the echo of his mother's warning and wondered whether he shouldn't be planning to confess his double identity instead of planning to take Sarah to bed.

Nope, the last thing I want now is to spook her.

Once she understood how much he cared, she'd be much more likely to forgive his silly charade. He had a chance to take their relationship to the next level, and it was a miracle he'd finally gotten this far after almost a year of watching, hanging around, and hinting. Plus, every guy knew that women liked them much more after they'd had sex. He'd discussed it with his buddies many times. That was why women got so freaked out if they didn't call them the next day. After the sex, they were totally hooked.

Blake stopped in the hallway to check his hair in the mirror again.

And on the hook is right where I want her, he thought, smiling at himself. *Only for the best possible reasons, of course.*

Blake would take excellent care of her heart if he was lucky enough to win it. He wanted nothing more than to fall in love, settle down with one amazing woman, and make a family. From where he stood, Sarah and Devon looked like the cornerstones of happily ever after.

He looked at the clock on his phone and decided an hour was plenty of time for her to primp, so he led Hershey outside. After putting him in the truck, they drove off down the street.

SARAH SAW BLAKE PULL into the driveway as she stood between the stove and the granite island, stirring the risotto, a big white dish towel wrapped around her waist over a rosebud-print cotton sundress. Her long hair was loose and still damp, and she was barefoot. Acoustic guitar music played quietly in the background. Everything on the list was done, and when he came in the door carrying a big bouquet of sunflowers and a brown paper bag, she welcomed him with an easy smile.

Hershey and Kahlua danced a hello to one another and took turns lapping water from the stainless-steel dog dish in the corner. Sarah turned the heat to simmer and set down her spoon to walk around the island and let both dogs out into the fenced yard. She paused to give Blake a bold kiss on the cheek as she passed. He smelled like soap, and his face was smooth and soft. She was tempted to let her lips linger but pulled back. His hands were both full, so all he could do was stare longingly.

She laughed at his frustrated expression. "Welcome," she said, squeezing his arm. "Wow, these are gorgeous! Thank you." She took the flowers to the sink. Her hair swung to one side as she bent to take a large vase out of the lower cabinet, and she felt the air touch her back where the low-cut sleeveless dress exposed her skin and knew it was obvious she wasn't wearing a bra.

"Hope they're okay. I didn't know what kind you like," he mumbled, sounding a little choked up.

She heard the catch in his voice and turned around slowly to face him with her pulse racing. "Yes, they're lovely. So cheerful, summery."

His face was flushed, and his eyes glittered. A shadow of panic lurked in her belly, but then he smiled the most tender, heart-melting smile she'd ever seen, and it was all okay.

He really cares for me, she thought.

She added water to the vase and took the flowers to the island, where she had laid out a plate of cheese and crackers. Salmon fillets were marinating, a salad was in the fridge, and a box of fresh chocolate éclairs sat on the counter. Check, check, and check. Dinner could be served in ten minutes, whenever they were ready. Sarah relaxed her shoulders, looked up at him, and smiled into his eyes, cocking one hip as she leaned against the counter.

"I brought something else I know you'll enjoy." Blake held the eye contact, hesitating with a sly smile. Then he pulled two bottles, a little white box, a carton of half-and-half, and a cocktail shaker out of his shopping bag.

Safely behind the granite counter, she swiveled and took up her spoon again, stirring as the risotto softened and thickened. "What are we having? Sombreros?"

"Nope, chocolate martinis. Ever tried one?"

"Never. Sounds fabulous!" Sarah's chocolate addiction stirred like a sleeping dragon, and her mouth watered. "There's an ice dispenser in the refrigerator door. And here are some glasses that should work." She turned to reach high and pull them out of a cabinet, stretching up on tiptoes.

When she turned around, he was staring at her again, still holding the bottles in midair with a dazed expression. Then he hurried to get ice and measure the ingredients. He did his thing with the cocktail shaker while she removed her apron and turned off the risotto. Then they took the drinks and snacks out to the patio, where she had already set the table and lit lanterns.

The outdoor speakers carried quiet music into the cool, green space where blue hydrangeas and purple bee balm made a border under the shade trees. Cedar armchairs with padded seats surrounded a matching table, where Sarah arranged the food and flowers. Blake poured the martinis and garnished them with chocolate truffles on toothpicks, reminiscent of the olive in a traditional martini. He carefully passed one of the glasses to her and held his up for a toast.

Blake leaned close and captured her eyes. "To us, Sarah. And I mean it." He nodded solemnly, and she mirrored his expression, raising her glass to meet his. The aroma of cacao and alcohol wafted into her lungs, mixed with the scent of his powerful pheromones, and a reaction began to stir deep in her belly.

They drank the smooth, dark, frothy concoction, and she thought how adorable he was to put this together for her, even adding the chocolate garnish as a finishing touch. He would probably have been happier with a cold beer. As for Sarah, the kick of chocolate liqueur and vodka went straight to her head in seconds, and after the third sip and a few nibbles on the truffle, a pleasant heat radiated from her core.

Blissful sensations pumped into her awareness with every heartbeat, and her lips began to throb. Licking them, she tasted truffle, and a *frisson* of pleasure brought goose bumps on her skin. This was the point when she usually got up and exited, but tonight, she gave herself permission to ride the wave of endorphins wherever it might go.

Sarah crossed her legs, settling back in the chair, and saw his eyes follow the line of her calf down to her pink-polished toenails. If she looked anything like she felt right now, there must be a seductive grin on her face. One strap of the sundress had fallen off her shoulder, and she glanced down to see the top curve of her breast. She left it that way and watched his face when he noticed. As she raised her glass for another sip, he reached over and took her free hand, playing with her fingers. When he touched her, there was a snap like static electricity.

"I hope you understand," Blake started, a hesitance in his voice and a little pucker between his eyebrows. "I've been trying not to move too fast. Like you asked. Following your lead." When she started to speak, he went on, "No, don't say anything. You're just about the most beautiful, smart, funny, wonderful woman I've ever come across, Sarah." He examined her face, as though checking her reaction. "And I'm amazed by how you juggle work and family so well. I really admire you."

Sarah heard his words through a haze as he refilled her glass and added another skewered chocolate truffle. "Oh, no, I don't think—" she objected but then reached to pop the truffle into her mouth. "Mmmm, so good." She saw him watching her and returned to the conversation, though most of her attention was on the field of energy that radiated between them. "Blake, I know what I said before, but now, well, I guess I feel differently. About you, that is. I know you're a good person and you'd never lie to me or hurt me. I was just scared because of what happened before. But I can't let it ruin the rest of my life, or Devon's." Letting it all out in a rush, she leaned toward him and felt his heat, every skin cell in her body yearning to be touched.

Blake gave her hand a warm squeeze, and she felt it all the way to her toes.

He looked relieved but flustered. "You can't imagine how glad I am to hear you say that, Sarah, but maybe we should think about—"

Distracted by his hand, she interrupted. "No, Blake. Let's not ruin this. It's very simple. I like you, and you like me, right? No stupid hangups, no misdirected anger, no hidden agendas. A clean start, okay?" She laced her fingers through his and gave him a long look, smiling.

He hesitated but nodded, his eyes cautious.

"So, how about that salmon? Why don't you start the grill while I get things out of the fridge?" She pulled her hand away, took a deep cleansing breath, and stood up to go inside.

"Okay, whatever you say." He still looked worried.

She gave him a reassuring smile. "Let's grill. I'm starving. I could eat a brontosaurus."

Now he grinned. "Yes, ma'am! Me too."

"Be right back." She went inside to get the salad, rice, and fish then stopped at the mirror by the back door to check her makeup and fluff her hair. So far, so good. They were past the awkward part. She felt confident and powerful. After putting the food on a tray, along with the bottle of red wine and two glasses, she carried it out to the patio, and they began to chat comfortably about work, friends, and family.

Everything was going great. Why had she been worried? Being with Blake was so easy, like hanging out with someone she'd known all her life. Sarah let go of her fear and opened wide, pushing all of the dark and bitter feelings out into the fresh air. Watching him enjoy himself, looking at her with such admiration, was like cold water in the desert. She felt herself melting, softening, as the scars that had held her rigid for so long began to dissolve.

It was a beautiful night, and something magical was finally happening in her life.

THE SUN HAD SET, AND shadows under the trees deepened as the sky turned pink then lavender then navy blue with a few stars beginning to wink. Hershey and Kahlua had eaten in the kitchen earlier and were sitting like a pair of bookends on either side of the table, watching for scraps that might fall.

Blake had a moment to think when she took the dishes inside, telling him to stay seated. He watched her through the windows while she moved around the kitchen, graceful and efficient. It was dark outside on the patio and lit from within the house, like a stage. He was the audience. The skirt of her dress swayed around her bare legs, and a flash of skin showed her naked back when her long hair swung to one side. He felt like a voyeur, and it was incredibly sexy.

Totally enchanted, he watched as Sarah took a pastry box out of the refrigerator and brought it, with two plates and forks, to the table. She opened the lid and showed him four chocolate éclairs dripping with fudgy frosting.

Her eyes shone. "Two each!" she said, her voice husky. Then she dipped her finger into the frosting and brought it to his mouth.

He licked the fudge from her finger and was about to lean in for a kiss when she pulled back, focused on the pastry, and put the éclairs on two plates. Taking a fast bite, she closed her eyes in a mock swoon.

"A really great meal," he said, nodding in admiration as he downed both of his pastries in a few swift mouthfuls. She polished hers off and wiped her mouth on a napkin, watching him appraisingly. "Terrific dessert, by the way. Paisley's handiwork?"

"Yes," she said, gathering up their dishes. "But dessert isn't finished."

He raised one eyebrow and stood to move a chair out of her way.

Sarah deliberately brushed against him as she slipped by, whispering, "Come with me!" She led him to the kitchen door, glancing back over her shoulder to make sure he followed. "Let the dogs in too," she said then kicked the door shut behind them. She put the dishes on the counter next to the sink and beckoned, flipping off the kitchen lights.

He moved in for a long kiss, bending her back against the smooth granite and thinking about taking her right there, or on the floor. But she wriggled out from underneath him and slipped away toward the stairs, beckoning again with her finger.

"Come up to my tree house, Tarzan," she said. "I'll make it worth your while!"

Blake didn't have to hear it twice. He bounded up the stairs behind her, watching her sway as she went. All thoughts of his mother's advice fled as his mind shut down for the night and the combination of alcohol, chocolate, and testosterone drugged him into a state of mindless passion. Like a human sacrifice too thoroughly hypnotized by bliss to anticipate the fall of the knife, he took her to bed without further consideration of truth and lies or right and wrong. All he knew was the touch and smell and taste of her, and the crashing waves of passion that eventually brought them both to rest on her soft white sheets, twined in one another's arms.

Chapter 19

The neighborhood was still quiet when Sarah woke up the next morning. She lay on her back and watched shadows move on the bedroom ceiling. Soft sunlight bounced off the green walls and cast a celery glow above her, contrast for the flickering silhouettes of sickles and stars. Crack and curve shifted with each shake of the wind that rustled through the huge maple tree outside the window.

Last night, she thought, remembering.

Her impulse was to leap out of bed and run to the bathroom for her robe. She felt him lying next to her, a column of warmth along her side. His breath came and went with a quiet whistle, in the easy rhythm of sleep. Turning her head, she sniffed his scent mixed with the clean smell of her pillowcase.

Blake turned his head and sighed, his long legs stretching out beyond the foot of the bed as he rolled onto his back. She watched his profile. Strong, even features, with full lips that curved deliciously into a little smile.

He was such a happy person, even asleep. It was his nature. The optimism was contagious, tempting her to let down her guard. He'd been very sweet to Devon too. But the thought of her son brought a vague sense of discomfort, and her stomach clenched.

What was I thinking? How could I let this happen?

Sarah glanced at Blake again then carefully peeled back the sheet on her side of the bed. Swinging one bare leg over the side, she shifted her weight to stand up.

"Morning, beautiful." His voice was deep and full of sleep. She felt it rumble in the quiet space, shaking her thoughts into a dialogue, putting her on the spot. She'd have to answer now. She'd have to turn around.

The palm of his hand ran across her naked back, making her shiver. Then his arm slipped around her waist and pulled her back into bed, up against him under the sheets. His body heat slid over her, and she melted into a loose curl. He snuggled his face into her shoulder and kissed the side of her neck.

"Blake, I don't want you to..."

He continued the kisses around her shoulder, turning her onto her back.

"Get the wrong idea..."

He leaned over to cover her with his body, looking down into her eyes.

"I mean," she said, staring into the color of summer leaves with the sun behind them, floating away from logic. "I don't really do this kind of thing, you know."

He smiled and bent his head and kissed her. Images from their lovemaking the night before flooded into her mind—smooth limbs entwined, breath whispering—as he took the kiss deeper, and she completely forgot what she'd been trying to say.

She'd get up and find her robe in a little while. They could talk over coffee. Plenty of time before Miki and Devon got home. Swirling into a flow of heat and sparks, with that peaceful green light shining through her translucent eyelids, Sarah let herself relax and receive.

Maybe it wasn't a mistake. Maybe she could trust him. Or maybe she was being stupid and had forgotten what she had to lose.

AS IT TURNED OUT, THEY didn't have time to talk afterward. The morning passed in an intoxicating sensual blur, and when he gave her one last kiss and got into his truck, it was almost time to go pick up Devon from the sleepover.

Sarah cleared away the breakfast dishes and went upstairs. The twisted bedsheets confronted her accusingly, and she tried to push the images of what had happened between them out of her mind. After pulling the covers taut and fluffing the pillows, she tucked the bedspread in neatly and smoothed it into place. Now everything looked normal, as it should.

It didn't seem to help much, though. She could still see the ghosts of their bodies tangled together and feel the silk of his touch. Her body missed him already. But her mind spun with the usual worries, and as she showered and dressed, that critical internal voice reminded her how unreliable her judgment was when it came to men. But a tiny, hopeful voice answered, rising up out of the fear that had kept her alone for so long.

Maybe not this time. Maybe it'll be different.

She took Hershey out for a quick stroll around the yard then grabbed her jacket. Just as she was about to leave, she heard the mail fall through the slot in the front door and land on the floor. She gathered the envelopes and set them on the kitchen counter to sort through later, but one of the letters caught her eye.

It was a fat, heavy envelope with a Florida return address and looked as though it came from an accounting firm or law office. She ripped it open, unfolded the documents inside, and scanned them, her face growing hot as her emotions threatened to explode.

Her ex-husband had hired a new team of lawyers and was taking her back to court. Jim contended that the financial settlement was not equitable and should be renegotiated. Now that she was working at the restaurant and had become a full partner, she no longer needed his financial support. The language was hard to understand, but it sounded as though he was actually claiming that she should pay him alimony, since she had emptied their savings and initiated their legal separation.

There was also a carefully worded threat that custody of their son might be renegotiated as well if a compromise couldn't be reached.

Sarah's hands shook as she folded the papers and stuffed them inside the fancy embossed envelope. She sat down on a barstool and tried to breathe, dark splotches blurring her vision. She lay her head down on the granite countertop and felt its coolness against her cheek.

How can this be happening all over again? Just when I think the monster is dead, he comes back to life and attacks! It's the nightmare that never ends.

And just when she'd been considering the possibility that living happily ever after might be a real option for her. How stupid could she be? It was obvious that was never going to happen.

Sarah stood up and straightened her spine, fear transformed into blazing anger. No way was any man going to take advantage of her ever again. Not Jim, and certainly not Blake Harrison, no matter how sweet and cute he could be when he wanted to have sex with her.

Relationships were simply too risky. She had been right to think that being alone was the safest path, for her and for Devon. Grinding her teeth as her jaw clenched, she went out the back door and headed off to collect her son.

Her son. All hers. And that was how it was going to remain if she had anything to say about it.

WHEN SARAH GOT TO WORK around noon, Jerome and Raoul were busy in the kitchen, and Paisley was in the dining room, carefully transferring her newly finished chocolate creations from the rolling rack into the glass-fronted display case.

"Hey," Paisley said, glancing at Sarah as she squatted to rearrange the lower shelf. Then she stood up and turned her head for a second look.

Sarah tipped her face away, but it was too late.

"What's up?" Paisley followed her behind the bar. "You okay?"

Sarah took off her jacket and slung it over a stool, still not meeting her cousin's eyes. Then she sighed, giving in to the inevitable. "I'm fine. Sort of. You always know, don't you?"

Paisley grinned and patted her shoulder. "What happened?"

"Got a little present from Jim's attorney in the mail. He's taking me back to court about the money again." Sarah reached for a rocks glass and poured herself some water from the tap.

"*Merde.*" Her cousin scowled, her fists clenched.

"Exactly. And to top it off, I was a total fool last night and let Blake Harrison spend the night. You'd think I'd learn a lesson, at least occasionally, right?"

Paisley put her arm around Sarah's waist and hugged her. "Oh, sweetie," she said. "It's not your fault, none of it is. And you really can't let one bad apple spoil the whole crate. Jim is a complete jerk, but that doesn't mean Blake is too."

"I know that, intellectually, but something inside me is just not buying it." Sarah hung her head to rest it on her petite cousin's shoulder. Her nervous jitters subsided as the reassuring scent of cocoa and baked goods floated into her awareness.

Paisley reached up and patted her on the back. "I suppose you noticed his truck across the street. He pulled up right when I heard you come in the back door. I really think he's serious about you, Sarah. Very persistent, anyhow."

Sarah looked out the front windows and confirmed that Blake was indeed parked outside, apparently talking on the phone. "Why is he here? We just said goodbye a couple hours ago!"

Paisley let go of her, and they both went to the front entrance, peeking around the lowered shade to watch Blake, who was gesturing with one hand while the other held his cell phone to his ear. Kahlua sat in the passenger seat, his head hanging out the open window. His red tongue lolled out of his mouth as he panted and watched a pigeon strut along the sidewalk.

"That is one good-looking man," Paisley said. "Sure you want to throw him away with the rest of the trash?"

Sarah stared while he flipped his sunglasses up onto his forehead and seemed to make an emphatic point, pounding the steering wheel with the palm of his hand. "No, of course I'm not sure. We had a wonderful evening, and morning too. But look at him—he's a man! Can any of them be trusted, really? Or what's more to the point, can I be trusted?"

Her cousin laughed and stepped back from the entryway. "Sarah, it's about time you snap out of it. Get real, woman!"

Sarah puckered her eyebrows, a lump in her throat. "What do you mean? Snap out of what?"

Paisley pulled herself up onto a barstool. "You can't let fear ruin the rest of your life. You're the same person you were before your ex-husband revealed his true colors. He's the one who made the mistake, not you. Don't let him have this power over you. Don't play the victim role." Her dark eyes showed a controlled flare of anger as she gestured with her hands.

"But," Sarah stammered, "I trusted Jim. Now look what's happened. He just keeps coming back to take more and more away from me." She looked across the street, where Blake was letting the dog out of the truck, Kahlua's leash in his hand. They strolled down the sidewalk toward the river.

"But Blake didn't do any of that, right? He's the nice guy, the friend from a family we've known for years. What do you really have to be afraid of? Look, he even loves dogs! Can't get much better than that for you, can it?"

"Maybe," Sarah said, watching the pair disappear in the distance. "But that's what I thought last time."

"Just give the guy a chance. You could be pleasantly surprised. And that's all I'm going to say about it." Paisley got up and walked into the kitchen.

Sarah went behind the bar and held her head in her hands, trying to think clearly while emotions swirled in her thoughts. Then the phone rang, and she answered to take a dinner reservation, putting her problems on hold for now to focus on the job at hand.

AT SOME POINT DURING the busy afternoon, Blake's truck disappeared from its parking spot across the street, so Sarah assumed he'd gone back to work without stopping to visit. She didn't know whether to be grateful or disappointed. She didn't know how she felt about him in general, and for the moment, avoiding the whole issue seemed like a good plan. She needed time to think. After the latest entry in a long list of nasty interactions with Jim, she wanted to roll into a little ball and hide. Men were not to be trusted, that much was clear. One minute, they were reasonable, and the next, they were stabbing her in the back.

Just as she was coming to that conclusion, the bell over the front door rang, and she turned to say that they wouldn't be serving dinner for another hour. There he was, of course, all cleaned up in a soft-looking purple corduroy shirt, with his hair slicked back and his face flushed, holding out a single long-stemmed pink rose. She smiled and stepped forward to reach for it, then a bolt of sheer panic shot through her and she stumbled, pulling back her hand and stuffing it into her pocket.

He looked startled, then his forehead wrinkled with concern as he followed her over to the bar, where she took cover behind the mahogany barrier. She started polishing wine goblets with a towel. He put the flower down and sat on one of the stools across from her.

Ducking his head and running a hand over his hair, he tried to catch her eye. "Um, Sarah? You all right? Is everything... okay?"

She quickly glanced at him and saw he was watching her, reaching across the bar toward her hand. She pulled it away. "I'm fine, Blake. Everything is fine. What makes you ask?" Making her tone cool and matter-of-fact, she kept her gaze focused on her work.

His breath came out in a whoosh, as though he'd been holding it. "Oh, that's good. I brought you this, beautiful. A rose for my rose." He picked it up and held it out toward her. Hope showed in his eyes.

"What makes you think I'm *your* rose, Blake?" She stared at him with a deadpan expression, fear creeping up her spine to burst in her head like a cloud of angry bees. She scowled, pushing him away with her mind.

His happy face shattered and turned into a frown. "So we're back to that, eh? Nobody's trustworthy enough for you, is that it, Sarah?"

Blake stood up and reached for her. She stepped back despite the barricade between them, intimidated by the energy. His hand trembled.

"We're involved now." His face twisted with emotion. "This is real life, and you can't just hit backspace and erase it." A green flash shot from his eyes as he strode to the door. "I'll give you some time to get used to the idea, but I've had enough playing around. I know your heart *much* better than you think. In fact—" He started to say something else but seemed to reconsider. With one hand on the doorknob, he turned and looked back, sadness and anger in his defeated expression. Then he yanked open the door and walked outside.

"Blake, wait," she whispered uselessly, watching him disappear down the sidewalk. She picked up the rose and held its smooth pink petals to her face, inhaling the sweet, sensual scent.

Chapter 20

Blake had to walk around the block three times before his breathing slowed down and his clenched fists uncurled. He kept circling back toward the restaurant but managed to stop himself from going inside to apologize. He told himself that he had a perfect right to be angry, and she was jerking him around. At the same time, a wounded ego throbbed in his chest.

It wasn't supposed to be this way. He'd done everything right. He'd been a gentle and generous lover, though all he wanted was to rip her clothes off and take what he'd desired for so long. The day after sex, women were usually all over him, calling to set up the next date and sending him text messages with smiley faces and hearts in them. He'd been single for a long while now, too depressed to get out much. Was it possible he'd lost his touch? Blake's mind filled with pain and confusion.

How could she turn on me like that, after last night? Was she faking all that ecstasy?

He swallowed hard and crossed his arms to hug his chest. He sat on a bench in the park by the river, leaning forward to rub his face and rest his head in his hands.

Maybe I deserve this. After all, I've been lying to her for weeks.

He moaned, drawing concern from two elderly ladies who were walking their poodle. After assuring them that he was fine, Blake walked back to his condo. He clipped the leash on Kahlua and automatically reached for the battered leather satchel he used for paperwork then locked up and left for the factory. Before he pulled out of the parking lot, a ding told him that a message had arrived on his phone.

He glanced down and saw it was from CocoLvr, via the online dating site. He stiffened, and his eyes narrowed.

CocoLvr: *Meet me tonight? Need your advice.*

He sighed. *Great. Now she wants to complain to me, about me. I can't take this anymore.*

But he would. He'd take it and be grateful. Because while they were still talking, online or in real life, he still had a chance. Now that Blake knew for sure how amazing it really was between them, he was more determined than ever to win her over.

WHEN BLAKE AND KAHLUA got to the office, his two siblings were in the middle of a friendly brawl. Carrie was balling up copier paper and pelting Jordan with crumpled white projectiles, while he sat on his side of the partners' desk and shot rubber bands at her from behind a barricade of file folders. They were both shouting and hooting, with sheer joy on their faces. In other words, it was another typical day at the office.

Blake picked his way through the litter of debris to his side of the desk, while Kahlua trotted over to Carrie and wagged his tail expectantly, eyeing the paper ball in her hand.

"Good boy," she said, rubbing his head. "Fetch!" She abandoned the battle with Jordan and started to play with the dog.

Jordan smoothed his rumpled hair and returned his files to their usual location. Blake still hadn't said a word and sat slumped in his chair, staring at a stack of mail. A rubber band sailed over from across the desk and hit him on the head. He raised his eyes.

"Whassup?" Jordan had on jeans and a Grateful Dead T-shirt, with his leather jacket slung across the back of his chair. Blake deduced that he didn't have any sales appointments. "You look beat, bro," Jordan said and raised one eyebrow, turning the observation into a question.

Blake frowned. "Just tired. And I need a break, in more ways than one."

"That's so sad, you're breaking my heart." Jordan fired another rubber band at his brother. He waggled both eyebrows, the traditional Harrison family challenge.

Blake picked up the rubber band and fired it back, successfully hitting the bull's-eye he imagined on Jordan's forehead. "Yeah? What you goin' to do about it?" Cheering up, he almost grinned.

"It's a gorgeous day. Why don't you guys go for a ride? I'll take Kahlua for a walk then take him back to your place," Carrie offered, reaching for the red leash. "I don't have to work at the restaurant until tonight."

"Yeah," Jordan said, brightening. "Why don't we?"

"Now, that is a brilliant idea. You're both on." Blake stood up and strode to the door. "Meet you over there," he said to his brother. Their motorcycles were garaged at the family home, along with their riding gear.

Jordan waved and nodded. "One quick call, then I'll be right behind you." He picked up his mobile phone.

Blake went to the parking lot and got behind the wheel of his truck then took off in a cloud of dust. He noticed he was gripping the steering wheel so tightly that his knuckles were white, and he tried to relax. Sarah had really messed with his head. Some speed and a stretch of open road were just what he needed to blow the thought of her right out of his mind.

Chapter 21

When the menus were printed and everything was organized for that night's dinner service, Sarah went up to Emile's apartment to change into the clothes she had dropped off earlier—a cornflower-blue silk blouse that matched her eyes, a slim black pencil skirt, Grandma Annie's long pearls, and a pair of strappy heels that made her six feet tall. She parted her hair in the middle, smoothed it perfectly straight with a flatiron, and was careful with her makeup. She would need the boost in confidence for her afternoon rendezvous with Carlotta Maria Del Monte, aka the Chocolate Bride. They were going to visit the banquet hall together, sample several chocolate wedding cake options that Paisley had prepared, and hopefully make important decisions.

Carlotta had been fairly undemanding so far but had a tendency to change her mind. Sarah's job today was to get her to commit. They needed to move things along. The wedding date was coming up fast, and Sarah couldn't put off this meeting any longer, even though she felt far from ready to pose as a chocolate expert and seasoned caterer.

When the happy couple had first contacted Emile, they'd already booked a location for the wedding. Sarah wasn't surprised to hear that it was the most over-the-top, insanely expensive place in the area. She'd be staging the event in the ballroom at the Ashford Country Club, which had a bar and restaurant and a full banquet kitchen and normally catered its own weddings.

Sarah's eyes had opened wide when she'd heard the news, but Carlotta had just shrugged, waving her left hand so the spectacular marquise-cut diamond perched there flashed blinding rays of light. "Don't you worry," Carlotta said, patting Sarah's arm. "Teddy figured they might be a little miffed we were bringing you in, so he called the manager and asked him to make sure they're all real friendly to your people. He worked something out, you know?" She winked, and Sarah wondered just what kind of deal the Chocolate Groom had struck. "We'll go over there together and check it out. Have a little picnic. Try the cakes. It'll be fun! My girlfriends want to come too. I'll pick you up at three o'clock on Sunday, in front of your restaurant. Watch for the white car."

On her way out, Sarah stopped to kiss Emile. He was ensconced in his chair by the window, with notepads, newspapers, and cookbooks scattered around him. He pushed his reading glasses up onto his forehead to look at her, throwing her a kiss with his fingers in the classic French gesture.

"You look wonderful, *cheri*. Beautiful!" he said, tipping up his cheek to meet her lips. "Don't worry about a thing. You will be *absolument parfait*."

The wash of sunlight coming in the window behind him glowed brighter for a moment. Sarah imagined her grandmother standing next to Emile's chair, looking on as they spoke, and felt reassured.

"I hope you've managed to stuff enough information into my head," Sarah said. "And I hope Paisley keeps an eye on her cell phone in case I need to secretly text her with questions. You too!"

"It's right here." He gestured toward the lamp table next to him. "I'll be waiting, and I've practiced my thumb typing, just in case. It's not easy with these clumsy old sausage fingers."

Sarah collected the cake boxes waiting downstairs and made her way to the sidewalk in front of the restaurant. She heard a muffled pounding noise that seemed to be coming closer and closer. A white stretch limousine turned the corner, pulling up at Sarah's feet. When the driver jumped out and went around to open the rear door for her, music blared out into the street.

Carlotta and two of her bridesmaids were already celebrating the big event. Dance music pulsed as they swayed and sang along, wineglasses in hand. Carlotta beckoned Sarah inside as the driver carefully loaded the cakes. She waved at her friend to kill the music and grabbed both of Sarah's hands.

"Here she is, the woman who is literally making my dreams come true, Sarah Dumas!" The two girls cheered, and Sarah didn't bother to correct them on her last name, which was actually still Westwood, the same as Devon's. "These are my BFFs, Kayla and Nicole."

They both sang "hi-iii" and smiled, waving their glasses. The three had obviously been to the salon together, as they all sported intricate hairdos and matching hot-pink manicures. Kayla poured a glass of white wine for Sarah then passed it carefully as the limo began to roll down the street.

"Carlotta, your hair looks amazing!" Sarah examined the complicated series of braids and twists. With the bride's black hair, tanned skin, and light-gray eyes, she made a striking picture.

"It's the Viking look," Carlotta said, running her hand lightly over the crown of her head. In the front, hanging down over her shoulder, one longer braid was adorned with a rustic silver bead. "I'm trying out different options for the wedding. What do you think?"

Kayla and Nicole showed Sarah their braided hair too, and by the time they arrived at the club, they were all chattering away.

The banquet hall at the Ashford Country Club was available for members only, but the Chocolate Groom, aka Theodore Wilson Hamilton III, aka Teddy, had been a member since birth, so that wasn't a problem. Sarah had been there once before to attend the annual chamber of commerce holiday party. When the four women walked into the enormous lobby, she saw that the restaurant straight ahead was filled with families having Sunday-afternoon dinner, and the golfers' bar to the left was packed. A discreetly uniformed assistant manager immediately approached Carlotta and welcomed her then took them to the closed double doors that Sarah knew led into the ballroom. He held them open briefly as the women went inside.

It's perfect, Sarah thought. For the first time since she'd been handed this project, a thrill of creative excitement touched her. She looked around the room and imagined it set up for the event. Carlotta had chosen cream calla lilies and white roses for her floral theme, to complement her ivory silk gown, which fell in a long slim column. Sarah pictured flowers on the tables, on the stage, and edging the dance floor, with table linens of chocolate brown layered with crisp white, to match the staff uniforms. The bridesmaids would wear frothy mocha lace, and the groom and his men would be in dark-brown tuxedos. The walls and flooring in here were perfect, in earth tones with white marble trim and accents. Long brown velvet draperies tied back by heavy silk sashes framed the tall windows and French doors leading to the patio. It would be gorgeous, a chocolate lover's dream. Add the amazing menu that Emile and Paisley had put together, and the ultimate chocolate wedding fantasy would come true.

Carlotta stood in the middle of the room and rotated, pointing and dictating. Sarah stood beside her and took notes, trying to keep up.

"I want the bars there, there, and there. And we'll cut the cake in front of the windows, over there. When it's time to go home, you can set up the little cakes and ice creams right outside the door here, so people pick them up after they get their things from the coat room. You're bringing some kind of little refrigerator, right?" She turned to Sarah, who was scribbling madly on the rough floor plan she had sketched.

Sarah nodded. "Blake, the ice cream guy, is bringing a portable freezer. He's going to be here in person to serve when you cut the cake and afterward, when people take their goodies and leave." This was something she could say with confidence, since he had told her so when they were raiding the refrigerator around three in the morning.

"Hmm," Carlotta said, giving Sarah a quick, curious look. "Good for him. The dedicated, hard-working type, eh?"

"Very." Sarah felt her cheeks warm, thinking of his extremely dedicated behavior last night.

Carlotta grinned and winked.

Oh dear, Sarah thought. *It's that obvious?*

The assistant manager brought out the three white pastry boxes and set them on a table with plates, forks, and serving knives. The women gathered around and sampled tiny slices of each cake. Everyone agreed that the dark chocolate studded with semisweet chocolate chips, marbled with streaks of chocolate pudding, and enrobed in chocolate ganache was the winner, hands down.

"Are you sure she can do this in a multitiered cake?" Carlotta wanted to know. "It won't be too heavy and squash the bottom layers? Seems like the cake is pretty soft, and the ganache would be hard to cut. I love it, though. Yum!"

Sarah wrote down the questions. "I'll explain all that in just a minute, if you don't mind," she said and whispered, "Ladies' room?" Carlotta smiled and pointed the way. "Be right back," Sarah called as she scooted into the hallway.

She pulled out her cell phone and speed-dialed her cousin at she entered the bathroom. "Can we do the pudding cake in tiers? Won't it collapse when they try to cut through the ganache? Help! I have no idea!"

Paisley sounded serene, always the eye of the storm. "Calm down, Sarah. Yes, of course we can. That's why I sent a sample. I have a way of supporting the layers, and after they cut the ceremonial first slice, I'll do the rest myself to make sure it's perfect. I use a warm knife. It works fine."

Sarah could hear kitchen noises and people talking in the background and glanced at the clock on her phone. "Wow, it's so late. I didn't realize."

"Why don't you take the night off?" her cousin suggested. "Carrie's coming in a minute, and the reservation list looks pretty light. You could use a break."

"Really?"

"We'll be fine. Get some rest, Sarah."

"Okay, thanks."

She washed her hands and checked her hair then went back to the ballroom to report her findings about the cake as though she'd always known the answers. Carlotta asked the assistant manager to box up the remaining cakes and put them in her car. Then the ladies trooped into the bar for a glass of champagne, which turned into two when the golfers found out what they'd just been doing. By the time they got back to the limo, Sarah was a little woozy, but since Devon was safe with Miki tonight and someone else was driving, she wasn't too worried about it. She'd been flirting with the men and laughing with the women, silly fun she hadn't enjoyed in ages. It was the kind of relief she needed with so much on her mind. The client seemed happy and relaxed too, which had been Sarah's goal for the day.

The driver started the engine and took them gliding into the night. Darkness closed around them and turned the softly lit limo into a magical, intimate space. They traveled in silence for a few minutes, then Carlotta slid the cake boxes across the seat.

She pulled a handful of plastic forks out of her purse and challenged them with a raised eyebrow. "Ladies? Little snack?"

Carlotta cranked up the music, and they all attacked the cakes. Before she realized what had happened, Sarah had eaten way too much chocolate for her own good. The chemical high and intoxicating aroma had seduced her again. Her head began to buzz, and she couldn't stop laughing. When Carlotta opened another bottle of champagne, a loud pop sounded, and Sarah felt certain tonight was a lost cause for them all. They were in Cocoa Fantasy Land, and it was truly a paradise.

Sarah felt the vehicle glide to a stop.

Kayla rolled down her window. "We're here! Woo-hoo!"

"Really?" Nicole said, scrambling up to see. "Woo-hoo!"

"Woo what?" Sarah looked at Carlotta, who was struggling out of her jacket.

"Too hot," the bride muttered, yanking at her sleeve. "Won't need this inside, anyhow."

"Where are we? I need to go home." Sarah rolled down the other window. They were in the parking lot at Weepin' Willie's, the raunchiest bar in the county, and from the looks of the other vehicles parked nearby, there was a gang of bikers inside getting smashed. Sounded like it too.

"Oh no," she said, a big danger sign flashing in her brain. She tried to grab Carlotta's arm as the woman slid across the seat and out the door. "You really don't want to go in there." Sarah lost her grip on the bride and slid out into the driveway, somehow managing to land on her feet.

"Yes, I do," Carlotta said, linking arms with her BFFs and heading toward the door. "We come here all the time, don't we, girls?" They laughed and kept on walking.

Sarah tripped along behind like somebody's kid sister. "You do? For real? 'Cause I don't think it's the right kind of place for someone like you guys, you know? Or like me, for that matter. Couldn't we just get back in the—"

She looked yearningly at the limo then turned and followed the others in time to hear Carlotta sing out, "Party! Tequila shots for everybody."

Then there was a loud cheer, and Sarah followed them into the bar as she tried to get Carlotta's attention. "Stop, please! This is a really, really bad idea."

BLAKE AND HIS BROTHER leaned against the bar with a couple of cold beers in green bottles and watched as three crazy females all tried to squeeze through the door at the same time with their arms linked then gave up and entered one at a time. Then, after the third one, trailing along with a familiar scowl on her face, came Sarah.

She teetered on spindly little ridiculously high heels. Without thinking, he stepped over to hold her up so she wouldn't break an ankle in those idiotic shoes. She was reaching out toward the woman with the strange braided hairdo and calling, "Wait! Stop!" Then she recognized him and swayed on her feet. Concerned, he folded her under his arm and swung her up onto the barstool next to Jordan so the brothers stood on either side of her. When Blake registered the pungent scent of chocolate and alcohol, he realized why she seemed out of it.

"You! What are you doing here?" She frowned and leaned away from him. "And what are you wearing?" She examined his leather riding gear with obvious surprise. Then she noticed his brother and raised one eyebrow.

"Whoa," Jordan said. "If it isn't Little Miss Chocolate. Slumming, babycakes?"

"Watch it," Blake growled. "None of that."

"I am most certainly not," she said, blinking. She centered herself on the stool and crossed her legs. "I'm meeting with a client, actually."

Jordan snorted. "Ri-ight, that's a good one."

"I am too. That's the Chocolate Bride over there, Carlotta, the dark-haired one by the pool tables who's buying drinks for everyone."

The bartender was pouring tequila shots and passing them around. Blake and Sarah declined, but Jordan grabbed his and downed it in one swig. He looked toward the three women, who were now dancing. "Who are your pretty new friends?" His eyes wandered over to watch Carlotta kick off her Jimmy Choos and pick up a pool cue then chalk the tip. He put down his beer and started walking in her direction.

"Oops!" Sarah wobbled on her perch, and Blake steadied her, rotating the stool a bit so he could hold her in place. She gave him a dirty look, and he quickly held both hands in the air with an innocent smile. Obviously she was still mad at him, for whatever reason, but he wasn't going to just walk away. Maybe this would be his chance to get back into her good graces. He signaled to the bartender for a glass of water and offered it to her.

She accepted it and automatically sipped but seemed more interested in what was going on across the room. "I warned them," she muttered, shaking her head.

Laughter and cheers erupted from the pool tables, and Blake glanced over to see Carlotta lining up a shot. It looked as though she was playing against Jordan and some of his buddies. Her two friends sat on the laps of a couple of big, burly guys he'd seen at Willie's lots of times, regulars. Everyone watched avidly as the game proceeded, and the reason was soon obvious. Carlotta had apparently invited them to a game of Strip Pool. Instead of playing for money or drinks, they were playing for clothes.

It started with shoes, socks, and jewelry, but soon things got more serious. Several rounds of drinks were called for, and the noise volume escalated. The crowd got rowdier as Carlotta stripped down to her matching black lace bra and panties, and a couple of the guys were left wearing boxers. Jordan was doing pretty well and had managed to keep his pants on.

Sarah watched the whole thing while sitting with her legs crossed in a ladylike pose, her eyes wide and rarely blinking. Blake was a little worried about her.

"What were you ladies doing today, anyhow?"

"Oh, scouting the banquet hall and tasting cakes." She kept close attention on her friends, a worried pucker between her eyebrows. "I think they had too much chocolate and champagne," she whispered behind her hand.

He laughed. "You think so? They do seem to be having an interesting evening."

"Not me, though." Sarah glanced at him and folded her hands in her lap. "I know when to stop, especially around so many men."

"Oh, I see. Can't trust them, right?"

"No, of course not." She waved one hand. "Things can get out of control, you know."

"Yes, I remember."

She thought for a minute then raised her eyes. "I do too. Shouldn't have done that. Stupid of me to, um... lead you on. Sorry."

He watched her face cycle through several expressions, from embarrassment to sorrow. She lifted her chin and looked him in the eye.

"I just can't do it, Blake. Every time I let down my guard, it's a disaster."

"Sarah, I'm not like him. I'm one of the good guys."

"I know, but really, it's just impossible. My heart isn't normal anymore. You should find someone else." A tear slipped from her eye and ran down her cheek.

Blake wiped it away gently with his thumb, frowning. "What if I don't want to? What if I want you? Give us a chance. I won't let you down." He put his arms around her shoulders and kissed the side of her head. "Please trust me."

She shook her head then hesitated, gazing at him wistfully.

"I love you, Sarah," he whispered in her ear, but he wasn't sure she heard him. The crowd was getting louder and rowdier, and now it sounded as if a fight was breaking out. Out of the corner of his eye, he glimpsed the bouncer coming out from behind the bar, holding a baseball bat. Blake's brain flashed, warning him to pay attention.

"Uh-oh," he said, setting Sarah on her wobbly feet and urging her toward the door. "Time to go, missy." He half carried her away from the bar as they pushed through the crowd.

She clung to him, looking back over her shoulder anxiously. "But wait, my friends. Shouldn't we do something?"

Blake looked over and saw Jordan taking charge, herding the three women toward the rear exit, his arms full of discarded clothing.

"I think those girls can take care of themselves, honey. Let's meet them outside."

As they slipped toward the exit, he saw a woman's hand rise above the crowd, swinging a black lace bra round and round. Then a man's hands appeared, grabbed the bra, and shot it across the room like a rubber band.

Blake grinned and steered Sarah out the door.

Chapter 22

When Sarah woke up the next morning, she could tell that the room was bright, but when she cracked one eye open experimentally, a white flash seared her throbbing brain like steak on a grill. She buried her head under the pillow and tried to sink back into sleep, but a quiet click like the sound of a door closing made her wonder whether she ought to see what was going on. Maybe Devon needed her.

She pushed the pillow away and slowly sat up before swinging her legs off the side of the bed. It was a big mistake. Her headache slipped into her stomach, and she started to feel nauseated. Gripping the side of the mattress with both hands, she kept her eyes shut, hung on tight, and waited for the spell to pass.

Ohmigod. I will never drink champagne ever again. Please, please, someone just shoot me. In the head, preferably.

Shading her eyes with her hand, she sneaked them open, bit by bit, and was astonished to discover that she was wearing an unfamiliar oversized T-shirt, sitting on the edge of an enormous bed with a black leather headboard, alone in a room she didn't recognize.

This was enough to set her head pounding in a wild frenzy, and she bit back a groan as she peered around the room, her eyes squinting. A couple of framed prints hung on the slate-gray wall behind the headboard, and a bookcase next to the bed held an assortment of magazines and books. At the foot of the bed, a closet door stood ajar. Inside hung a row of men's shirts and slacks. So, it was a man's bedroom, the man she had apparently slept next to last night—and she was wearing his T-shirt.

Sarah cringed and struggled to remember what had happened the night before. There was something about riding in Carlotta's limo, then following the girls into a bar, then a crowd of people... nothing very specific. Had Blake been there too? And Jordan? A series of random images passed before her mind's eye, growing more and more crazy. But whose bedroom was this, and where was he now?

How utterly humiliating. This is a new low, even for me.

Waking up in a strange bedroom with a vicious hangover was not a welcome addition to her dating repertoire.

Sarah found her clothes lying in a wrinkled jumble on the floor next to the bed and took them with her into the adjoining bath. After she'd hosed herself down from head to toe, she toweled off and put on her dirty underwear and the wilted silk shirt, which had a splotch of something sticky on the sleeve, and her rumpled black skirt, which now had a torn slit opening up one side seam to the top of her thigh. This rang a distant bell. Had she ridden behind some man on a motorcycle last night? Her shoes and purse were missing.

She sniffed. The spot on her sleeve was chocolate ganache.

Now, that definitely sparks a memory. Hmmmm... wedding cakes... the white limousine and Carlotta! And that awful bar, ohmigod.

She couldn't quite hook the rest of the story, which floated just out of reach.

Sarah opened the bedroom door a tiny crack and peeked out into a hallway. Nobody appeared, so she opened the door wider and stuck her head out. A door across from her was closed, so she tiptoed past it silently and headed toward the top of a staircase at the end of the hallway. Looking over the bannisters, she saw below her a large L-shaped kitchen and open living space, filled with browns and autumn colors. Something moved, and her eye zoomed in on the man sitting at the kitchen island, his face hidden behind a newspaper. He had dark-brown hair and wore jeans and a white T-shirt. She caught her breath as he turned the page and his identity was revealed.

Ohmigod. I spent the night with Jordan Harrison!

Her gasp drew his attention, and he lowered the paper and looked up at her. A mischievous grin slipped onto Jordan's face. "Morning, sweetheart," he said. "Ready for breakfast? Come on down." He patted the empty stool next to him.

Sarah took a step toward the stairs and hesitated, her fingers trembling as they touched the handrail. Her face grew hotter by the second.

What will Blake think? How could I have done this?

She saw her bag sitting on the coffee table in front of the sofa, with her shoes on the floor nearby. A quick escape was definitely on the agenda, but she'd have to pass him on her way to collect her things.

What will Paisley say? He's her old boyfriend... totally out of bounds.

Smoothing her hair back with one hand while she steadied herself on the railing, she walked down the stairs, trying to look casual. "Yes, good morning. Wow, that was, um... quite a night. I think, that is. It's all a bit fuzzy." She arrived at the bottom step and slipped over to the living room area, where she stepped into one shoe before she realized the other had a broken strap. "Oh!" she said, wobbling on one foot. She sat down and stared at the shoe, another glimpse of memory shooting through her mind. Something about rushing into the dark, away from... something. She looked over at Jordan, her brow furrowed with confusion.

Jordan Harrison, her savior? It didn't seem right. He'd never struck her as the type, for one thing. And he'd never seemed interested in Sarah, not *that* way. There he was now, grinning as though waiting for her to... what? To get the joke?

What joke? Is it on me? What did he do to me last night, anyhow? And why is it so damned funny?

Sarah frowned, curiosity transforming into anger.

The door rattled and opened. Kahlua came rushing inside, running over to greet her. He was followed by Blake, carrying a cardboard tray filled with tall coffees and a bag of what looked like pastries. He set the tray on the table, one hand on her shoulder as he leaned close and kissed her on the cheek. "Good morning. How did you sleep?"

Kahlua lay his head in her lap, and she stroked his silky ears. "Um... like the dead?" she said. She studied Blake's expression, which seemed relaxed and happy.

How much does he know? Why isn't he mad at me? Am I in trouble?

Blake laughed, passing her one of the coffees. "Here you go. Tall mocha latte with a chocolate cream doughnut. Is that okay? Go lie down, Kahlua. No begging."

The scent of coffee and chocolate filled her consciousness, and she reached for the cup. One large gulp and a bite of the pastry began to clear her head as stimulants rushed into her bloodstream. Kahlua padded over to a large red cushion on the floor near the fireplace and collapsed onto it, staring at her food with a hopeful yet resigned expression.

As she stared at the dog lying on his bed, the light dawned, and Sarah turned to look at Blake, who sat next to her, dipping a cruller into his black coffee.

"This is *your* condo, isn't it?"

He nodded, mouth full and eyes curious. He swallowed his food. "Yeah, sure. You don't remember?"

He looked concerned, but Sarah just giggled, snorting latte up her nose in the process. She put her cup down on the table, and all the tension she'd been holding melted out of her body, leaving her draped across the cushions like a limp noodle. Blake still looked worried, but he reached down and stroked her hair while his eyes softened and he leaned in for another kiss.

She closed her sore, tired eyes and spun into the world of his kiss, the deep, sweet, velvety darkness, with sparks of tingling explosions around the edges. She floated, losing her sense of gravity. Her head didn't hurt anymore, and she felt ridiculously happy until she remembered she wasn't supposed to do this anymore.

Jordan cleared his throat. "Public space and all. Just saying."

Blake pulled back and glanced at his brother over his shoulder. "Want your coffee?"

"Yeah." Jordan walked over and picked up the last cup that remained in the tray. "Thanks, bro. Guess I'll head home. Those girlfriends of yours are a hoot a minute, Sarah. Too bad the brunette is getting married soon." He exited with a wave.

Sarah simmered, her temper rising as she sipped her coffee and the memories returned. Blake had taken full advantage of her inebriated state, of course, to bring her here and take off her clothes. Typical man.

He knows how I feel about sex, and relationships, and, well... sex!

"How dare you?" She turned on him, setting her cup on the table with a smack. "It's all coming back now. How dare you bring me here and... *you know* when I told you it's not going to be that way between us, Blake? You had no right, considering the condition I was in!"

"What?" His eyebrows shot up, and his jaw dropped. "Sarah, I slept down here on the couch, in case you've forgotten. Jordan took the guest room."

She pulled back and shot a bolt of scorn at him with her eyes. "Do you expect me to believe that, Blake Harrison? Don't be ridiculous!"

After gathering her purse and shoes in her arms, she walked out the door with as much dignity as she could summon, considering her bare feet and the state of her clothing.

Blake watched with a forlorn expression. "Can't I give you a ride home? Will you be all right?"

"My car is parked at the restaurant, but thank you." She avoided eye contact and closed the door behind her.

She had time to change into sweats and a T-shirt, beat Devon and Miki to the kitchen, and start breakfast so they would never know she'd been out all night. Not that there was anything wrong with that. After all, she was a single, healthy adult. Didn't she deserve a social life like everyone else?

Maybe not. Maybe it was safer to stay home and chat on the internet. She'd missed another date with HotNCold last night. The last time they'd met online, he'd encouraged her to talk about Blake. Sarah wondered what her faceless friend would have to say when she told him the latest developments.

Chapter 23

Blake watched Sarah leave with the hopeless feeling of a man whose engine had just quit in the middle of the desert. He moped around the townhouse alone for most of the morning, taking care of business emails and trying to decide what to do.

One side of him wanted to surrender. If Sarah could think such negative things about him, if she didn't recognize who he really was, then trying to build a relationship was doomed. He couldn't talk her into it. She had to see the truth. Even if she gave him another chance, the way things were now, he'd always be waiting for her to accuse him of something awful, and she'd constantly be expecting him to let her down.

He should walk away and find someone else, as she'd suggested. If only he didn't care so much. But it was inescapable. In a way, he was addicted. Already, in the background, his devious mind was cooking up ideas for how to get her back.

For a while there, he'd connected with her on a deeper level. They'd been together in a whole new way, a beautiful, compatible joining. Not just sexually intimate but in a "kindred spirit" manner. She'd let down her guard, and they'd looked each other in the heart. It was like nothing he'd ever felt before, and he wanted it again. Craving Sarah was almost a physical sensation like hunger or thirst. He pictured her as she'd been when he snuck upstairs to get clean clothes that morning, lying asleep under the top sheet of his bed. One long bare leg had been exposed, her blond hair spilling over the pillows. His chest actually burned with longing. He clutched at it, trying to breathe calm and serenity back into his mind.

All the cheesy old songs are true. I'm totally hung up on her, and my heart... aches. I told her last night, at the bar. I wonder if she heard me.

Blake texted her a funny little apology, even though he didn't know what he was apologizing for. She didn't reply, though the message was marked "delivered." Then he tried email, with the same nonresult. Then he went on Facebook and shared a cool recipe for chocolate popsicles to her page and sent her a private message begging her to let him explain what had really happened. He could see she was online around lunchtime, since her icon was on the list of active users, but she still didn't respond. At least she hadn't unfriended him, though. There was still hope.

By the time he was ready to put Kahlua in the truck and drive over to the factory and check on the day's orders, he had become a desperate man. Sitting in the parking lot, he caved in and sent her a message.

HotNCold: *I'm sad and lonely, I need a friend. How are you? Hope all is well.*

Then he sat and waited, staring at his phone until a few minutes later, when he turned the key to start the engine, and a miracle happened.

CocoLvr: *Hi HotNCold! I miss U. Meet tonight? Lots to talk about. xo Coco*

Blake's eyes opened wide as he read her text, and the rush of relief was dizzying.

HotNCold: *Sure thing! Miss U 2.*

Then he fist-pumped and startled Kahlua with a joyous hoot. The dog grinned, tail wagging, and jumped over to head-butt him and slip under Blake's arm to lick his face, wriggling with excitement.

So much for the idea of sitting her down and confessing my double identity.

That was no longer an option, anyhow, since she basically wasn't speaking to him. The real him, that was. But maybe he could finagle this differently. He had an idea that might work. It was worth a try, since he didn't seem to have any other choices.

What the hell, I'm going for it.

Blake turned the radio up and drummed on the steering wheel as he drove down the road.

LATE THAT NIGHT, AFTER Sarah came home from work and checked on Devon, she changed into her nightshirt, got into bed with her laptop, turned out all the lights, and went to meet the only man she currently trusted, except for her grandfather and her son.

HotNCold's letters appeared on the screen.

HotNCold: *Hi sweetheart. How R U?*

It glowed green and reminded her of the green glow she'd seen through her closed eyelids when she lay right here in this same bed just two days ago, with Blake.

CocoLvr: *Not great.*

Her lip quivered. *No more crying, please,* she scolded herself and sat up straighter, bunching up a pillow to support her back.

CocoLvr: *I did something really stupid, and then, just to make sure I'm the biggest idiot in the world, I did it again.*

HotNCold: *LOL!!! You are too much.*

He added a cyber-hug emoji.

CocoLvr: *Really. All true.*

She felt like such a jerk, but the gloom did brighten a bit from confiding in a friend.

HotNCold: *It can't be that bad. Tell me all about it, girl? <Pats her hand and pours them each a cup of tea>*

He added a couple of teacup emojis.

CocoLvr: *<Sips her tea> Thanks, cute and delicious! Well, remember that guy I told you about? The one who likes me?*

She pictured Blake's face looking down at her, inches away, his green eyes hypnotic, and despite her melancholy mood, she smiled.

HotNCold: *Whatever happened, it's going to be fine, Coco. You need to relax, baby. <Massages her shoulders gently, forcing her to unclench>*

CocoLvr: *Mmmmm...*

She shrugged and heard her shoulders crackle.

CocoLvr: *Wow, I am a little tense.*

HotNCold: *<Continues to massage> So, what terrible horrible awful thing happened with the guy?*

Sarah relaxed her shoulders, pretending she could feel his virtual magic fingers, and it actually seemed to help.

CocoLvr: *Well, first we had sex, and then we had sex again. Several times.*

HotNCold: *Uh-oh. Doesn't sound much like you, does it? The chick who's embarrassed by cybersex?*

CocoLvr: *No. Not like me at all.*

She wondered if that was a good or a bad thing.

HotNCold: *Maybe doing something different is what you need.*

Her eyebrows shot up.

CocoLvr: *That's exactly what I was just thinking! Are you inside my head or what? I'm pretty confused. Let me explain...*

So Sarah typed out her story, bit by bit, starting at the beginning. She told him about her father, and about her ex-husband, and about Jim taking her back to court. HotNCold commented here and there but mostly let her ramble. He said things weren't as disastrous as she thought and urged her to give her new suitor another chance.

HotNCold: *Sounds like you're prejudiced against him for stuff he had nothing to do with. He's probably a good guy, someone kind of like me.*

CocoLvr: *Yes, he's good and sweet, a kind person. I'm just so freaking vulnerable all the time. It's ridiculous, how I overreact. It's... me.*

HotNCold: *Geez, woman! You need to chill.*

Sarah laughed out loud, for real.

CocoLvr: *Yup.*

HotNCold: *Don't give up on the new guy. It's not like you have someone better waiting in the wings. Being alone is no picnic, or we two wouldn't be chatting right now. We would never have joined the site. You and I are lonely people, Coco. I'd come over right now and hold your hand in person, if I could.*

CocoLvr: *Where are you located, anyhow?*

She'd never thought to wonder before and pictured him somewhere tropical, near a beach, where they didn't wear many clothes.

It took a few minutes for his reply to appear, though the row of moving dots showed he was typing something.

HotNCold: *I'm in a little town in Massachusetts, Ashford. Never heard of it, right?*

Sarah sat straight up, as if a bolt of lightning had struck her, and stared at the screen. She bent over her laptop. *Quick,* she thought, *lie!* Her heartbeat raced, and she started sweating.

CocoLvr: *Sure. I'm down in New York. Not too far away.*

She racked her brain for who HotNCold could actually be. *Maybe it's someone I know. Can't let him find out that I'm me.*

HotNCold: *It's raining here now. Kind of gloomy.*

She looked outside and listened to the gentle rushing sound.

CocoLvr: *It is here too.*

She needed to find out who he was.

CocoLvr: *Hey, what do you do for work, anyhow? We never spoke about that.*

Again, there was a slight pause before his answer came through.

HotNCold: *Don't laugh. It's kind of a weird career. I make ice cream. My brother sells it, and I run the factory.*

Sarah's jaw dropped, and she held her breath, shaking her head in horror.

HotNCold is Blake Harrison? Ohmigod!

Chapter 24

After she typed an abrupt goodbye and slammed her laptop shut, Sarah sat in the dark and held her head. Hershey got up from his pad and came to her bed, wagging a slow tail as he laid his head on her arm and looked at her lovingly. She reached down to stroke his silky head, and her mind raced as she tried to assess the potential damage.

How much trouble am I in?

It seemed, on reflection, that Blake might have no clue who she was. Nothing he'd ever said hinted at it, and she'd been so paranoid about online stalkers that she hadn't given away any clues. When she'd mentioned "the new guy," it had been in very general terms. Maybe she was safe, unless he'd added two plus two when he read her user name. They had always conducted business in person, so there was a fairly good chance he'd never checked out the restaurant's email address.

Anyhow, if he knows I'm CocoLvr, wouldn't he have said something?

Sarah's breathing returned to normal, and she stopped trembling. She broke her usual rule and patted the mattress next to her. Hershey jumped onto the bed and rolled onto his back to have his tummy rubbed then stretched his legs up in the air and grinned at her. She found it comforting to have his warm, furry body pressed up against her. He always seemed to know when she was upset. She slid down to put her head on the pillow and snuggled him while she listened to the rain and tried to relax.

So, while Blake's been trying to have cybersex with a complete stranger online, he's also been chasing me around in real life? The rat!

Of course, it was pretty much the same thing Sarah had been doing too. But that was different. Sort of. Oh, it was too confusing. She'd been drawn to Blake from the start, both in person and online. Appar-

174

ently, it had been the same for him. She liked that, a lot, though she was still mad at him for virtually two-timing her. Was it her own fault for being so hard to get? She had made him jump through a lot of hoops. He was a desirable quantity, bachelor-wise, and any sane single woman in her thirties would have leaped at the chance to get close to him.

That raised an important question. Why was he wasting time with CocoLvr online when he could have easily gone out with nearly anyone he wanted, right here in Ashford?

She could understand why he'd checked out the online dating site, just as she had, out of curiosity. She could even understand why he'd initiated conversation with CocoLvr, especially considering the attention-getting profile Paisley had posted. After all, he was a man. But he'd gone further... led her on, made her trust him, and encouraged her to think he was her friend. He'd turned a silly night of experimentation into an actual relationship. *Why?*

Sarah couldn't come up with an answer. Or stop being angry with him for tricking her. Not to mention, the fact she'd told him all her darkest secrets and could never, ever face him again if he found out that she was CocoLvr! She sighed, tossing and turning in the bed so often that Hershey gave up on her and went back to his peaceful corner.

She could never forgive Blake for putting her through this embarrassment. Never.

She knew who he was now, but unless she'd guessed wrong, he didn't know that she was Coco. She had the advantage. She wasn't sure yet what to do with it, but one thing was certain. She was going to teach Blake Harrison a lesson. If he thought she'd been bitchy before, wait until he saw what was coming next.

Sarah lay in the dark, listening to the rain pour down outside. Her head hurt, her eyes ached, and her nose was stuffy. Maybe she was getting a cold. Or maybe, she thought as she wiped the tears away again, it was a serious case of regret. A condition she couldn't seem to shake. It had followed her like a shadow through most of her life, and here it was still, a familiar ghost in the night.

Life isn't a fairy tale, Sarah. Everybody doesn't get a happy ending.

She heard her father's discouraging voice in the back of her mind and drifted off into a restless sleep.

SARAH OPENED HER EYES, surprised to see it was still dark. Hershey was downstairs, barking his head off.

"Mom?" Devon's voice came closer, shaking as he bounded across the hall and leapt into her arms. "Why's he barking? Is it raccoons again?"

"Probably, sweetie. Or the neighbors' cat. Let's go see." She pulled on her bathrobe and tied the belt.

They got up and found Miki in the hallway, carrying a big flashlight and a pink can of mace.

"You can't be too careful," she said when she saw Sarah read the label. "I got it at my self-defense class. Let's sneak up on 'em! Come on, team."

Miki turned off the flashlight, and the three of them crept down the stairs in the dark, peeking through the bannisters into the kitchen. Hershey stood in the middle of the floor, facing the back door, barking steadily, his ears and tail both up and on alert. Sarah couldn't see anything outside in the blackness, so she motioned for the others to stay put and sprinted across the floor to flatten herself against the wall next to the light switches. With one quick motion, she flipped all the exterior lights on.

Hershey wagged his tail once and barked again before running toward the door and whining. He looked at Sarah urgently, begging to go out.

Sarah ran her gaze across the deck, the yard, and the back porch. Nada. Then she stepped away from her safe nook and looked out at the driveway and garage. Nothing out there, either.

Devon ran from the stairway and threw his arms around her waist. "Do you see something, Mommy?"

"Nope." She shook her head. "But let's all go out together and see, okay?"

She figured it was probably raccoons again but knew they'd all sleep better after a thorough investigation. They pulled on jackets from the hooks by the door and slipped their bare feet into the shoes that stood under the coatrack. Then Sarah put Hershey on his leash and opened the door. Miki switched on her flashlight and gripped it tighter, the can of mace ready in her other hand.

For the next twenty minutes or so, the three of them followed Hershey while he sniffed a trail all the way around the foundation of the house, dodging behind bushes and ducking under low-hanging tree limbs. He paused under every first-floor window to wave his tail excitedly and sniff the ground, as though something or someone had been looking inside. Sarah didn't see any evidence of an attempt to break in, though, and everything was closed up tight. When they circled back to the garage area, Hershey veered off down the driveway toward the street, where a dark-blue car was parked in front of the empty house, exactly where it had been on the rainy night Sarah first noticed it. Now, it appeared empty, but the sight still spooked her, and she stopped, pulling back on the leash.

"That's enough, boy. I think we've seen plenty."

"Yeah!" Devon patted the dog and hugged him. "You did a good job. Didn't he, Mom? He checked all the windows for us to make sure they were shut."

Miki and Sarah exchanged uneasy glances, both of them apparently having interpreted the dog's behavior in another way. They nodded, silently agreeing to let Devon believe his version.

"Okay, pardner, let's mosey into my saloon for a drink, on the house!" Sarah draped her arm around his skinny shoulders and propelled him toward the kitchen entrance.

"Yes, ma'am!" he piped and reached for Miki's hand, drawing her closer too. Sarah could see that he was still nervous. "We hunters got to take a break after all this hard work, tracking the wild raccoons."

They went inside, and Sarah made hot chocolate while Miki and Devon gathered pillows and blankets from upstairs, then they opened the sofa bed and camped out together in the TV room for the rest of the night. Devon was out cold after the first fifteen minutes of *Charlie Chan at Monte Carlo*, and after Sarah switched off the television, Miki settled down in the big armchair. Hershey, however, still lay on the kitchen floor, watching the back door with his head resting on his paws, ears perked.

A while later, as Sarah dozed, she heard an engine start. She got up and tiptoed to peer out the window at the front of the house. Sure enough, the blue car was gone now.

She shivered and quickly climbed back into bed with her son, holding him close as she watched him sleep.

Chapter 25

The next morning, on her way to work, Sarah called the local police and told them what had happened. The officer asked several questions and said she'd warn the cars patrolling Sarah's neighborhood to be on the alert. Sarah gave her a rough description of the blue car, kicking herself for not getting a look at the license plate. The officer said Sarah was lucky to have a dog, since most burglars would rather not mess with a house where dogs lived. If it was a prowler, he'd probably been scared off by Hershey's barking. She thanked Sarah for the report, saying it might help prevent a break-in for one of her neighbors. And that was that.

Paisley met her at the back door of the restaurant with a big, excited smile. "You'll never guess who called!"

"Okay, then why don't you just tell me?" Sarah teased and led the way into the office to hang her jacket over the back of a chair.

Her cousin stood there grinning. "The *Boston Globe* is doing a story on the chocolate wedding! They're sending that snooty food writer to interview us!"

Both cousins squealed with joy and grabbed each other's hands, jiggling up and down like kids. It was a brief moment but long enough to get Jerome's attention. He beckoned to Raoul, and they came and stood in the office doorway.

"All right, girlfriends, going to share the bliss?" Jerome dried his hands on the dish towel that habitually hung over his shoulder while he worked.

"What happened?" Raoul asked. When Paisley repeated the news, he looked thoughtful. "Their food critic will probably come for dinner and write us up," he said. "We'd better be ready! I hear he usually doesn't identify himself so he won't get special treatment. He wants to experience the real deal."

Sarah came down to earth and nodded. "You're right, I read that somewhere too. We need to be on our toes the next two weeks leading up to the wedding, just in case. When is the interview scheduled?"

"Next Friday. We're meeting him for lunch at the country club so we can show him the venue and talk about the setup plans."

"At least then, we'll know what the guy looks like. Did you Google him to see if there's a photo posted?" Sarah tried to catch the elusive thought that was flitting around in her mind. Then it landed. "Ohmigod! Will he be at the reception too? Does Carlotta know about this?" Paisley shrugged, so Sarah pulled out her cell phone and started dialing.

If there was one thing she'd learned from hanging around with the Chocolate Bride, it was to respect Carlotta's need to be in charge. She left a friendly voice mail with details and questions and asked for a return call. She had a feeling Carlotta would be delighted.

Paisley watched with admiration, her hands on her hips. "That was smart," she said. "I never would have thought to include her, and she would have had a hissy fit! You're good at this, Sarah."

Sarah felt her cheeks flush. "Aw, thanks, P! I love you too." She pulled a yellow legal pad off Emile's desk and sat down at the table, grabbing a pen. "Let's put our heads together on this now, while it's fresh."

Paisley nodded and took another seat. "Boys? How about coffee all around and a fast brainstorm? Can you take a break?"

Raoul nodded and turned, untying his immaculate white apron and lifting off his *toque* to park them at his workstation. Jerome brought four mugs and a pot of coffee into the office. They all sat down and strategized, planning to offer their best dishes for the next week, and Paisley's most popular desserts. The all-you-can-eat-buffet idea was put on the back burner. An hour later, they all had their assignments and were ready to get back to work.

Just what I needed, Sarah thought, scanning the list in her hand. *Something else to worry about!* But Paisley and the sous chefs all seemed so happy and jazzed about it, she didn't have a right to complain. After all, it was the kind of opportunity they had dreamed of.

"Does Grandpa know yet?" she asked her cousin, who was already at the computer, making shopping lists.

Paisley glanced at her. "No, I was waiting for you. Didn't want him to imagine he's going to do any of this work. Period."

"Right. Good idea. Shall I go up?"

Paisley nodded, absorbed in her work. "Yep. It's what you do, my silver-tongued salesperson. Convince the unpersuadable that it's all his idea and he's managing us from his armchair."

Sarah saluted and turned to go. "Piece of gâteau, darling."

AS THE NEXT WEEK PASSED, Blake was careful to stay away from Sarah, both online and off. When he'd given her the last piece of the puzzle, he knew she'd realized who he was. It was confirmed by her hasty log-off. He suspected she didn't know he'd recognized her and was glad to keep it that way for now. She was probably in shock from the revelation of his true identity. He didn't want to push her too far. He'd said what he did when the right opening in the conversation came along, because he wanted her to see that the attraction between them existed mind to mind, no touching required.

Not that the physical stuff wasn't heavy-duty too, because it definitely was. But what was going on between them was so much more important. He'd been trying to get up the nerve to confess, but the way it worked out was much better. She had time to consider her reaction in private and with no dramatic confrontation. He might never have to tell her that he knew she was Coco all along and had pursued her on-line because he was already crazy about her in real life.

Women are weird about that kind of thing, he thought. *She might even get mad instead of taking it as a compliment.*

Blake walked his dog by the river, worked long hours, read the en-tire *New York Times* and did the crossword puzzle on Sunday, and went over to his parents' house on family dinner night. He played endless games of Words with Friends online with his sister, Carrie, who was still working part time at Sarah's restaurant and kept him posted on the news. He was waiting. Something would happen, and the right path would appear. Until then, he wasn't going to mess things up even worse by being impatient.

The chocolate wedding was coming up soon. He'd be right there beside her, helping it go smoothly. Should score some brownie points for that. He couldn't wait until she got a taste of the orgasmic hot fudge sauce he'd perfected to go with the cake and ice cream. He planned to be nearby when she tried it, knowing as he did how Sarah reacted to chocolate. His creation had lots of potential uses, some of which he'd experienced only in his imagination. Blake looked forward to correct-ing that situation in the near future.

He whistled, and Kahlua came out of the river with an orange ball in his mouth, shaking off sheets of water. Blake stepped out of the way then snapped on the leash. They started down the sidewalk toward home. Strolling along slowly with the sun setting behind them, turn-ing the sky flamingo pink, they were two amiable companions enjoy-ing the evening. Three blocks down, across the street, he spotted the brown awning and potted topiaries in front of Sarah's restaurant. The brass sconces were lit in the entryway, and the door opened as a cou-ple emerged and walked away, arm in arm. When he walked past the big window that said The Three Chocolatiers in distinctive gold script, Blake turned his head to peek inside.

It was a slow night, he could tell. Only eight o'clock, and there were two empty tables in the window, which meant the first seating was over and there wasn't much of a second, if any. Not unusual for a weeknight in summer, when so many people were out of town on vacation.

He laughed. How did he know so much about the restaurant and its customers? From watching obsessively from the sidewalk across the street, as he was right then, while he pretended not to be looking for Sarah. Behind the bar, or coming out of the kitchen, or— there she was—serving a bottle of wine to a couple in the back of the room.

Looks like red. Ah, they like it. Good girl! Nice pour, very elegant twist of the wrist.

Blake smiled, happy at the sight of her. Glad to give her the space she needed now, if it meant that in the end, he'd win her back. Live and in person. The real him. Letting her discover his secret had been dangerous, but it was the only way forward. It was a huge relief. He'd been honest, admittedly in a screwed-up, chickenshit kind of way. Now it was up to Sarah to decide how she felt about it.

Next time around, I'll get you, and you'll never run away again.

He turned to look back over his shoulder for one last glimpse as he walked on, the pavement as soft as air.

SARAH AND PAISLEY CHOSE their most sophisticated clothes and their most sadistic high heels, and they'd painted their mouths and fingernails red. Paisley's were a purplish red, and her eyes were shadowed with smoky gray. Sarah's was a clear, cherry red that made her eyes a startling sky blue, and it matched the sleeveless V-neck linen dress that was a little too short, but what the heck. Paisley wore black, her signature color, and looked like a sexy evil pixie. Together, they drew every eye in the room when they walked into the restaurant at the country club and waited to be shown to their table.

The hostess found their names on her reservation list. "Right this way, ladies. Your third party hasn't yet arrived, but we'd love to serve you a drink while you wait. Yes?"

They ordered Perrier.

With a smile, the waiter handed them menus. "Have a look while you're waiting?" He came back in a moment and poured their sparkling water.

Sarah ran her eyes around the room, taking in the décor and the clientele. She recognized many of the customers. In the corner, she spotted a couple she'd served last night, and next to them was Blake Harrison, sitting with his back toward her, across the table from the most beautiful woman she'd ever seen in Ashford.

A little gasp escaped her lips when she recognized him as he turned his head to speak to the waiter. He hadn't seen her yet.

"What?" Paisley asked, reading her menu.

"Over there. It's him, Blake. What a total freaking jerk! Didn't take him long to find somebody else, did it?" Sarah sipped her water then set it down too hard. It spilled a little when it sloshed. Her eyes sent stabbing knives of fire across the room at his back.

"Where?" Paisley looked up. "Oh! Wow, who is that chick? She is gorgeous."

"Exactly! Who the hell is she?" Sarah clenched her fists and tried not to grind her teeth.

"Never saw her before." Paisley stared. "And I would remember."

The woman was elegant and slender, with long limbs, amazing eyes in a perfectly symmetrical model's face, and a shining updo of dark hair. She looked like Audrey Hepburn in *Breakfast at Tiffany's*, without the white streak. She laughed at something he said, and a sound like bells rippled across the room. Sarah hated her guts.

"Well, isn't this just peachy?" she said. "Here I am, working my way through total humiliation and trying to get up the nerve to call him, and he's having lunch!"

Paisley put her hand over Sarah's, about to speak, when the hostess came over to their table, followed by a tall man in an expensive-looking suit. When she stepped aside, they saw it was none other than Alonzo/Hercules/Tarzan, the mysterious customer from the restaurant who Sarah had imagined might be her cyber-lover, stalking her.

He saw that she recognized him and smiled. "Hello again, Sarah. I hope you'll forgive my not introducing myself correctly the other night." He took her hand and held it in both of his for a moment, European style. "I get a much better idea of what a restaurant is really like if I don't identify myself." His brown eyes twinkled, and he turned to Paisley. "The extremely talented Ms. Dumas, I presume? Your reputation preceded you, but I was still completely delighted by your creations. I spoke to my editor, and she insisted we also cover the amazing chocolate wedding." He took her hand then and repeated the ceremonial gesture.

"You are a naughty boy, Alonzo," Sarah said as he seated himself. "Or... what should we call you? The newspaper said Marco Romano. Is that your real name?"

"Yes," he admitted, shaking out his napkin and putting it in his lap. "And I'm not in the heating and cooling business. I just said that because it's so boring, most people don't want to talk about it and leave me to enjoy my meal." He leaned toward Sarah and lowered his voice. "Not that I wanted you to go away! You were very hospitable and absolutely charming, as indeed you are right now."

His eyes ran down her body and up again very quickly, taking her all in, and she reacted to the blatant appraisal with a regal lift of one eyebrow. He nodded, acknowledging her superior authority. It was all for show, not the least bit threatening, and they both knew it. Paisley watched with amusement.

Sarah laughed but was distracted by Blake gesturing broadly with his arms, across the room. The Audrey Hepburn woman smiled at him with her sweet, irresistible turned-up eyes, and Sarah forgot what was going on at her own table for a minute. There was a pause, an odd silence, and she looked back to see the food writer staring at her *expectantly*. Under the table, Paisley poked her.

"Um, don't worry a bit, no offense taken," Sarah stammered. "Shall
we talk about the chocolate wedding? Paisley can fill you in on the
menu, which is outrageously fabulous. I know Carlotta has sent you an
invitation. You'll be able to experience it for yourself. She was really the
inspiration for the whole idea. It's her dream wedding."

"I'm very much looking forward to it. We'll have a photographer
at the reception too. The paper is going all out on this." He summoned
the waiter with a flick of the finger, ordered more water and a bottle of
wine, and requested to hear the specials.

As they worked their way through lunch, which Sarah thought
was mediocre, she paid less attention to the conversation going on between her cousin and the reporter than she did to what was happening
across the room. Blake and his companion finished their meal. When
he stood up to escort her to the door, he turned around and saw Sarah
watching him.

He was startled. He actually blushed. But he kept his eyes riveted
on hers and barely paid attention to the woman at his side as they
walked through the dining room toward the exit. As they approached
her table, Sarah realized Marco had just asked her a question.

"Pardon?"

"I said, has it been difficult to work out a system for how your people will work with the club's staff? They'll be serving a full menu in here
that night too, won't they?"

Sarah froze, watching Blake walk right up to her, a casual smile on
his face. She had no idea how to answer the reporter's question, and her
cousin hadn't chimed in. Blake, who was close enough to hear, seemed
to realize it. His eyes flashed her a warning as he reached out his hand
toward Marco.

"Hello, chocolate lovers! Nice to see you here today, ladies. Blake Harrison," he said as the two men shook hands. "And this is my friend Lydia Maxwell, accountant extraordinaire."

Lydia smiled and nodded at everyone as they greeted her.

Oh, really? His accountant? I'll bet. Wait. She's wearing a wedding ring and a big honker diamond. Because she's married. Ha! And I'm an idiot.

Relief washed over Sarah like a cool breeze, but she still had another problem. The reporter was waiting for his answer.

"We've just been talking about the famous chocolate wedding these ladies are putting on. I'm sure you've heard about it," Marco said.

Blake nodded. "My company is supplying ice cream to complement Paisley's wedding cake. I'm sure she'll be coordinating in the kitchen. Right, my friend?" He patted Paisley on the shoulder, deflecting Marco's attention toward her. Sarah realized Blake had just rescued her, again.

She treated him like crap and wouldn't speak to him for weeks, but he was still treating her as though she were someone important in his life. Someone he cared about. Maybe he hadn't been such a jerk after all. Maybe he really was what he'd said to Coco, "a lonely person." Looking for more than a shallow physical relationship, as she'd assumed. Frustrated that Sarah kept pushing him away. Maybe he'd been looking for someone to talk to late at night online. Just as she was. Sarah remembered what he'd told her online about his girlfriend dumping him, when he'd thought they were headed for marriage and a family. He'd sounded so sweet and sad.

"We must be off," Lydia said, looking at Blake. "I have a three-month-old in day care who wants his lunch, and I'm it! This guy is my ride, so—"

"Oh." Sarah laughed, impressed that someone who had given birth so recently could already look so trim, since it had taken her a year to recover from carrying Devon. "Well, don't let us keep you from that! Nice to meet you."

"Bye-bye!"

Blake took Lydia's elbow and steered her through the crowd, pausing at the door to look back at Sarah, catch her eye, and wink.

Chapter 26

The next few weeks went by in a whirlwind of planning, phone calls, scheduling staff, meetings with the florist and Carlotta's wedding planner, plus a million last-minute details. In the way things usually went, the restaurant was also packed, with sold-out reservations every night. Sarah and Paisley were on the run, trying to get everything done without their third chocolatier.

Sarah's idea about a fixed-price dinner was a big hit. The special deal drew in their regular customers in droves. Profits were up, and everyone was happy. Every Monday, Paisley slipped copies of the previous week's paperwork into a FedEx package and shipped it off to her brother with a sigh of relief. Carrie was doing a terrific job in the dining room, charming people with her bubbly personality. She was going to stand in for Sarah as hostess on the night of the wedding.

Under the circumstances, it was relatively easy for Sarah not to think too much about Blake. Exhaustion put her to sleep at night. Now and then, a flash of green sunlight as she drove down the street would spin her into a memory of the world inside his eyes, but most of the time, she was happy to procrastinate in trying to understand her emotions. She knew he was out there, waiting. She'd seen him lurking along the sidewalk with Kahlua in the evenings, peeking into the window as he passed. She'd stood up straighter and pulled in her tummy, sliding her eyes to watch him secretly from under her lashes. But she wasn't finished feeling angry and humiliated by all the personal things she'd said to him online, under false pretenses. And all the extremely personal things they'd done to one another right in her very own bed, where she had to try to sleep at night.

Taking some time is a good thing. Too busy to think about it right now, anyhow.

The cousins shielded Emile from most of the chaos, giving him "assignments" that required a lot of waiting by the phone for certain information to be received or researching sources for supplies on the internet. They made time for a daily meeting in his apartment every afternoon to bring one another up to date. His laptop and cell phone were the tools of his trade these days, Emile told the cousins with a wistful tone.

"Be patient. It won't be like this forever," Paisley said with a shrug.

Sarah agreed. "Grandpa, you're healing fast, so don't blow it now." She gave him a stern look. "Listen, I've been thinking. What if you and Paisley present the cake to the bride and groom together? Photographers from the media will be there. Someone can drive you home right afterward. All three of us really should be there. What do you think?" She watched him and waited. The doctor had warned her that some people in Emile's situation were a little afraid to resume their normal lives, even after improving their exercise and eating habits and getting a green light from their cardiologists. He seemed eager to go along with her suggestion, though.

Emile was steadily getting stronger and had dropped twenty pounds. He walked all the way to the river and back with Hershey every other day. The girls still wouldn't let him work in the kitchen, but some nights, Sarah served him dinner at the bar, and he was allowed to brag about his granddaughters to the customers while he sipped sparkling water on the rocks.

Paisley gathered their tea things onto a tray and took them into Emile's kitchen to wash up.

"I have to go pick up Devon at the Y," Sarah said, tucking her notes into a folder and standing up. "Miki is visiting her sister for a couple days. She'll be home tomorrow. Until then, I am with child." She gave Emile a hug and kiss then stuck her head around the kitchen doorway to talk to Paisley. "I'll be working from home, so please call me with whatever. Carrie's going to hostess tonight, and Raoul's nephew is covering the bar, so I'm good to take off. Bye!"

"Au revoir, *cheri*." Emile looked up and waved as she passed through the living room. A brilliant glow from the window silhouetted his white hair with a bright wispy halo, swelling to cover his shoulders like two arms of fuzzy light holding him in an embrace.

Thanks, Grandma! Sarah thought of Annie, watching out for Emile as always.

Sarah took the back stairs down to the parking lot and headed for home.

SHE UNLOCKED THE BACK door, and Devon burst into the house ahead of her, racing straight to the bathroom. Hershey said his usual enthusiastic hello, and she opened the patio door for him to go outside then turned back to the island to browse through the stack of mail she'd picked up at the end of her driveway.

There was a nudge on her leg, and she swung around, startled. Hershey was still standing next to her rather than chasing squirrels around outside as he always did. And he looked funny. The dog stared at her meaningfully then walked over to the foot of the stairs and sat.

"Okay, what's up, boy?" Sarah followed him, preparing herself for gutted couch cushions or a deluge of garbage. When he was a puppy, there had been some nightmarish moments.

Hershey waited until she reached him, looked up at her, and wagged his tail twice, almost bashfully. He looked up the stairs then back at her.

"Ah. You've done something dreadful, have you? Let's see it." Sarah started up the stairs, and he followed then pushed past her to the top, where he turned and went into her bedroom. She groaned. "Noooooo. Couldn't you barf in the bathroom for once?"

She went to the doorway and looked inside. At first, she didn't notice anything out of place. There was certainly no dog vomit on the floor or in the middle of her bed, which had been her worst fear. Hershey sat looking at her, hanging his head a little.

"What's the matter, good boy?" She knelt to put her arm around him and stroke him. He was trembling. "Now, now, it's okay. Calm down, now."

He raised his head and licked her face, then ran over to her dresser and looked up at the jewelry box on top, then faced Sarah with sad eyes. She noticed the lid was slightly open, but that wasn't unusual. She walked over to flip the lid up and had to look twice to be sure what she saw. Her everyday jewelry was all there, hanging on the little hooks and in the square compartments, but the Chinese silk bag that held her most precious things was gone. Vanished. It usually sat in the bottom of the box, filling the space. Now, she was looking at solid cherry, the bare wood. Her Chinese bag had disappeared.

Her paternal grandmother's diamonds, much too fancy for any occasion in Sarah's life except her wedding, and the opera-length strand of perfectly matched pearls. Two pairs of earrings one might see on the red carpet, and a platinum bangle bracelet channel-set with diamonds all the way around. It was Devon's college education, carefully preserved in a beautiful padded bag.

Tears came to her eyes, and her throat ached. It was the last really valuable thing she owned, and it had come from her family, passed down through generations. She hadn't sold the jewels even when things looked their darkest, because it never seemed as though they really belonged to her. They were her son's future. It was the most she'd ever be able to give him, or rather, it had been, before some sneaking slimy creep had slithered into her bedroom and taken them.

She knew one thing for sure. It was not a masked man in a cape.

Sarah looked at Hershey, who was watching her warily. "Who did this, boy? Who came in here? How did he get in? Show me, show me, boy!"

Excited, Hershey jumped up and ran to the window seat. He leapt onto the cushions and pawed at one of the screens. Sarah saw it was in place but slightly bent, and small slits had been cut near the fasteners that held the screen in place. Hershey wagged his tail, proud of himself.

"Good dog! You're just like Lassie, aren't you?" She pulled him back down onto the floor and made a fuss over him, petting him and scratching his ears. He grunted with pleasure, sneezed, and shook, flinging a little spit around the room. Then he panted and perked his ears at something Sarah couldn't hear, like the distant sound of squirrel laughter, and he was off, racing down the stairs.

Sarah turned the two metal fasteners that held the screen in its frame and lifted it out. The casement window was cranked open all the way, as were the other two in the reading alcove, as she had left them that morning. She looked out the window and down at the ground. The giant maple tree that shaded her window reached its limbs toward her. Several of the branches brushed right up against the house, and she realized it was like a ladder of sorts, certainly a path that someone athletic could have easily traveled. Two slits with a pocketknife, pry open the screen fasteners and push it inside, then swing inside and get past the dog.

The barking, growling, vicious, terrifying ninety-pound ball of muscle with teeth. The dog she'd just been hugging and kissing but who would never put up with a strange person climbing in the window. No freaking way. Where was the blood? Where were the pieces of bone and hair? Because that was all that should be left if Sarah knew Hershey.

Sarah cranked the windows shut and fastened them. Tomorrow she would call the tree service and have them cut off the encroaching limbs. She paused to wipe a few tears away, sorely disappointed that unless there was a miracle, her plans for Devon's future were a complete washout. She went downstairs and found the note where she'd written the nice officer's name and number and dialed.

THE POLICE WERE RESPONSIVE and sympathetic. A man and a woman, both careful not to scare Devon. She let them in and explained then went out in the yard to play catch with her son while they looked upstairs and dusted around the windows for fingerprints. Luckily, the pieces were covered by her homeowner's insurance, and she'd had them appraised. The officers took the documents to make copies. They said estate jewelry rarely showed up in local pawnshops, since it was so easy to spot. They didn't hold out much hope for Sarah ever recovering the jewelry. It had probably been taken apart, and the stones would be sold separately.

The officers asked Sarah who had known she had valuables in her bedroom. She couldn't think of anyone at first. The police looked dubious, pointing out that nothing else was disturbed, and the window screen was left in place, as though someone hoped Sarah wouldn't notice right away what had happened.

"Has anyone been in your bedroom recently? Anyone new, who might have had a few minutes alone to snoop around?"

Sarah immediately thought of Blake.

But that's ridiculous. He would never do that.

"No," she said. "Nobody at all."

The officers exchanged meaningful glances.

"Really! Well, there was one guy, but he's an old friend, and I know his family, and he would never, never... wouldn't even need to. He has his own money and a successful business, and—" Sarah stopped to take a breath.

"Ma'am," the woman officer said. "You never know about people. They can have money troubles or other problems you'd never guess. You want to give us this guy's name?" She held her pad and pen ready to write.

"No!" Sarah said. "I do not." Her heart raced, and she worried they might not give up.

The woman put her things away. She shrugged. "Okay. Listen, you need to be more careful, you understand me? I don't want to get another call to come back over here because something much worse happened. You need to think about why your dog let someone break in here, unless your burglar was waving a nice juicy steak. Which sometimes does work, by the way. It's a possibility."

Sarah swallowed hard and nodded. "Okay."

"And get that tree limb lopped! It's not safe." The woman looked at her with a stern expression.

"Yes, Officer."

"Have you thought about installing an alarm system?" the male officer suggested.

"That's a good idea. I'll check into it right away. And thank you."

Sarah walked them to the door and let them out. Devon sat at the island with a glass of almond milk and some gluten-free cookies. His eyes were the size of an owl's.

"Hey, pardner, how you doin'?" She put her arm around his shoulders, wondering exactly how much he'd heard.

"Okay, Mom. Did you see their guns?"

"Yes. And their radios too."

"Yeah, and they both had, like, these miniature baseball bat things hanging from their belts. To hit bad people with. Did you see that?" His voice rose higher and higher, and he started to tremble, tears gathering in his enormous eyes.

She surrounded him with her arms and held him.

"Mommy?" His lip quivered. "I don't want them to ever come back, okay?"

"Okay. Nothing bad is going to happen, so they won't need to come back, right?" She tipped up his chin and kissed his nose.

Devon smiled, squeezing a few tears out of the corners of his eyes. "Right. Thanks, Mom! Are you going to work soon?" He looked worried.

Sarah stroked his fine, fair hair. "No, honey, I'm staying here with you tonight."

"I wonder... can we have macaroni and hot dogs for dinner and maybe watch a movie?" He tapped his mouth with an "I'm thinking" gesture, sneaking a look at her. A smile was lurking around the edges of his mouth.

"You've got it, pardner," Sarah said. "Step into my saloon with the widescreen entertainment center. Let's see what we can find to watch."

Devon grinned and ran into the TV room, where he jumped on the sofa and held out his arms to her.

LATE THAT NIGHT, SARAH sat in the dark on her window seat, wrapped in a quilt, and watched. She couldn't sleep. She might never sleep again. Every time she'd tried, lying down and closing her eyes, she imagined a faceless burglar climbing up to her window and silently sneaking inside. Her eyes flew open, expecting to see something terrible, only to find everything as usual except for the sound of her heart beating superfast and loud in her ears, and the sweat on her upper lip. After experiencing this several times, she stopped closing her eyes and stared at the ceiling. She wondered if someone could have a heart attack from scaring themselves with their imagination. She got up with her blanket and settled down at the window to stand guard over her home. She promised herself to call the home security system installers in the morning.

Devon had gone to bed willingly, asking her to read him a story. He'd wanted to hear all his old favorites, from when he was tiny. She'd read them in their traditional way, with all the right pauses and tones of voice. The ritual always seemed to reassure him. It definitely made Sarah feel better.

After Devon had fallen asleep, Sarah went to her own bed, finally let go, and all the emotions that had been building up in her came pouring out in a furious crying and punching attack on her pillows. Anger at the way she'd been victimized, yet again. Frustration, because she wasn't able to stop it from happening. Fear, because she felt so vulnerable. Afterward, she'd rolled onto her side, defeated and empty, staring into space as she tried to recover from what had happened.

Hours later, camped out on the window seat, she was still trying.

It was quiet outside, just crickets and some peepers in the distance. Clear and cool, with a little breeze, and a quarter moon floating in a sky full of stars. She heard a car go by a few blocks over, closer to the center of town. She distinguished canned laughter coming from the house diagonally across the road, where a border of green television light showed around the edges of a pulled shade. She saw something move in the streetlight shadows below her. The neighbor's cat, as quick as a cheetah, caught a mouse and stalked away into the bushes with the legs and tail all sticking out of the edges of her mouth, still wriggling. Out in the street, nothing moved for a long time. Leaning over and craning her neck, she glimpsed a sliver of her backyard, as dark as a black hole in outer space.

Sarah cleared her throat and noticed it was getting scratchy. Her nose wasn't just sore from all the crying. She poked around and confirmed that her tonsils seemed swollen.

Ohmigod, just what I needed. Maybe if I drink a lot of tea with honey and eat those disgusting zinc lozenges, I can stave it off.

She pulled a pillow around so she could rest her head while she watched the driveway and stayed curled up there until nearly dawn. Finally, she fell asleep.

Chapter 27

Sarah spent most of the next day in bed. She fought to get rid of the nasty bug that was trying to take control of her body. Miki came home and took charge, feeding her tea and chicken noodle soup. She took Devon and Hershey to the park. Sarah left a message with the home security company, and the owner was going to call back with an estimate. Paisley dealt with the staffing issues at work. Emile worried, but Sarah tried to convince him it was nothing.

It wasn't nothing, though. Her voice went from husky to scratchy, and it hurt to talk. She made her last phone call at three o'clock, confirming that the chocolate-brown table linens had been successfully delivered to the country club. After that, she didn't speak a word for the rest of the day. She moped and read a romance novel, thinking about all the reasons the burglar couldn't possibly have been Blake. She was dead asleep by eight o'clock.

When the morning of the chocolate wedding dawned, Sarah woke up and realized with horror that her strongest asset, the ability to talk anyone into anything, was fast disappearing as she teetered on the brink of laryngitis.

She dressed in dark-brown pants and a white tuxedo shirt and loaded everything else she needed into her car. She had all the staff's long brown aprons in the back seat, fresh from the dry cleaners and bagged in plastic. Miki and Devon wished her luck. Then she was off to the country club, where setup was already well in progress.

The ceremony in the club's rose garden was scheduled for four o'clock. There would be a champagne toast on the patio afterward then cocktails and hors d'oeuvres. This would be followed by dinner in the ballroom, wine, dancing, the chocolate wedding cake presentation and another champagne toast, more dancing, more drinking, and chocolate treats for the guests to take home at the end of the evening.

Sarah was relieved that the day had finally come. And by the fact that Blake Harrison was currently rolling his portable ice cream freezer into the ballroom, looking around for the best place to plug it in.

"Here," she croaked and cleared her throat. "Over here." She beckoned, flapping her hands, and led him over to the cake table, where a power strip was waiting.

He plugged in the freezer, looked at her with raised eyebrows, and pointed at his throat. "You okay?"

Sarah shook her head, grimaced, and mimed choking herself.

He nodded. "That bug is going around town. You poor thing!" Blake patted her on the back then let his hand linger and rubbed her shoulder.

She jumped away, remembering she was supposed to be mad at him.

Why was that again? Oh yeah, he chases women online while he's sleeping with me in real life. Not cool.

Sarah scowled, glancing around at the staff busily setting the tables. She pointed at the doors, beckoned, and walked over to fling one open and march out into the hallway. They'd have more privacy there. They had to talk about it sometime, so why not just have it out with him right now and clear the air? No time like the present.

BLAKE WATCHED HER WALK across the ballroom and thought how little things had changed over the past few months. She was still running away.

Why hadn't she caved in and let him catch her? They'd had terrific sex, several times. He'd been so careful to do everything just the way girls liked it, according to what he'd learned from *Men's Health* magazine.

She should be head over heels for me by now. What the hell went wrong?

He racked his brain for an explanation. He knew she'd enjoyed it too. She'd moaned and bitten him and shuddered when they'd climaxed together. He didn't get it. He'd given her plenty of space, knowing he'd see her today. He'd saved her ass at lunch that day, when the food reporter caught her off guard. Again, at the biker bar. He'd revealed his double identity and let her see how vulnerable he really was. And now, she was acting all pissy again and dragging him out into the hallway for a spanking.

Hmmmm... not a bad idea. Maybe she can get it out of her system?

Blake had hoped that when he let her figure out he was HotNCold, she would realize that he was her true friend. Someone who wanted the whole package. Because he definitely was smitten, and nothing she said or did seemed to make any difference. Even now, when she was murdering him with her eyes, he obeyed like a man bewitched.

In the hallway by the cloakroom door, Sarah turned, with angry tears on her red cheeks. His heart cracked open when he saw how upset she was. He stood in front of her, his hands dangling, helpless to do anything useful. She started to talk, but her voice broke, so she used a combination of stabbing gestures and vehement whispers.

"I know," she hissed, glaring at him. "It's you!" She pointed, hard. "No respect!"

He stretched out his hand toward her, trying to interrupt, but she made the "stop" sign with hers and stepped back.

"No!" She winced and clutched her throat. "I know what you've been doing, HotNCold!"

Blake pursed his lips and looked at her warily, wondering how much she'd figured out. "Um, how'd you know about that?" Did she realize he'd recognized her too? Maybe he should have told her. It felt wrong now to be holding anything back.

"Oh, please," she croaked and waved her hands. "You should be ashamed, Blake Harrison. I know, because it was me you were trying to seduce online. I'm Coco."

His eyebrows shot up. He was shocked she would confess if she thought he didn't already know. "You... you are?" He played along, buying some time to think.

I feel... guilty. That's it, guilty. Crap!

Sarah was crying, and it was his fault. Blake panicked. He had to do something, fast. He regretted ever starting the whole cybersex flirtation with her. It had seemed like a harmless prank at the time, but he should have known better.

She nodded, wiping away the tears with a tissue she pulled from her pocket and blowing her nose with a loud honk. Now her voice sounded a little better. "I had to tell you. It wasn't fair for you not to know, since I was doing pretty much the same thing, but you—" She shook her head, crossing her arms in front of her chest. "You were so into it! You led Coco on, Blake. You never told her there was someone else in your real life. Never told me about Coco. Online, you had a whole different thing going on. It wasn't honest. And the whole thing belittles me, as Coco and as Sarah. You took the power of making a rational decision away from both of us, both of me, by hiding the truth." Her broken voice had dwindled to a squeak.

"No, no, you don't understand," he said, desperate to apologize now, aware of his mistakes and totally mortified, despite all his excuses and good intentions. He felt his face flush, and he tensed then spat it out. "I knew it was you."

There it was. He watched her face display a series of emotions as the meaning of his words dawned. "From the beginning, I knew you were Coco," he continued, though her cresting reaction was scaring him.

She shook her head, her eyes totally enraged, her mouth stretched open in a soundless scream. He worried for a second that she wasn't breathing, then she inhaled in a long gasp.

Blake stuffed his hands in his pants pockets and went for broke, since there was no turning back now. "I wasn't flirting with just anybody, Sarah. I was flirting with *you*. At first, it was just for fun, and I recognized your starfish necklace, so I messaged you. When you wouldn't see me in reality, I couldn't stop meeting you online. By then, things were complicated. You know what I mean, don't you?"

"Ohmigod!" she wheezed, hanging her head and hiding her face in her hands. Her shoulders heaved.

"I meant to tell you, really, but then we hooked up, and I thought, well, maybe don't risk it by making her mad again." Blake rattled on while he rubbed her back, trying to calm her down. "I'm sorry, Sarah. I'm really, really sorry. If you'll give me the chance to prove—"

She cut him off, raising her tear-stained face and waving her arms. "No more, Blake," she rasped. "No manipulation, no lies, no games. No 'us.' The client is paying at the end of the reception, with a cash tip, and I'll give you your share right then. After tonight, just leave me alone."

Sarah shot a look of sheer poison at him, then she spun around and went off down the corridor, headed for the ladies' room. Blake stared after her with a painful throbbing in his chest, as if a piece of him had been torn away.

Chapter 28

"Ready? Everyone smile!"

The photographers pointed their cameras, and a score of blinding flashes went off, all within seconds. Posed in front of the cake table, Carlotta and Teddy stood on one side while Sarah, Paisley, and Emile lined up on the other. With their tall white chef's hats and crisp white aprons over brown shirts and pants, Sarah's cousin and grandfather looked sensational. The cake stood five tiers tall. It was enrobed in glossy dark-brown ganache and garlanded with white chocolate roses. The bride and groom were splendid as well in their color-coordinated wedding attire. The guests clapped and cheered, taking pictures with their cell phones. The photographer from the newspaper asked for one more shot. When the flashes went off again, Sarah saw blue lights dance before her eyes. She had to blink several times before she dared move.

Everything had gone without a serious hitch. A good thing, seeing as Sarah's voice was completely unavailable and nothing came out when she tried to speak except a breathy croak.

"I'll cut the cake now." Paisley sidled up to her and said discreetly, "Will you take Grandpa into the kitchen and make him go home? A driver is waiting outside."

They glanced over to where Emile chatted with Carlotta and Teddy, holding one of the bride's hands between both of his and bowing. He was obviously exercising the famous Dumas charm. Sarah nodded. She hooked her arm through his with a smile, slowly steering him out of the way while Paisley moved the couple into position for the ceremonial cutting of the first slice. When all eyes were on them, Sarah gently pulled Emile through the service doors.

He beamed, giving her a loving hug. "Don't try to speak, *cheri*. I know it hurts. Thank you so much for allowing me to take credit for the magnificent job you girls have done today. I'm proud of you."

"Me too," she mimed. One of the waiters from the restaurant lingered in the doorway to the parking area, and she pointed him out to Emile. "Go," she urged, shooing him with a flap of her hands and a smile.

"All right, all right. *Bon soir, ma petite.* I love you, sweetheart."

He followed the young man outside, and they disappeared. Sarah waited a moment to make sure he didn't wander back then straightened her shoulders and went into the ballroom to make herself useful.

Paisley had removed the top tier and boxed it for the bride and groom to take home. According to tradition, they would save it in the freezer to enjoy on their first anniversary. She was busily slicing the next layers. Sarah handed plates of cake to Blake, who garnished them with scoops of ice cream and drizzles of fudge sauce, then placed them on trays for the waiters to distribute. They worked together quickly, an efficient assembly line.

She avoided meeting his eyes or touching his hands when she passed him the plates. Her head was pounding, and her throat ached. The event was a huge success and would be all she had hoped for in terms of publicity for the restaurant. But a dark cloud of gloom hovered over Sarah. She longed to be home in bed. All day, while she'd been working, Blake's confession had rotated in and out of her thoughts. She was furious at him, yes, but on the other hand, she didn't know what to make of it. He hadn't been two-timing her after all. He'd lied about who he was, but everything else was the truth. He'd told her real secrets about himself, just as she had told him hers. Did that mean her feelings for the man she'd known online were genuine or fake? It was hard to merge the two Blakes in her mind. She still thought of them as two separate people.

After the cake had been cut and served, Paisley stepped away to work the crowd. She accepted congratulations and passed out business cards. Blake rolled his freezer into the hallway to plug it in there and get things ready for the guests' departure. He gave her a long, searching look as he left, but she turned her head away.

Sarah stood behind the cake table, most of which was covered with adorable little shiny brown boxes bearing the restaurant's logo in gold foil and containing slices of cake for guests to take home. Those who were single and superstitious would sleep with these under their pillows tonight, to dream of the man or woman they would marry. Or so the ritual went. Sarah wasn't planning to follow it. She had survived the excruciating day by using a lot of hand gestures and trying not to think about her disastrous life. Now she couldn't wait to get into a hot tub.

Carlotta danced in her direction, dazzling in a column of cream silk. She threw her arms around Sarah's neck and kissed her on the cheek. "Thank you so much! What a perfect day! I adored everything. Are you pleased?" White and chocolate diamonds twinkled on her left hand.

Sarah smiled and nodded for the umpteenth time that day.

Carlotta leaned closer and said into her ear, "Teddy said to tell you to meet him in the cloakroom. He has something for you!"

Sarah raised her eyebrows and smiled, giving the thumbs-up sign. "Thank you!" she mouthed.

The Chocolate Bride scooped a finger of filling from the cake carcass on the table then popped it into her mouth with a naughty grin as she slipped back into the crowd and danced away. Never one to keep a client standing with his wallet open, Sarah hurried into the hallway and entered the cloakroom through the open door.

He was waiting, bent over the service desk and writing with a slim golden pen. He smiled, stood up, and handed the check to her then shook her hand.

"I hope this is correct? My... wife is very pleased, so I am too." Teddy tucked his pen away, reached into his jacket pocket, and pulled out a fat banded stack of bills. "Twenty percent? I've never paid for a wedding before. Is that sufficient for your gratuity?" He handed her the money.

Sarah nodded, thanking him in her scratchy voice. "Very sufficient! And cash is appreciated too. Easier to divide up among the staff." She slipped the money into the front pocket of her apron, where her order tablet usually rested when she was at work. "Thanks again for the business. We're very grateful!" They shook hands. Teddy said goodbye, accidentally dislodging the stopper holding the cloakroom door open as he was on his way out. It slowly swung shut while Sarah checked her hair in the mirror on the wall. A moment later, the door opened again.

Blake stood in the doorway. "Everything okay in here?"

Sarah nodded, unable to struggle anymore. "I'm fine," she whispered. "Really can't talk."

He reached for one of her hands. "I hope you didn't mean what you said. Don't blame you for being mad, but—"

"I know," she whispered. "Don't know how I feel." She counted out some bills from the cash Teddy had given her. "Here, this is what you quoted, plus twenty percent for your service today. Thank you."

He folded the money into his pocket without looking at it, watching her with an anxious crease between his eyebrows. "Okay. Be careful driving tonight. I'll call you soon."

She nodded, too tired to object.

One way or the other, things were approaching a conclusion. Should she say goodbye forever or forgive him? Sarah had no idea which way to turn.

Chapter 29

S arah drove home from the country club slowly. Her tired eyes were having trouble focusing on the road. Paisley would supervise the breakdown after the bride and groom made their ceremonial departure, and she'd make sure nothing was left behind. It was a good thing Sarah didn't have to do it. She could barely hold her head up, but still, it buzzed with thoughts. She couldn't decide what to do about Blake. Her contradictory feelings flitted like a cloud of butterflies, and she couldn't quite get ahold of any of them.

It kept coming back to deep insecurity about her ability to make a solid judgment. She reasoned it out step-by-step and thought she understood what was going on but then got paralyzed when it came to moving forward an inch. She hated being so wishy-washy. When managing accounts at the advertising agency, she'd made major decisions impacting tens of thousands of dollars every day without batting an eye. Where was that woman? What happened to the clear thinking and rational behavior?

Sarah was disgusted with herself. Even if Blake was totally sincere and truly did love her, as he'd whispered at the biker bar, she couldn't think of a single reason she deserved a happy ending. She was emotionally crippled, and it was her own fault. She'd allowed herself to be humiliated and deserted by a total jerk, and she'd set Devon up for trauma that would last a lifetime. Floating along in her romantic dream world, she'd turned her back on the signs.

Her cell phone rang for the third time on her drive home, and she picked it up to glance at the screen. It was Blake again. He was tuning in on her thoughts, eavesdropping on her mind. She let it ring and go to voice mail, but this time she didn't hear the "ding" that meant he'd left a message. It figured. He'd probably given up on her.

Her weakness was incapacitating, and the last thing Blake needed was a helpless female to drag him down. Sarah was cursed, and the disease was probably contagious. A sob caught in her throat as self-pity overwhelmed her.

When she pulled into her driveway, these negative thoughts vanished as something much more important swept them from her mind. A dark-blue car was parked in front of the back door. It looked like the same one she had seen across the street and reported to the police. A rush of adrenaline coursed through her body. She was awake and alert in a flash.

Through the windows, in the brightly lit kitchen, she saw a tall man sitting next to Devon on a barstool at the end of the island. When he turned to watch her car pulling into the garage, she saw his face. It was Jim, the sleazy weasel himself! Up from Florida to make her life miserable again. Now it all made sense. The prowler, the stolen jewelry, the reason Hershey hadn't ripped the burglar apart. If she hadn't thought he was a thousand miles away, she would have figured it out sooner.

Sarah went in through the kitchen door like a mama bear whose cub was sniffing a bobcat. Her eyes blazed. Tossing her things on the floor in the entryway, she beckoned to Miki, who stood nervously shifting her weight back and forth while Devon spoke to his dad in a high, excited voice. Hershey sat at Devon's feet, his body a barrier between Jim and the boy.

"And I always get A-plus in spelling too," Devon said, waving his hands in the air. "Just ask Mom. Hey, here she is now." He turned, his eyes dazzled and distracted, his cheeks flushed, and pointed at Sarah. "Don't I, Mom? I always get A-plus, right? Hey, my... dad is here. Did you see? He came to see us!" His excited smile made her want to cry.

She smoothed back the wispy hair from his hot forehead and kissed him, shooting a dangerous glance at her ex-husband. Jim watched with a bored expression. His fingers fidgeted with a large brown envelope sitting in front of him.

"It's time for bed now, Devon. Miki? Please take him upstairs to brush his teeth and read him a book or two. I'll be along soon." Her voice was still low and scratchy, but the utter panic in her heart seemed to have done it some good.

Miki looked relieved and nodded as they exchanged glances. "You'll be all right down here?" She glanced at the telephone on the hall table, raising one eyebrow. Sarah knew Miki was offering to call the police.

"Of course," Sarah said, subtly shaking her head. The cell phone in her jacket pocket began to ring again. She switched off the ringer and put the phone near her hand while she leaned on the other end of the counter. "We're going to have a little chat." The anger welling up inside was just below the surface, bubbling and hot.

Miki gently pulled Devon from his stool and offered him a pony ride on her back. He climbed on board, and with a yearning look at Jim, he waved and said, "Bye, um... Dad!" They trotted up the stairs and out of sight.

Sarah looked across at Jim. He had aged considerably since they'd last met in person. His hair was thinning and speckled with gray. Deep creases ringed his eyes, and his cheeks sagged at the jowl. When he shifted in his seat, his sweater pulled over a rounded paunch. She wondered what she'd ever found so attractive about the man. He was still in his early forties, but he looked ten or fifteen years older. *Life must not be so great in the Sunshine State after all,* she thought with a flash of satisfaction.

"What do you want?" She got straight to the point. "You already took everything worth money, didn't you?"

He didn't answer her question, his eyes roaming over her body. "You look good, Sarah. Real good."

"You don't," she said. "Why are you here?" Her tone was impatient, but she was holding herself back.

"Now, now, little girl. No need to get nasty. Wouldn't want to piss me off, would you?" He grinned, a glint of evil pleasure in his eyes. "I came to make sure my attorney's letter got here. And to discuss terms."

Sarah's cell phone vibrated, a low hum. She glanced down and saw it was Blake again. He obviously wasn't giving up, but this was not a good time for interruptions.

"Yes, the letter arrived. I prefer to have the attorneys handle it. You should go now. Before I call the police and they match your prints to the ones they found in my bedroom." She shot a poison arrow flying from her eyes to his.

But he just laughed, not the least bit intimidated. "I wouldn't do that," he warned, "until you've seen what I brought to show you." He patted the brown envelope, teasing her. "You know, things have changed since you sweet-talked that judge into giving you alimony and child support. Neither one of us is in the same position, financially."

"What do you mean by that?" She slitted her eyes, wondering what was up his sleeve this time.

"My last three expos didn't do so well. I had to go bankrupt. Luckily, in Florida, you get to keep your primary residence. But that bimbo I married kicked me out of the house, after... well, none of your business. Not so sure that last brat is even mine. I've been living in a little apartment near the beach. Great view of the surfer girls but not what I'm used to, you know?"

She laughed, a short, raspy sound. "Where's the sad music, Jim? You're breaking my heart."

He scowled, and she saw that wicked gleam in his eyes again. "And you, sweetheart, are up here living the life, aren't you? Full partner in that restaurant your family owns, eh? A mail-order nanny to take care of the kid? And this house"—he looked around the room—"all finished now and must be worth a fortune. You're sitting on a gold mine, lucky girl."

For the first time since she walked inside, a flicker of fear shot through her. "So?" She stared at him, brazen, her feelings hidden.

"So, I think the tables have turned. Maybe you owe me now."

"Ha! The mortgage on this place is enormous, you idiot. I barely make enough to get by. Miki works for room and board. I'd have to sell everything to—"

He waited, staring, as it dawned on her.

"You wouldn't." She shook her head. "You wouldn't be able to make me do that." Now she was filled with anxiety, picturing all kinds of horrors.

He smiled. She knew he'd seen the fear in her eyes. He patted the big brown envelope.

"Oh, wouldn't I? Just wait 'til you see what's in here, Sarah. I think you'll change your mind. How much do you want to keep that scrawny, pathetic little runt all to yourself, anyhow?"

Sarah's cell phone vibrated again. And again. And again, then it stopped.

"The boyfriend, Sarah? Pretty persistent, isn't he?" Jim grinned, opening the clasp on the envelope then pulling out some stiff white papers.

"What? It's just a friend. Why does that matter to you?"

"Well," he said slowly, savoring it, "I really don't give two craps myself. But a judge might, if he saw these. Wouldn't do to give sole custody to a loose divorcée who entertains men overnight with her kid at home, would it? Immoral, I'd say. A bad influence. Not even Christian, really. What would you say?"

He flipped over the papers and showed her the black-and-white photo prints. First, one of her on the patio, kissing Blake, with the strap of her dress falling off her shoulder. Her breast was nearly exposed. Then the next shot, obviously taken through her bedroom window. It was dark, but the image was clear. The two of them were in bed together, naked. Doing private and passionate things to one another. Her face was turned toward the window, ecstatic, wanton. The photos left nothing to the imagination, and there were at least a dozen. The photos made Sarah feel sick, and her hands began to shake.

"How much do you want?"

He slid the last photo out of the envelope and slapped it onto the counter right in front of her. "Five hundred thousand, cash, with no records for the tax collector. I'll give you two weeks to get it together. No more alimony, no more child support. When you give me the money, I'll sign papers agreeing to give you permanent custody and make the deal final. Your lawyer can draw them up."

Sarah gasped. To raise that much, she'd have to get a second mortgage on the house and borrow from her family. It was impossible. Suddenly the air in the room seemed too thin, she couldn't breathe, and black splotches throbbed before her eyes.

A knock on the back door startled them both. Sarah turned to see Blake standing outside with a suspicious frown, looking through the glass at Jim. He didn't wait for her to answer but turned the doorknob and walked in.

"Everything okay in here, Sarah? I worried when you didn't answer." He walked across the room, staring at Jim. "What's this?"

Jim had started to gather up the prints and stuff them back into the envelope, but Blake reached out a big hand to stop him. He grabbed one of the bedroom shots and held it up. "What's this, Sarah?" he snapped and turned to look at her, angry. But when he saw her devastated face, he turned back to Jim. "Who is this asshole, and what's he trying to pull?" His face darkened, and he took a step toward Jim, who shrank back.

"It's Devon's dad," Sarah said, her voice cracking as she told him Jim's demands.

Blake dropped the print and put his arm around her shoulders, his warmth reaching out to comfort her. She took a deep breath, and her head stopped spinning.

"What kind of stupid game are you playing, man?" Blake taunted him. "This is the new millennium. The Puritans landed here four hundred years ago, but they're all dead now. We're two healthy single people, and the kid was away at a chaperoned sleepover. Nobody cares, you asshole!"

Sarah started to calm down, realizing that Blake was right. It might be embarrassing if the photos got out but not the end of the world. Not enough to threaten her custody of Devon.

"Well," Jim mumbled, "a judge might care! Do you two want to see these pictures plastered all over the internet? Could be real bad for business."

Blake laughed. "Go ahead, jackass. You can post them from your jail cell. I'm calling the cops. They've got some fingerprints to match up, and I've got a feeling yours might be a perfect fit. Know what the time is for breaking and entering?" He squeezed Sarah's shoulders, and her head spun as a sense of relief rushed through her and she began to relax.

"I'm sure my lawyer will be interested to hear about all this," she added. "What do you think a judge might make of attempted blackmail and extortion, Jim?" She ventured a small smirk. "Who's the bad influence now?"

Jim flushed a dark red as he stuffed the last of the pictures into his envelope and stood up. "We'll see about that," he muttered, sliding off his stool and slithering toward the door.

"You can run, slimeball, but you can't hide. I got a clear shot of your license plate on my cell phone before I came inside." Blake sneered as Jim scurried across the room and out the door.

Jim jumped into his car and backed carefully around Blake's truck then zoomed out of the driveway.

"Ohmigod," Sarah moaned as the tears rolled down her face. "I was totally falling for it! How did you even know about the fingerprints? And how can I ever repay you?"

Blake turned her face toward his, wiping away the tears with a tissue from the box on the island, and kissed her. "Don't worry, sweetheart. We'll think of something." He smiled and took her into his arms. "Paisley told Jordan about the break-in, and he blabbed to me. That's why I rushed over to check on you tonight. We're all keeping a close eye on you, darling. Because we care."

She sobbed for a minute or two, then when it was out of her system, she pulled back and looked at him. "I'm such an idiot. Why do you put up with me?"

He shrugged, grinning. "Just hooked, I guess. I love you, Sarah. To me, you're the most perfect, beautiful, wonderful woman in the world." He kissed her again. "Now, I'm going to call the cops while you go upstairs and take a long, hot shower, okay?"

She nodded. "Okay. I mean, yes to the shower, and I'm kind of hooked on you too, Blake. I might even love you, though I'm scared to admit it."

"Well, it's about time," he said with a big smile. "I've been waiting a while to hear that. No more running away?"

She shook her head and smiled. "Promise. I need to work some things out, but no more running away. You can come to my rescue whenever you want. I'm good with it."

"All right! Now, get along and do whatever it is you females do when you spend an hour in the bathroom, and I'll be right here guarding the castle gate. I'll just bring Kahlua in from the truck so he can help."

She made her way upstairs with a lighter footstep than she'd thought possible.

Chapter 30

Sarah awoke the next morning when Devon jumped up onto her bed, bouncing with excitement.

"Mom! Do you know what? Mom, wake up!"

She opened one eye then decided it was safe to open the other one. "What? Okay, I'm up."

"Coach Harrison is here, and his dog too, and they're downstairs right now, and he's cooking something really good for breakfast. You gotta come see. Smell the bacon?"

She didn't have to sniff, since it was already making her mouth water. "I do. Yum. Are you hungry? I sure am." She grabbed him, and they wrestled as she tickled him under the chin while he giggled.

"But Dad is gone, I guess. I didn't see him." His happy face showed a flicker of concern. "At least we have bacon, though. Come on. Let's go!"

Sarah figured if bacon trumped Jim, then Devon wasn't going to be too upset that his father had disappeared again. She got up and pulled on a robe over her nightshirt then followed her hopping son down the stairs. He started running when he reached the ground floor and beat her into the kitchen.

Miki was already seated at the island, wearing Hello Kitty pajamas and chattering away with Blake. He stood in front of the stove, flipping what looked like latkes, pancakes made of shredded potato, on her cast-iron griddle. In his stocking feet and the sweatpants pulled from the gym bag he'd brought in from his truck last night, he looked right at home. His hair was fluffed up in the back, and he hadn't shaved. Sarah thought he looked cute. She went over and hugged him, kissing his stubble. His eyes beamed a hello, and he motioned toward the coffeepot with his eyebrows while he scooped up latkes and put them on a baking sheet, which he slid into the oven. She glimpsed a plate of crispy bacon warming in there too.

"Okay, who wants eggs? Everybody? Sunny side up or over easy?" He took orders and started cracking eggshells.

Meanwhile Miki continued the apparently long story she'd been telling him about her studies. Devon lay down on the floor between Hershey and Kahlua, stroking them both at the same time. They didn't seem to mind sharing.

Sarah took out plates and silverware then set them on the island near a basket of paper napkins. She poured herself a mug of coffee and watched while Blake expertly prepare the fried eggs, not breaking a single yolk.

Last night, he'd insisted on sleeping on the couch in the TV room. He'd called the police after she went up to shower, and the same two officers who had answered her call about the burglary were waiting in the kitchen to ask her some questions when she went downstairs. When they learned the details and Blake emailed the photo of Jim's license plate to them, they'd called in an all-points bulletin, directing all units to watch for his car. Then they'd headed out to check the local motels, where he might have been staying, though they felt there was a better chance he would head straight south and be picked up by the state police in Connecticut.

"Don't worry," the woman officer had said, a determined look on her face. "We'll have him in custody within twenty-four hours. But please, install that alarm system!"

"She will," Blake said. "I'm taking care of it first thing in the morning. My buddy owns the company. And I won't leave them alone here until it's a done deal."

Sarah had started to object then stopped and closed her mouth. Instead, she'd smiled at him and allowed herself to feel cherished and cared for.

Now, she watched as he served everyone, laughing along with Miki and teasing Devon about sprinkling dog hairs onto his food. They were all smiling and happy, even the dogs, who got to split one of the latkes. Sunshine streamed through the windows, and birds were singing outside. It was the most beautiful day Sarah could remember.

And to think that just last night, on her way home in the car, she'd experienced one of the lowest moments of her life. Amazing, how things could turn around so fast. All that was required, it seemed, was a sweet, honest man, a little faith, and the courage to believe her own eyes.

THAT EVENING, AFTER the security installation guys had finished, Blake took Sarah out for dinner, just the two of them. Paisley had offered her the night off and insisted on it after hearing what had happened.

"Now, I know it won't be as good as your cousin's cooking, but I've had some really good meals at this place," Blake said as they got into his truck and headed west. He'd reserved a quiet corner table for them at a terrific Italian place in Northampton, a neighboring town known for its many restaurants.

Blake was right. The food was extraordinary. They held hands, drank excellent wine, and ate spaghetti Bolognese with the best Italian bread Sarah ever remembered tasting. The desserts were a little disappointing, though. They decided to save room for a treat back at Blake's condo, where he'd stashed some of the double-chocolate ice cream left over from the wedding.

As they drove home through the star-sprinkled night, she looked at Blake, who was awfully quiet. "You okay?"

"I'm fine, just relaxing. It's so nice to look over and see you there. I love you, Sarah."

She felt the blush rising into her cheeks and was glad of the shadows hiding it. "Well," she said, "let's not talk about—"

He picked up her hand and kissed it. "I mean it. Please don't ever be mad at me again! I'm a knucklehead, but I'm *your* knucklehead."

She leaned over and kissed his cheek. "I was just scared. But especially now, I can see how different you are from him. It was silly of me to be so nervous. I'm flattered that you went to all that trouble to court me, twice! I officially forgive you. You're pretty terrific, Blake. I feel lucky."

"Sarah?"

"Mmmm?" She scooted over on the bench seat and nuzzled him, loving his scent.

"Got a jar of the wedding fudge sauce for you at my place. And some great ideas for what to do with it. The recipe was invented in your honor, you know. I call it 'Orgasmic Chocolate Fudge Sauce.'"

She looked at him in shock then grinned. "Well, then. What are we waiting for? Step on it!"

Sarah was looking forward to letting the chocolate have its way, releasing her inhibitions and enjoying its effects for a change. She suspected that from now on, she'd have a whole new attitude toward her sweet addiction.

Dear Reader,

We hope you enjoyed *Love & Chocolate*, by Gail Cleare. Please consider leaving a review on your favorite book site.

Visit our website (https://RedAdeptPublishing.com) to subscribe to the Red Adept Publishing Newsletter to be notified of future releases.

A Note About the Recipes

Your results can only be as good as the ingredients you use, so be picky.

Use the very best-quality chocolate you can find. Before you buy something familiar in the baking section of your grocery store, look in the imported foods and deli sections of the store. Then do a taste test. You'll be shocked at how different the flavor and texture can be.

Likewise, use a real vanilla bean instead of vanilla extract, or at least use the best vanilla extract you can get. The same goes for cinnamon, and consider grating or grinding your own so it's fresh. These key ingredients, used in small quantities to achieve big results, may be old and stale if they have been sitting on the shelf for a long time. The best may cost a little more, but it makes all the difference.

I happen to prefer Callebaut chocolate, which is usually available in the deli section of my local grocery store. They make white, milk, and dark chocolate that you can buy in big chunks that have been chiseled off a huge brick. It is simply "to die for." There are lots of other gourmet brands that are fantastic too. Most of these can be ordered via the internet if you don't have a local specialty foods store.

Recipes from The Three Chocolatiers

Better Than Cybersex Brownies
Ingredients:
4 ounces dark semisweet chocolate
1 stick butter
4 medium eggs
1/4 teaspoon salt
1/2 teaspoon cinnamon
1 vanilla bean (or 1/2 teaspoon vanilla extract)
2 cups granulated sugar
1 cup flour
1 cup coarse-chopped pecans
Directions:
Preheat oven to 350 degrees F.

Chop the chocolate into coarse chunks and put it into a small microwavable bowl with the butter, cut into 4 pieces. Heat in microwave SLOWLY on Low/Defrost for 2 to 3 minutes. Be careful not to burn the chocolate, and stop when it is not yet completely melted. It will continue to melt for a few minutes after you take it out. Stir to blend and expose any solid chunks to the warmer liquefied part. Set this mixture aside to cool slightly.

In a large bowl, beat the eggs with a wire whisk until well mixed and add salt and cinnamon. Slit the vanilla bean and scrape out all the seeds. Blend them into the eggs too. Add the sugar in three parts, stirring gently with a big spoon until it all dissolves.

Butter the bottom and sides of an 8-inch-square pan.

When the chocolate mixture is cool enough not to cook the eggs, pour it slowly into the sugar mixture and fold them together. Mix thoroughly. Gently add the flour, stirring it in slowly with a spoon. Last, add the pecans. Pour the batter into the baking pan.

Bake until brownies pull away from the sides slightly and a toothpick inserted in the middle comes out clean, about 45 minutes (depending on your oven). Let the brownies cool for at least 1 hour. They will be slightly cakelike and slightly fudgy, a perfect compromise, utterly delectable, about 2-1/2 inches tall.

Mocha Mint Madness Cocktails

This recipe works best if all ingredients are chilled in the refrigerator first so the ice doesn't melt too much when you put everything in the shaker.

Serves 2 generously.

INGREDIENTS:

 2 ounces crème de cacao

 1 ounce Kahlua coffee liqueur[1]

 1 ounce crème de menthe

 1 ounce vodka

 2 ounces half-and-half

 Garnishes: Mint leaves and dark chocolate shavings

 Directions:

Assemble all liquid ingredients in a cocktail shaker with ice cubes. Shake well for 1 to 2 minutes and immediately pour through strainer into martini glasses. Garnish with mint leaves and chocolate curls.

---

1. http://www.drinksmixer.com/desc292.html

Double Trouble Chocolate Ice Cream
Ingredients:
1-1/2 cups heavy cream
1-1/2 cups half-and-half
1/2 cup unsweetened cocoa powder
4 ounces semisweet chocolate, finely chopped
4 large egg yolks
3/4 cup granulated sugar
1 teaspoon vanilla extract or seeds from 1 bean
1/2 teaspoon cinnamon
1/2 cup mini milk chocolate chips or chocolate shavings
Directions:
Bring cream and half-and-half to a simmer in a large heavy-bottomed saucepan. Do not boil. Remove from heat and whisk in cocoa powder. Add chopped chocolate and whisk until completely melted. Set saucepan aside. Cool to room temperature.

Beat egg yolks in a large bowl, then add sugar and mix about 3 minutes until thickened. Slowly pour about a quarter of the chocolate mixture into the egg mixture, beating or whisking constantly. When that is blended, pour in half the remaining chocolate mixture and repeat, then blend in the last of it, always whisking constantly. (A stand mixer works well for this.)

Pour the chocolate-egg mixture back into the saucepan. Cook very slowly on lowest setting and stir until the mixture thickens and will coat a spoon, about 5 to 10 minutes.

Remove from heat and pour into a bowl, straining through a prepared fine-mesh strainer or cheesecloth to remove any lumps. Stir in the vanilla extract and cinnamon, then set the bowl over an ice bath to cool to room temperature.

Cover bowl with plastic wrap and refrigerate at least 3 to 4 hours. Cool completely, the colder the better. Churn in an ice cream maker according to the manufacturer's instructions. Add mini chocolate chips or chocolate shavings when ice cream is soft-churned—solid but still flexible. Mix in well by hand with a wooden spoon or rubber spatula, then transfer to a plastic container, seal tightly, and harden in the freezer for 6 to 8 hours.

Orgasmic Chocolate Fudge Sauce
Makes about 1 cup.
Ingredients:
3/4 cup dark chocolate, chopped
1 cup sugar
1/8 teaspoon salt
1/8 teaspoon cinnamon
1/2 teaspoon vanilla extract or seeds from 1 bean, scraped
1 tablespoon unsalted butter
1 cup heavy cream or half-and-half

Pour chopped chocolate into a heavy-bottomed saucepan over very low heat and stir until starting to melt. Stir in sugar, salt, cinnamon, vanilla, and butter and continue stirring as the mixture melts. Add the cream gradually, stirring constantly, as the chocolate mixture continues to melt. DO NOT BOIL!

You can keep this sauce in the refrigerator between uses. It will get thicker from the cold. Warm it up in your microwave, set on Defrost or Low, and stir to loosen. If it's still too thick, add a little milk or cream.

From the Author

Dear Chocolate Lovers,

For more great chocolate recipes, go to your favorite online bookseller and look for this novel's free companion piece. Available only in e-book, it includes a reading group discussion guide and is also posted in PDF format at: www.gailcleare.com[1].

Follow me on Facebook/GailCleareAuthor and let me know how your cocoa cookery comes out. I'd love to hear your ideas for new recipes to try, and we may even add them to the cookbook, with your permission.

Best,

Gail

---

1. http://www.gailcleare.com

Acknowledgements

The idea behind this story came from an event called the Chocolate Lovers' Festival, which I produced three years in a row in Western Massachusetts with a business partner, Jane O'Connor. She taught me much of the arcane chocolate lore included in this book. We also took turns writing a popular monthly column for America Online called "I Love Chocolate."

Thanks to Gary Schaefer of Bart's Ice Cream for his educational tour of the factory in Greenfield, which I have never forgotten. Years later, I was pitching literary agent Meg Ruley, and she saw the AOL job listed on my resumé. "Write about chocolate," she suggested. So, I drafted the first two chapters, developed quite a few original recipes, and then the project sat on the shelf for several years. I dusted it off and re-drafted most of the book in 2016 while participating in a twelve-week writing workshop at Patchwork Farm with Patricia Lee Lewis, who was delightfully encouraging.

My critique group, the Women's Fiction Critique Group (WFCG) on Facebook, was very helpful in identifying the manuscript's weak spots and suggesting solutions.

Thanks also to Red Adept Publishing and Lynn McNamee for bringing this book into the world.

Also by Gail Cleare

The Taste of Air
Love & Chocolate

Watch for more at gailcleare.com.

About the Author

USA Today Bestselling author Gail Cleare used to write for newspapers, magazines, ad agencies, and Fortune 50 companies. She wrote a monthly column for AOL called "I Love Chocolate" and hosted a popular live chat about cocoa cookery and its fascinating history.

Now she writes fiction and lives on an 18th century farm in Massachusetts with her family and dogs, cats, chickens, black bears, beavers, blue herons, rushing streams, and wide, windy skies. When she's not writing, Gail is usually working in her organic vegetable garden or stalking wild creatures with a 300mm lens.

Read more at gailcleare.com.

About the Publisher

Dear Reader,

We hope you enjoyed this book. Please consider leaving a review on your favorite book site.

Visit https://RedAdeptPublishing.com to see our entire catalogue.

Don't forget to subscribe to our monthly newsletter to be notified of future releases and special sales.

Made in the USA
Middletown, DE
15 December 2018